BOOKS BY BRENDAN DENEEN

Scatterbrain

Flash Gordon: The Mercy Wars

Flash Gordon: Invasion of the Red Sword

Flash Gordon: The Vengeance of Ming

The Ninth Circle

The Island of Misfit Toys

Night Night, Groot

The Chrysalis

THE
CHRYSALIS

THE
CHRYSALIS

BRENDAN
DENEEN

TOR

A TOM DOHERTY ASSOCIATES BOOK
NEW YORK

This is a work of fiction. All of the characters, organizations, and
events portrayed in this novel are either products of the author's
imagination or are used fictitiously.

THE CHRYSALIS

A Tor Book
Published by Tom Doherty Associates
175 Fifth Avenue
New York, NY 10010

www.tor-forge.com

Tor® is a registered trademark of Macmillan Publishing Group, LLC.

The Library of Congress Cataloging-in-Publication
Data is available upon request.

ISBN 978-0-7653-9555-9 (hardcover)
ISBN 978-0-7653-9556-6 (ebook)

Our books may be purchased in bulk for promotional, educational, or business
use. Please contact your local bookseller or the Macmillan Corporate and
Premium Sales Department at 1-800-221-7945, extension 5442, or by
email at MacmillanSpecialMarkets@macmillan.com.

First Edition: September 2018

Printed in the United States of America

0 9 8 7 6 5 4 3 2 1

This novel is dedicated to

comic books made before 1990

and scary movies on VHS

and the smell of old paperback horror novels

THE
CHRYSALIS

PROLOGUE

The basement gaped open like a mouth.

In the kitchen, the linoleum floor streaked with freshly spilled blood, a man and a woman struggled for control of a twelve-inch carving knife. The woman held it in a frenzied grip and tried desperately to plunge it into her husband's neck. The man, clawing at her hands, was bleeding from numerous wounds to his face, chest, and arms. His lips opened and closed like a suffocating fish as he wrestled with his wife, their battle silent except for an occasional grunt and the soft sound of midnight rain against the windows.

For a moment, he thought he was gaining the upper hand. They were about the same height, but he was stronger—normally. Tonight, her strength surprised him. As had the strange smile that wrapped itself around her face a few minutes earlier, when he'd told her he was sick of her secrecy and declared that he was heading down into the basement to get some answers.

As he'd made his way across the room, she started stabbing him.

Though his head was swimming as the life leaked out of him,

he managed to get hold of the knife handle, his fingers intertwined with his wife's in some kind of sick intimacy. He pushed the blade toward her. A sound bubbled up from the back of her throat, and at first he thought she was crying. Then he realized, his stomach dropping, that she was *laughing*. They'd been married for forty-six years, and he'd never heard her laugh like that: coarse, guttural, unnatural.

He remembered the last time he had heard her regular laugh: weeks ago, before her trip to the desert. He'd begged her not to go. She was retired, after all. Why was she volunteering for a high school trip? They were supposed to be spending their golden years together, finding new hobbies to enjoy and taking it easy. He just wanted to putter around the house during the day, maybe head into town now and then, and watch TV at night. But she had insisted. She missed her work, she said. The field trip was a way for her to reconnect with the woman she had once been. And he had relented. Of course he had. He loved her.

She'd returned from that trip a changed woman, clutching something wrapped in a dirty cloth that she refused to show him, babbling about the perverted nature of the students and other adults who had gone with her.

She hadn't laughed once since that day. Not with her real laugh, the one he missed. The one he used to hear all the time, before that visit to the desert and his wife's strange obsession with the basement. He glanced across the kitchen at the open door and the stairs that led down into pitch darkness.

That was all the distraction she needed.

"It's *mine*," she hissed, her fetid breath curling against his face.

She shoved him with the hand not struggling for control of the knife. The man's bare feet slipped on the blood—*his* blood—pooling on the kitchen floor, and he went down hard, the air knocked violently from his lungs. Before he fully registered what was happening, she was on top of him, stabbing over and over again.

"Mine, mine, mine, mine . . . ," she whispered.

As his vision dimmed, the man's gaze focused on the basement doorway. He'd read in a newspaper article years earlier that the moment of death was usually accompanied by an overall sense of peace, but his terror only increased as he stared at the dark entrance to the basement and his consciousness slipped away.

Soon, the only noises in the room were the knife repeatedly entering flesh and the woman's strange laughter rising above the growing sound of the storm.

MONTH ONE

Tom Decker looked haunted.

He stared at himself in the bathroom mirror, the weak light from the fluorescent bulb pulsing down on him as he attempted not to puke his guts out. Jenny was asleep in what passed as their small bedroom, cut off from the rest of the apartment by a flimsy room divider, legs tangled up in the whatever-thread-count cotton sheets they'd received from some cousin for their wedding a year earlier. Even though Tom had shut the door, he heard her heavy breathing through the thin walls. His long, greasy hair hung in his eyes, but he could still see himself—and he looked like shit. It was 2 P.M. on a rainy Saturday afternoon. Or was it Sunday? He honestly had no idea.

Racked by a violent cough, he spat, then ran the water to wash away the evidence. How many cigarettes had he smoked the night before? He felt even sicker just thinking about it. He really needed to quit. Then again, he'd been telling himself that for years. Ever since he was a teen and had started sneaking butts from his dad's never-ending packs. His father had died from lung cancer. It'd been ugly at the end. Tom blinked and shook away the memories of the man's sallow face, refocusing on the present. On the far different life he was trying to create for himself in New York City, away from his past.

He and Jenny had closed the dingy Alphabet City bar yet again, an easy task since he worked there most nights as the sole bartender. Easy to lock the door at 4 A.M. and stay inside with a few customer-friends and his wife and drink a couple more before he finally kicked everyone out.

It wasn't unusual for Tom and Jenny to stumble the few blocks to their apartment while the sun was coming up, to pass shocked, offended, or disgusted neighbors heading out for early-morning activities. The couple would laugh guiltily as they tripped up the stairs and collapsed into bed, sometimes too drunk to fuck, sometimes not.

Last night he'd switched from beer to bourbon a little after midnight, a rookie mistake. Now his head was pounding and his stomach was a gurgling mess, but he prided himself on throwing up as seldom as possible. Plus, he was a loud puker, raging-lunatic loud, embarrassingly loud, and he didn't want to wake Jenny.

Leaning over, Tom splashed water onto his unshaven face. It was a crapshoot at any given moment whether their tiny apartment would have hot water, but right now he welcomed the feel of the icy-cold liquid; it tamped down the nausea. How much sleep had he gotten? He didn't have a clue, but it felt as though he'd slept for about twenty minutes.

"Tom . . . ," Jenny called softly from the bedroom.

He pushed his straggly hair up and out of his eyes, exhaled, and blinked several times. The water droplets on his face, through his blurred vision, gave him an almost alien look. He smiled at himself without any real mirth and wiped the water away before shutting off the light, opening the door, and returning to his bed and his wife.

Jenny Decker sat at the dining room table and watched her husband through bloodshot eyes. Their apartment was a glorified studio, so calling the tiny piece of furniture a "dining room table" was a stretch, but they'd done their best to create areas that replicated the spaces of a larger home. Since this table was in the designated "dining room," it was the dining room table.

Rain beat against the nearby "living room" windows, making Jenny feel even sleepier. Shadows danced on the exposed brick above the small, nonfunctional fireplace.

The coffee that she was trying to suck down should have been delicious, especially considering how much sugar she'd dumped into it, but her hangover was bad enough that the heat flowing down her throat and into her stomach was all that mattered.

Tom looked as bad as she felt. He had that faraway expression on his face that told her he was trying not to throw up. He was playing with his Zippo, a habit she loved and hated at the same time. She loved the sound the lighter made but hated how much her husband smoked. Her grandfather, a colossally heavy smoker, had died from lung cancer when she was twelve. It was one of the things she and Tom had bonded over when they first met.

Still, the deaths of his father and her grandfather weren't enough to get him to quit smoking, and eventually he gently asked her to stop berating him about it, explaining that he needed to do it on his own schedule. She no longer brought it up, but it broke her heart every time he lit up.

Across the table from her, though pale and sickly, Tom still looked good to her, with his crown of dark, shoulder-length hair and ratty white T-shirt, his dark tattoos peeking out of the sleeves. She smiled at the sight.

It had taken them a little while to figure out that it was Sunday, which sucked because it meant she had to work the next day. But at least Tom had the night off. It was pouring rain out, so Jenny took solace in the fact that after drinking coffee and picking at the stale bagels that had been in the cupboard for at least two days too many, she and Tom would snuggle down on the couch and watch bad TV on their unintentionally stolen cable. When they'd moved in a couple of years earlier, they found what was clearly an antenna wire sticking out of the wall facing the street. Was it their fault that when they plugged it into their TV, they had almost every channel known to humanity?

Tom caught her looking at him and gave Jenny that crooked grin she'd first noticed a little over three years earlier, when he'd been tending bar at a coworker's going-away party in the same Alphabet City dive bar where he still worked. That was the first time she'd stayed at any bar after closing time. Tom's lips had tasted so good that night.

They'd dated for only a year before he proposed, getting down on bended knee at a restaurant, embarrassing and exhilarating her at the same time. He had said the most amazing things in that moment, things she had always wanted to hear from a man. He seemed to understand her perfectly. She had gotten down onto the floor with him, whispered yes, and hugged him with a fervor that surprised even her. The restaurant's other patrons applauded, and someone sent over a bottle of champagne. They never found out who had done it.

"Hey," he said softly, bringing her back to the present.

"Hey, what?" she answered, mock serious.

"I love you," he whispered.

"I love you, too, baby."

Monday morning was a little more forgiving.

Jenny was up early, as usual on a weekday, and had left for work before Tom woke up. He hated when he missed her getting ready. Watching her slip back into their bedroom after a 6 A.M. shower, pulling on her underwear and bra. Pretending she didn't know he was watching as she pulled her long dirty-blond hair into a ponytail and put on the designer track suit with that stupid corporate logo, which should have looked horrible but somehow made her even hotter than usual.

He often tried to coax her back into bed but failed almost every time. She was way too dedicated to her work to let some quick morning sex jeopardize her job, no matter how good it was. Tom didn't understand that kind of dedication to a nine-to-five job but respected it nonetheless. So he contented himself by watching her suit up for her day as a personal trainer to a bunch of douchebag investment bankers.

By the time he got up at nine thirty that Monday, Jenny had probably been at that fancy basement gym inside the Swiss investment bank for more than an hour. As if missing her morning routine wasn't bad enough, his hangover from the previous day was still lingering.

Fuck, he thought, climbing out of bed and making his way to the bathroom. *I must be getting old.*

Still, he had nearly a whole day in front of him, before he had to clock in at the bar, and could spend the time painting. He'd won awards in high school for his work and had dreamed of moving to New York City and taking the art world by storm. His teachers had told him he was destined for greatness, and he'd believed them.

What an idiot, he thought.

Jenny kept telling him not to give up. She loved his art. She believed in him. These days, he painted for her more than for himself, yet he still dreamed of somehow striking it rich through his art. Of giving Jenny the kind of life she deserved.

He would do anything for her. He would give up anything.

Jenny knew the old dude was looking at her ass.

He came down to the gym almost every day but barely worked out. Jenny suspected it was just a ploy so he could watch her while she guided his stretches and half-baked attempts at weight training. Still, the guy was a senior vice president in Mergers and Acquisitions, so if he got his rocks off by checking out her chest and backside for a few minutes each morning, so be it. So long as he kept his wrinkled old hands to himself and her modest check cleared each week.

After the perv finished his session and hobbled off to the locker room, Jenny made her way to the front desk, where her manager, Sean, was typing away at the computer. A short redhead, he was seriously jacked for his size, and was generally nice, though sometimes he acted as if he were saving lives, not catering to a bunch of entitled 1 percenters.

"Hi, Sean," she said, forcing a smile. He was constantly tell-ing her to smile. "I'm done with—"

"One sec," he mumbled, fingers blazing over the keyboard, updating his client database. Sean loved his database and labored over it for hours every day. Jenny kept the smile plastered on her face while attempting not to stare at the prominent, mildly disgusting veins that traversed his forearms.

"Ooooo-kay . . . what's up, Jennifer?" he said, sounding distracted. He glanced at her for only a second before looking back at the computer.

Since Jenny's grandfather had died, Sean was the only person who called her Jennifer, and she hated it. But he was her boss, so, much like the ogling banker, he got a pass.

"I'm done a little early with Mr. Schrum. Is there anything you want me to do, or should I go on break?"

"Let's see . . . Yeah, if you could mop the women's locker room, that would be super-helpful. Apparently, Mrs. Griffin had a little accident in there. At least that's what I'm told. I don't even wanna know!"

He laughed at his own joke without looking up, and Jenny laughed along through clenched teeth. It wasn't her job to clean anything—the building had custodians for that kind of thing—but she was in a good mood, so she let it go. After all, how bad a mess could it be?

Tom's art studio sucked.

In fact, calling it an "art studio" wasn't even close to accurate. Every once in a while, he'd retrieve a stack of newspapers from their building's garbage/recycling area, spread them on the floor of the apartment's tiny kitchenette, then set up his easel and stare at a blank canvas, waiting for inspiration. Technically, there was more space in the dining room or the living room or possibly even the tiny bedroom, but Tom liked how the light filtered in through the small window above the sink. It faced an adjoining apartment building, but the reflection of the sun against their neighbor's always-shaded window was often dizzyingly beautiful and inspiring.

Today? Not so much.

Tom's head still throbbed from Saturday's drinking. He held the paintbrush in his slightly trembling hand but couldn't figure out where to start, or even which color he wanted to start with. Honestly, he just wanted to go back to sleep. But if Jenny came home and found him in bed, he knew she'd be silently disappointed in him. Hell, he'd be disappointed in himself.

Maybe if he cracked a beer . . .

The blaring of his cell phone made him jump and drop the paintbrush onto the newspaper-covered floor. He laughed at himself, surprised at how on edge he was, then muttered, "Fuck . . ." The phone was on the couch, where he'd zoned out for an hour or so after dragging his ass out of bed. He caught the call on the last ring.

"What's up, Kev?" he said after a glance at the screen. He headed for the living room window, which led to the fire escape and a much-needed cigarette.

Kevin Jenkins was Tom's best friend, had been since they met in elementary school back in their tiny Pennsylvania town. They'd stayed in touch after high school graduation, no matter how much distance separated them, but these days, even living in the same city, they didn't hang out or talk as much as they used to. Kevin's bullshit corporate sales job, the kind of work they both used to mock, kept him far too busy, especially after a recent promotion.

"I'm surprised you're awake," Kevin said, the slight echo indicating that he was on his headset, something Tom also made fun of.

"Of course I'm awake," Tom answered. "Wait, what time is it?"

Kevin laughed but Tom pulled the phone away from his head and looked—11:42 A.M. At least it was still morning.

"When are we hanging out, man?" Kevin asked. Tom could hear the computer keys clicking in the background while they talked, another thing he found annoying about his friend's work habits.

Shit, he thought, *I'm in an awful mood.* He squeezed himself through the open window and sat down on the rusted metal fire escape, feeling the post-rain wind push through his hair. He fished the last cigarette from a crumpled pack, cupped it in one hand, and lit it with his Zippo. He gently tossed the lighter and the empty cigarette pack back through the window, onto the couch.

Four stories below, his fellow New Yorkers milled about, cabbies honking and cursing at each other. The streets glimmered with slowly drying rainwater. He suddenly felt inspired, knew which color he was going to use to begin his painting. Gray was always a good way to start.

"What are you talking about?" Tom said. He inhaled deeply; smoke trickled out of his mouth and nose as he continued, "You can come drink for free at my bar anytime you want. You know that."

"Ahh, fuck that. I wanna go *out*, man. You know, to someplace that's not a dive. No offense. Someplace where I'm not the only black guy and you're not walking away every five minutes and I can talk to real women, not underage NYU students or barflies with three teeth."

Tom laughed and took another deep puff. Kevin had a fair point.

"Okay, fine. I'll talk to Jenny and we'll figure out a date. Or

I'll come alone the next time she makes plans with Victoria. I'd rather hang out with you anyway. I'll text you soon to set it up."

"Yeah yeah yeah, that's what you said a month ago. I *told* you you were gonna get boring when you got married."

"Fuck. You." Tom smiled and tapped the cigarette, watching the ash float off into the wind before dispersing completely. He observed the people below entering and leaving buildings, like insects. The painting was continuing to come together in his mind.

"Ha, okay," Kevin said, the sound of typing increasing. "Well, let me know. And remember, anytime you want a real job, I could always use a new sales associate."

"No way," Tom answered, looking up into the sky and letting the sun temporarily blind him. "Never. Not in a million years."

Jenny choked down the last of her nine-dollar beer, feeling her stomach revolt.

That first drink after a weekend of intense boozing was always the toughest, but she could already feel the lingering hangover starting to recede. Her older sister, Victoria, stared at her with a blank expression. Blank but somehow deeply judgmental. She had barely touched her own drink. Of course.

"Lookin' a little green around the gills there, Jen," Victoria said, smiling. Not a mean smile, Jenny conceded, but sure as hell not a nice one either.

"Ah, you know, the perks of being married to a bartender."

Victoria raised her eyebrows at this remark and sipped daintily at her drink, some fruit-infused concoction that cost almost twice as much as the beer. "Speaking of which, how's his 'art' going?"

Hearing the quotation marks, Jenny bit back the urge to unleash an obscenity-laced retort. She was in no mood to hear her sister trash her husband. "Good, actually. He's probably painting right now. He loves working when the sun comes out right after it rains."

"Mm-hm."

"How's Lakshmi?" Jenny asked quickly, both of them knowing it was a loaded question. Lakshmi, Victoria's younger wife, was always moving from one entrepreneurial idea to the next, with Victoria usually acting as her primary investor. So far, nothing had panned out.

Jenny's older sister squirmed in her expensive business suit. "She's doing amazing, thanks. She has this new diet regimen that she created. It's pretty groundbreaking. I think it would make a fantastic book. She was actually hoping she could talk to you about it."

"Well," Jenny said, cringing inside, "I mean, yeah, I'm a personal trainer, but I don't think I'm any kind of diet expert. Maybe I can—"

Victoria laughed—that loud, bitchy laugh Jenny had hated her whole life. It usually preceded some comment that made her want to cry or punch her sister in the mouth or both.

"Oh, no, honey, not for diet advice. Obviously. In case someone you train at the bank might be interested in investing. You know, to pay for one of those *New York Times*-bestselling ghostwriters or something."

Obviously? Fucking obviously?

Jenny was about to unload on Victoria when their waitress reappeared. *Saved by the bell, sis.*

"Can I get you ladies another round?"

"No, thank you. I think just the ch—" Victoria started.

"I'll take a shot of whiskey and another beer, and then *she'll* take the check," Jenny interrupted.

The waitress clearly got the signal because she backed away without another word. Victoria raised her eyebrows at her sister again.

"How's work?" Jenny said, biting down on each word.

At first, Victoria seemed ready for a standoff, but then she sighed and looked away. Jenny saw the black circles under her eyes, and felt bad. She knew how hard Victoria worked, knew how much she had to fight to be taken seriously at her high-pressure, extremely high-paying marketing job, where most of the other executives were older men. Victoria had overcome a lot of sexism and general disdain to get where she was. She was tough, yes, maybe sometimes downright mean, but she was a strong woman, a great role model for a younger sister, and Jenny respected the hell out of her. Not that she'd readily admit it.

"Oh, you know," her sister said, almost dreamily. "Never enough hours in the day. Or night. Lakshmi says I work too much. That I need to relax more. That we need to take more vacations. Like I have time for any of that. How about you? How's the gym?"

"Oh, you know," echoed Jenny with a grin, and saw Victoria's expression soften. They'd fought constantly growing up, and still did often, but were fundamentally a tight unit, especially when dealing with their aging, increasingly obnoxious parents. "Nothing better than having a ninety-year-old corpse trying to paw your tits with his zombie hands." Jenny held up her arms like the undead and swiped at her sister's chest, and Victoria burst out laughing in a rare moment of pure emotion. Flooded with affection, Jenny laughed, too.

"I needed that," Victoria said.

The waitress returned with the shot and the beer. Jenny pounded the former and chased it with a huge gulp of the latter while her sister shook her head. But there was still a smile on her face.

Jenny walked into her apartment building vestibule, tripping slightly on the uneven floor—she was nowhere near as drunk as she'd been two nights earlier, but certainly wasn't sober. She'd convinced Victoria to stay and have a couple more drinks, then splurged for a cab after hugging her sister goodbye—two things she rarely did. Both felt great.

Approaching the row of small metal mailboxes built into the far wall, she tried to ignore the large cockroach she could see scuttling across the floor out of the corner of her eye. The building was fairly clean, especially for Alphabet City, but the dark, smelly garbage room was directly across from the mailboxes, and you could never really get away from the vermin in New York City. Shortly after she and Tom moved in, they'd heard scratching sounds in the walls and realized they had mice. They'd set out glue traps, and to this day Tom still refused to tell her how he'd disposed of the writhing, still-breathing, terrified rodents. He'd always looked pale and upset afterwards. He hated killing anything.

It was a struggle to maneuver the tiny key into the lock of their mailbox, but Jenny eventually succeeded, opening the metal door with a clang. There was rarely anything good in there—once in a while an envelope from her father, full of news clippings and comic strips from their hometown paper in Upstate New York. Otherwise, all they got were bills and junk mail.

As she riffled through the envelopes, she came upon one that wasn't junk or a bill or a letter from her dad: something from the building's management firm. Probably about renewing their lease, which was expiring soon. She hoped the rent wasn't going up too much. A year earlier, around the time they were shelling out money for their wedding, it had jumped up a hundred dollars a month. Which was doable, but they'd had to cut back on booze and eating out, two of their absolute favorite things.

Leaning against the wall, cradling her purse in the crook of her elbow, Jenny ripped open the envelope and scanned the letter. She cocked her head in confusion and then read it again, more slowly, forcing her eyes to focus through the haze of alcohol.

"No . . . no . . . no . . . ," she repeated as she slid down the wall, landing on her ass, reading the letter for a third time. Finally, she closed her eyes and let out a shaky breath. The letter slipped from her fingers and fell to the floor as her eyes filled with tears.

"Fuck . . . ," she whispered.

The letter from the management company, which Jenny had ripped into shreds, was splayed across their dining room table, as was most of the Chinese food that they'd had delivered, one of those extra expenses they almost never indulged in anymore. Chopsticks jutted out of barely touched white boxes like strange sculptures. Though neither Tom nor Jenny had much of an appetite, they'd polished off a bottle of white wine and were halfway through a second. Tom had rushed home as soon as he closed the bar.

He looked back down at the screen of his crappy laptop, its case covered with stickers for obscure indie rock bands. They'd been looking at real estate websites for at least an hour, with little success.

"We're fucked," he muttered. "Even the shitty parts of Brooklyn have gotten too expensive for us."

"I told you," Jenny said, "we can look at the Br—"

"No way," Tom interrupted, shutting the computer angrily. "I am *not* moving to the Bronx. Or to Queens, for that matter. I'd rather just give up entirely and move back to Pennsylvania. I can work in my cousin's coffee shop, sweeping floors and taking out the garbage, and slowly shrivel up and die."

Jenny knew he was kidding but could still see the look of enraged desperation in his eyes. Tom wasn't always great under pressure, something that continued to surprise her considering how cool and collected he normally was.

"I just don't get it. How can they jack up our rent so much? It's almost tripled."

"It's the end of our lease and this place isn't rent-controlled," Tom answered. "They can do pretty much whatever the hell they want. They're putting up all these new buildings . . . closing all the cool old-school stores . . . more room for fancy fucking wine bars and high-priced coffee shops and lame-ass Wall Street yuppies. It's how they get rid of the undesirables."

He chugged the rest of his wine and refilled his glass. Silence descended on the apartment. It was dark outside and weirdly quiet for Alphabet City. They looked at each other, neither sure what to say, how to proceed.

Jenny sipped her wine, weighing her next words before deciding to blurt them out.

"I can call Victoria."

Tom stared at her for a long moment, unmoving. Jenny felt a ball of panic beginning to form in the pit of her stomach but forced it out of her system, knowing this was their only logical way forward.

"And why would you do that?" he said, barely audible.

"*Tom,*" Jenny said quickly, knowing how much he hated when she used his name like that, "We don't make anywhere near enough for us to get another apartment like this. We got lucky last time and we both know it. And, whether you like it or not, Victoria is very well connected. She must know at least one Realtor who will help us out. If not a bunch of them.

"Trust me, I don't love the idea of going to her, begging for help. It kind of makes my skin crawl. Do you think I want to give her more ammo? I just don't know that we have much choice. Neither of us knows the first thing about real estate, and who knows which of these sites we can even trust.

"We're probably missing a bunch of opportunities. We've only looked for an hour. Who knows how many cheap, great apartments are right under our noses? I think calling Victoria is the best thing we can do."

Tom stared at his wife. She had so much more that she wanted to say, but she held her tongue. She knew how her husband's thought process worked. She had presented her case and now he had to convince himself. A long moment of silence passed.

"Fine," he said finally, looking down at the floor.

Tom and Jenny pulled the rental car up to yet another tiny house in New Jersey.

Chelsea, the unbelievably positive and thoroughly made-up real estate agent whom Victoria had gone to college with, was already there. Standing next to her immaculate white minivan in her bright-blue power suit, she beamed at them with a smile that looked painted onto her face.

"I don't know if I can do this again," Jenny muttered. It had been a long day already. Each house they'd seen was worse than the one before.

"Yeah," Tom agreed. "I mean, that last one was obviously a crack den at some point. Did you see that mattress in the backyard? And some of these neighborhoods . . . I thought Alphabet City was bad."

They both looked at the still-smiling Chelsea, who hadn't moved, and grinned back. The smile standoff lasted for a few moments, then Tom sighed and pushed the car door open, unfolding himself up and out of the rental. Jenny joined him on the sidewalk in the warm June sunlight and growing wind.

Chelsea approached, pushing a strand of bleached platinum hair off her face and trying to tuck it back into her shockingly tight bun.

"So," she said, waving her arm toward the small red house as if she were a game show hostess, "what we have here is a delightful two-bedroom ranch. It's a little small compared to the last few I've shown you, but it has the cutest yard and the taxes are very reasonable. I think you're going to like it a lot!"

Wrinkling her nose in what she probably thought was childlike cuteness, Chelsea sashayed up the walk to the almost nonexistent concrete porch. Jenny looked at Tom, and they locked hands.

"The city was a bust and New Jersey isn't exactly stepping up. Pennsylvania is looking better and better . . . ," he said with the crooked smile she loved.

She laughed and squeezed his fingers, pulling him forward. "Oh, shut up. This one is going to be perfect for us. I can feel it."

The smell of stale cat urine assaulted them even though all the house's windows were cracked open.

"The layout is supremely functional, it has great feng shui," Chelsea was saying. It had taken very little time to walk through all the rooms; the ground floor wasn't all that much bigger than their apartment, and the upstairs was even smaller. "There's a jitney stop a couple of blocks over, and the shuttle drops you off right in back of the train station. Which is terribly convenient!

"Now, let me show you the backyard. It's actually much bigger than it looks at first glance."

"Um . . . Chelsea?" Jenny interrupted.

"Hm, yes, Jenny?"

"Isn't there a . . . bit of a problem here?"

Chelsea stared at her with a blankness that Tom found kind of impressive.

"Problem? No . . . no, not that I can think of . . ."

"The smell, Chelsea," Tom said after a moment of awkward silence. "I think my wife is talking about the fact that this entire house reeks of cat pee. Not exactly the kind of smell that goes away . . . you know . . . ever."

"Oh," Chelsea answered, seemingly shocked by the idea that one of the houses she was showing could be considered somehow less than perfect. "I hadn't noticed."

"Yeah, okay, but we noticed," Tom continued, his bullshit meter going off. "I think—"

"We realize our price range isn't the most competitive," Jenny interrupted, stepping closer to Chelsea, "but the apartments and houses we've seen so far haven't really been . . . our style. I mean, we really appreciate your time—Victoria said you squeezed us in at the last minute. Which is *so* nice of you. But is there anything else you have . . . maybe something affordable but with a bit more . . . personality?"

Chelsea's face went slack and Jenny could see her nostrils flare ever so slightly. Then the Realtor blinked several times, as if she were rebooting, and the mask went back up.

"Personality . . . personality . . . hmm. Actually, now that I think about it, I do know about one house that you might *adore*. It isn't *officially* listed yet, but trust me, it has a *lot* of personality."

Tom's left hand was raised in a futile attempt to block the sunlight from his eyes, the late-day clouds having parted and then vanished during the drive over. Jenny stood next to him in the reverse pose, her right hand shielding her eyes as the two of them stared at the large, 112-year-old house.

"Sorry I'm late!" Chelsea nearly shouted from close behind them, making them both jump. "My husband called, there was some kind of emergency with my youngest. . . . Isn't there always? Apparently, multiple adhesive bandages were required!" She laughed.

Jenny wondered what was so amusing about one of Chelsea's kids getting hurt. A parent's prerogative, she decided.

"*This* house is almost in our price range?" Jenny asked, focusing on the large structure in front of them and shaking her head in disbelief. "It's gorgeous."

The house at 79 Waldrop Street, in Springdale, New Jersey, one of several homes in a rounded cul-de-sac, was a big Victorian with large bay windows, a slate roof, and a huge porch with iron railings and wide front steps. The third floor boasted a single small, stained-glass window. On the porch, a wooden swing rocked gently in the breeze. The yard was overgrown but clearly had a lot of potential.

"Shall we?" Chelsea intoned, smiling at them like a cat staring at a couple of mice. She led them up the steps, unlocked the door, and ushered them inside.

Jenny was sure they were in the wrong house. There was no way they could afford a place like this. On top of that, the place was a mess, practically overflowing with stuff—all of it tacky as hell, in her opinion. A thin layer of dust covered everything.

The entry opened directly into a dining room. An enormous wooden table with lion's-paw feet filled most of the floor; a lighter-colored wooden china cabinet stood along the closest wall. Another wooden china area, this one built into the wall to their left, was closed off by small glass doors. An antique-looking wooden display table squatted in the far corner, covered in random bric-a-brac.

Another doorway across the room and to the left opened into a small bathroom. A doorway directly in front of them led into the kitchen, and a small door with a brass knob stood to the left of that, between the other two doors, oddly placed in the far wall, cut into the painfully bright wallpaper.

"Whoa," Jenny said quietly.

"Is this . . . does someone live here?" Tom asked, confused.

"Not anymore," Chelsea answered, walking around the table and spreading her arms out with a bizarre amount of pride, as if she had decorated this disaster herself. "The house is what we call 'as is.' A friend of a friend of a friend who lives in Europe inherited it like this. I don't know *all* the details but he is *very* eager to get it off his hands, so it's less expensive than it might otherwise be . . . *much* less expensive. On the condition, of course, that whoever buys it will have to deal with all of the stuff left behind."

Jenny and Tom followed Chelsea around the giant wooden table and into a room through yet another doorway directly to the left. This space was clearly intended to be the living room, judging by the matching floral-pattern upholstered couch and love seat, both shrouded in yellowing plastic. An ancient rocking chair sat by itself against the far wall. An awful red-and-black rug covered the floor, and above the furniture hung an ugly, angular chandelier that was too low—it would be hard to walk straight across the room without having to duck, or risk having your eyes gouged out. An old-school stereo system hunkered in the far corner, complete with a turntable, double cassette player, and an eight-track.

"When you consider the . . . extremely cluttered nature of the house, you begin to understand why it's so affordable. The rooms don't have to stay as is, of course. Who wants to walk straight into a dining room from the outside?" Chelsea said with an offended laugh.

"You can make the place your own! How much fun would *that* be!" She lowered her voice slightly. "Of course, the house does need some work, some overall upkeep, another aspect that may have turned off some buyers, though the foundation is more than solid. Are you handy, Tom?"

"We both are, actually," Jenny said, put off by Chelsea's casual sexism, though she wasn't exactly proficient with tools.

"Well, good," Chelsea said with a smile that seemed to be calling Jenny a liar. "This might be perfect for you, then, if you're up for a project. And who knows what kind of cool things you'll find hidden here!"

"Where does that door go?" Tom asked as they walked back into the dining room, pointing to the small one with the brass handle.

"Ah yes," Chelsea responded. "That goes upstairs. I love this little door. These Victorians have all kinds of cute touches. A tiny door! So quaint." She opened it and walked quickly up the carpeted stairs. The carpet was a pretty awful dark pink. Tom half expected the stairs to creak and groan as Chelsea walked up, but her ascent was silent. *Maybe she's right,* he thought, *maybe this house really does have a solid foundation.*

He grabbed Jenny's hand before she went up. "Well?"

"I . . . I kind of frickin' *love* it, Tom."

He laughed and put his arm around his wife, kissing her cheek gently. "Let's see the rest of this haunted house before we jump into the deep end."

"Of course," she whispered as they walked up the steps. "But I know you like it, too. I can see it in your eyes."

Tom didn't answer, but he didn't have to. She was right. He kind of frickin' loved it, too.

The second floor was fairly unremarkable, the three bedrooms and bathroom all large and cluttered, but Tom and Jenny loved the small, winding staircase at the end of the hallway that led to the compact third floor, which had only one room, as the house narrowed. When Chelsea opened the small door, Jenny marveled at the sunlight pulsing in, multicolored, through the stained glass.

Surprisingly, unlike the rest of the house, this small room was empty of furniture. The walls were decorated with a half dozen large, framed black-and-white photographs of desert settings, including two that featured the gaping maw of a dark cave. The photos themselves were a little hard to see, since someone had taken a red marker to the glass, covering each image with illegible scrawls, what looked like crude maps, and somewhat disturbing drawings of monstrous faces.

"Whoa . . . ," Tom muttered, "postmodern."

"This room gets beautiful light, as you can see," Chelsea said cheerily, ignoring the pictures. "Might be nice for an office . . . or a nursery?"

Jenny felt blood immediately rush to her face and could sense Tom tensing next to her. This was a conversation they'd had many times, and it never ended well. Tom was open to the idea of having kids but it was something that made him extremely nervous. He thought his parents had been emotionally abusive, to him and to each other, and he didn't want to make the same mistakes they had. And honestly, Jenny didn't feel ready for kids either, but lately, when she saw cherubic little faces in strollers or a toddler asleep on a parent's shoulder, she'd started feeling those "biological clock" pangs she had always dismissed.

A long moment of uncomfortable silence stretched out until Tom clapped his hands together, a little too loud for the small space.

"So . . . is that it up here?"

"I'm glad you asked!" Chelsea said, her eyes lighting up. She headed toward the far wall, to the right of the window. Jenny looked at Tom quizzically and he shrugged in reply. "Like I said," the real estate agent continued, "these old houses are full of all kinds of cute touches." Tom cringed at her repeated use of the phrase, as though she were reading out of a brochure permanently etched in front of her eyes. "Check this out."

Chelsea pushed her fingers against the wall. Tom noticed the thin, tall, rectangular outline in the wall just as the hidden door swung open.

"Okay, you got me," he admitted, laughing. "That *is* cool."

Jenny and Tom stepped forward and peered down into the darkness of the open doorway as Chelsea moved aside. "A . . . secret staircase?"

"Exactly! I'm thinking a servant used to live up here, back when the house was first constructed."

"What makes you think that?" Jenny asked.

"Come on down and I'll show you," Chelsea said, and whisked past them, walking daintily down the steep and rickety wooden stairs.

"This is pretty sweet," Tom said to Jenny, smiling.

"You always did love the Gothic stuff," she responded, pushing him into the stairwell ahead of her.

As they walked slowly down the stairs, Jenny wondered how many people had used them in the last hundred-plus years and felt goose bumps race across her flesh. Something about this gloomy staircase and the stale smell of the air made her feel light-headed.

Chelsea had already opened the door at the bottom, flooding the space with light from below. She stared up at them with an anticipatory smile on her face, as if she'd sneaked them dessert before dinner.

When Tom reached the bottom, his face contorted in surprise.

"What's down there?" Jenny called out, unable to see past either of them.

The kitchen looked like the 1970s had thrown up in it. Repeatedly.

Polished bronze and white lacquer were everywhere. The

stained wooden cabinets, which Tom and Jenny glanced through, were still full of supplies, including half-full spice containers, plates and bowls, dust-covered glassware, and knives and other utensils. On the far side of the kitchen, Tom saw a well-stocked pantry through an open doorway that was right next to a closed door.

"Wow," Jenny said, taking in the room.

"It's got a lot of personality, that's for sure," Chelsea agreed.

"Where does that go?" Tom asked, pointing at the closed door.

"Ah yes, that's the basement," Chelsea said through her unnaturally white teeth. "A great space, but it needs some work. Maybe a man's touch." Something in her tone drew Tom's attention; she wasn't as ebullient or friendly as she'd been earlier. He noticed how tired she looked and that her smile was starting to really look forced. He felt bad for how unenthusiastic he'd been all day. *Maybe she's not as bad as she seems,* he thought.

"Why don't you and I check out the backyard while Tom looks at the basement?" Chelsea said to Jenny.

"I could use some fresh air," Jenny admitted.

"Sounds good to me," Tom said, absentmindedly pulling an elastic band off his wrist and pulling his hair back into a ponytail. It was warm in the kitchen and he was starting to sweat a little.

As the two women went outside, Tom moved toward the basement, then stopped, noticing a large, somewhat faint stain on the linoleum floor. He'd never seen that particular shade of gray before. Some sort of horrible pasta accident, he thought with a chuckle as he walked over to the closed door.

The metal doorknob was cold and his entire body shivered when he touched it.

Turning the knob, he pushed the door open and was greeted by a dank, moist odor, like upturned earth after a particularly bad storm. Images of his parents' funerals flashed through his mind . . . how they had died so close to each other, how Tom had been forced to go through the process twice in the same year when he was in his early twenties . . . but he forced them away. Spotting a light switch to his left, he flipped it; a dirty, naked bulb sputtered on overhead, accompanied by an intermittent ticking noise that seemed to emanate from the bulb itself. The wooden stairs that led down to a cracked, gray concrete floor were old, worn, and not altogether safe-looking. Tom felt dizzy—a familiar sensation he often experienced when entering a new place, somewhere potentially exciting or terrifying.

He walked down the stairs slowly, the wood creaking and even buckling slightly in places. At the bottom, he found and flicked another light switch. Fluorescent ceiling lights hummed to life, crisscrossing the low-hanging drop ceiling. There were a few scattered windows down here, but, Tom saw, they had been painted over. He stared at the contents of the basement for a few seconds in slack-jawed wonder.

Every inch of the enormous space was packed with stuff . . . boxes, black garbage bags filled to near explosion, stacks of books, sports equipment, what must have been hundreds of gardening tools, bags of seed and dirt, camping equipment, at least a dozen old television sets, and who knew what else.

His eyes started to water from all the dust as he surveyed the space. The piles stretched off into the darkness, a lunatic maze of seemingly infinite proportions. Tom took a deep, panicked breath, as if he'd been drowning and surfaced at the last possible moment, then laughed at himself.

"Fucking hoarders," he said out loud. Jenny would probably love going through all this. She was obsessed with crappy little flea markets and secondhand shops.

He turned to go back upstairs, but a strange noise from the distant shadows stopped him.

"The hell?" he murmured, turning to once again peer into the darkness. After a few seconds, he heard it again. God damn if it didn't sound like breathing. Watery breathing, as if a sick animal were hidden down here.

Plumbing problems? Tom wondered as he cautiously moved toward the sound, wary of the precarious towers of junk. It got darker the farther he walked, as though the basement were somehow absorbing the fluorescent light, but he was able to discern a kind of path through the piles, like someone had walked this route before. Looking ahead, he squinted at something large and shadowy against the far wall. His breath hitched in his throat, his steps faltering.

A person, huge and hunched, stood facing him.

No, that was ridiculous. What would someone be doing down here, waiting in the dark? Fighting the urge to turn and run, Tom reached shaking, sweaty fingers into his beat-up jeans and withdrew his phone, which he immediately dropped. It landed with a hollow thud. Hoping the screen wasn't broken, he bent down to pick it up. A huge millipede-type insect ran out of a nearby pile of junk and skittered across his fingers—Tom flinched, yelled, and fell back onto his ass. Terrified, feeling like an infant, and hating himself for his reaction, he hit the button on the side of the phone and it blazed with light. He held it up, aiming it toward the person or whatever the hell it was in the corner.

The horrifying "person" was actually an old refrigerator. A very old refrigerator. It had probably been white once, but now it was mostly brown and yellow. A rusty metal handle dangled off the door.

"Get a grip," Tom mumbled. At that instant, the light went out and his stomach dropped. He quickly hit the button a second time.

Moving closer to the fridge, he noticed markings on the floor in front of it, scrapes in the concrete and shifted dust. He shook his head, intrigued even though a knot was forming in his gut. *Someone moved this refrigerator back and forth*, he thought, cocking his head as he studied the ground. *A lot.*

Tom shoved the phone back into his pocket, plunging the corner back into darkness, and took hold of the fridge. Slick with sweat, his fingers slipped. He quickly wiped them on his shirt and grabbed the antique appliance again.

It was heavy. Really heavy. He smiled at the challenge, then tightened his grip and pulled with all his strength.

The refrigerator inched forward, then seemed to find its path, swinging to one side as if it were the door to yet another hidden passageway, opening into darkness like a toothless grin.

Panting slightly from the exertion, Tom squinted into the shadows.

Stuck to the wall, previously hidden by the refrigerator, was a dark pulsating mass about the size of a baby.

"Jesus . . ." Tom whispered. It resembled an oversized chrysalis, reminding him of days spent in the woods when he was a kid. Back when he had parents, had a family. But he'd never seen anything quite like this—the size, the color, everything about it seemed somehow *wrong*.

Despite the fear nestling in his stomach, he leaned closer, his eyes having adjusted to the darkness. Black and dark-purple veins covered the object, and he realized that the slow, rhythmic breathing noise he'd heard earlier was coming from the chrysalis. So was a rancid smell, like days-old garbage or the scent of a body after it gave up the ghost. The thing was covered in a thick, shiny mucus that caught what little light reached back here.

Disgusted, Tom looked around for something he could use to get rid of whatever this was, the same way he handled cockroaches or spiders or even mice in their apartment. If they ended up buying this house, he didn't want Jenny to inadvertently come across whatever this thing was. His gaze came to rest on a short-toothed metal rake. The teeth were incredibly sharp looking, making the tool resemble a medieval torture device more than a suburban gardening implement. He picked it up and tapped it against the floor a couple of times, liking that the bars of the rake were stiff, unbending. Strong enough to be used the way he intended. The splintered wooden handle felt comfortable against his palms, reminding him of working in the backyard with his dad when he was a kid. Some of the only good memories he had of the man. Maybe Tom could get used to living in the suburbs again.

Turning back toward the chrysalis, he raised the rake, ready to destroy this bizarre object stuck to the wall. Just before he swung, he paused. Had the "breathing" increased, or was that his imagination? The veins also seemed to be pulsating. Tom stared at it, makeshift weapon still raised. *What* is *this thing?*

He dropped the rake, which clattered onto the floor, and stepped forward. He could feel something intangible radiating off the chrysalis. Blood pounded in his ears, and a wave of excitement swept through him as he reached out. Before he could even question his actions, Tom carefully placed his hand on the dark mass. It was warmer than he expected, soft and spongelike. It pulsed, shrinking away and then expanding back into his grasp, as if frightened and then accepting, pulsating into his palm over and over and over again.

After a long moment, Tom pulled his hand away. Mucus stretched between his fingers and the still-throbbing chrysalis, arcing through the air, connecting them.

He stared at his glistening fingers. They seemed very far away, as if they were falling to the floor while the rest of him stayed in the same place. The entire basement brightened, went black, then lit up again, darkness and light oscillating in a regular rhythm. The chrysalis grew larger, its shape morphing, human hands and faces reaching out toward Tom from beneath its surface, beckoning him closer.

Voices whispered his name. His skin seemed to slough off in the same instant that his blood was absorbed by his bones, which turned to dust. He blew away in a sudden gust of wind, only to re-form in the same spot, the lights above him flickering, his eyes opening and closing even though, he knew, his lids were completely gone. He disintegrated and reappeared once, then multiple times. Time stood still.

Holy fucking shit.

"How was the basement?" Chelsea asked as Tom joined them outside, striding through the long grass.

"And what took you so long?" Jenny added, staring at him.

"It was . . . uhh . . . pretty crazy down there," Tom said, avoiding eye contact with Jenny. He could only imagine what he looked like after what had just happened. Or had it even happened? He wasn't sure. He fought an urge to head back inside and go down those rickety stairs again.

"Like I said, the basement needs a bit of work," Chelsea admitted. "'As is' means 'as is.' But who knows what treasures are down there!"

"Yeah . . . who knows . . . ," he mumbled, feeling Jenny's gaze burning a hole through his face. He fought to keep his composure, mind still spinning. "There's a ton of dust, that's for sure. What have you two been up to?"

Jenny's face softened and she smiled. "I've been grilling Chelsea about Victoria's college days, but I'm not getting much out of her. Something about a sorority sister 'code of silence.'"

"That's right!" the real estate agent chirped. "Just trust me when I tell you that neither of us will ever drink tequila again!"

Jenny looked out at the passing houses while Tom drove them back to the car-rental place. They had taken a train out to New Jersey to see what the commute was like, and were surprised to discover how little time it took.

Tom was almost done with his second consecutive cigarette, blowing the smoke out the slightly open window. He'd been quiet since the backyard.

"So," she said, turning away from her window as the cute little town receded behind them, "what do you think?"

"About what?" he said, eyes fixed on the road. Dark clouds were starting to gather in the sky.

"All the houses. But especially the last one. It's kind of ridiculously big for us, right?"

"Yeah, it's hard to imagine living there," he said, speeding up to make it through a yellow light. "But . . . it's pretty great."

"Right?" Jenny agreed, putting her left hand on Tom's arm. "I mean, it costs a bit more than we were hoping to spend, but for that price, we are getting a major deal. Victoria says she'll lend us as much as we need for the down payment and the first couple of months, and we can pay her back whenever. We'll have to sign some extra paperwork at closing but it'll totally be fine." Tom looked at her, but she pressed on. "I know, it's not optimal. . . . I feel the same way as you do about having to borrow from her . . . but this is an amazing opportunity. We could really grow into it. And Sean was saying we'll all probably get raises soon, membership has been going through the roof."

"You deserve a raise. Putting up with those handsy old pervs."

"Seriously." She laughed, pulling her phone out of her purse. "Awesome. I'll email Chelsea and tell her we're interested in moving forward."

"Nice," Tom said, his voice distant as he concentrated on making a left turn across traffic and into the car-rental place.

"So . . . admit it," Jenny said, tapping an email into her phone, "you totally smoked a joint in the basement."

"What? I did not!" he said, turning to look at her as he pulled into the CUSTOMERS ONLY parking spot in front of the storefront.

"Mmm-hm," she answered. "Then what took you so long? And why are your eyes so bloodshot?"

"I told you, it was crazy down there. Beyond anything you can imagine. And an insane amount of dust. Seriously. It's packed with wall-to-wall stuff. Once we get it cleaned out, though, it'll be amazing. It would make a killer art studio. . . ."

"That's fine with me," Jenny said, gathering up the rental documents. "I would love for you to have a space to really concentrate on your art. And you can finally have the man cave you've always wanted."

It wasn't often that they made love while completely sober.

But as soon as they got back to their apartment that night, exhausted, Tom led Jenny into the bedroom. No dinner, no alcohol, no words. He stripped her out of her clothes slowly and laid her down on the bed. He stared into her eyes for a silent minute as she unbuckled his pants. She couldn't remember ever being as turned on as she was right then. He didn't take off his clothes, just kissed her mouth gently as he entered her. Her senses buzzed with white light and they both came within minutes. He stayed on top of her for a little while and they kissed softly as the wind pushed against their tiny bedroom window.

"I love you," she murmured. "Almost as much as I love that house."

Tom cracked up and fell off his wife, landing next to her, still panting. She laughed, too, and curled up against him, and they both fell asleep.

"I can't believe you're moving to fucking *Jersey,* man."

Kevin shook his head at Tom and raised the half-finished glass of beer to his lips. It was nine o'clock on a Wednesday and they had just finished dinner at a recently opened Italian restaurant that was getting rave reviews, then moved to the bar to continue their conversation.

"Me neither," Tom said. "I always said they'd have to get me out of New York in a coffin. But you should see the house, Kev. It's incredible."

"Yeah, but it's in Jersey." He said the last word slowly, as if it were the name of some newly discovered disease. "You're turning in your New York City badge and becoming a commuter. A fuckin' bridge and tunneler."

"You're just jealous because I get to pay even more taxes now."

Kevin laughed and chugged the rest of his beer. Tom swept the hair out of his eyes and did the same. They signaled the bartender and ordered another round.

"How's Jenny feeling about this whole thing? You guys gonna settle down and have fourteen kids and go apple picking in matching sweaters? Start going to church every week?"

"Ha!" Tom barked as the bartender poured their beers, his pale face lit from underneath by lights on the floor behind the bar. The place was filling up quickly, a line of people waiting for a table stretching out the door, and it was getting loud. Some awful pop music blared in the background. A pack of twenty-something guys in suits pushed in around Kevin and Tom, jockeying for position and trying to catch the bartender's eye. "Not likely. Nothing is gonna change, other than how long it'll take me to get to work. I'll probably still be spending more time in Manhattan than the burbs."

"Suuuuuure," Kevin responded. "Keep telling yourself that."

"You're an asshole," Tom laughed.

"I learned it by watching you!" Kevin said in a high voice, a favorite joke of theirs from childhood, and the two friends cracked up as their beers appeared in front of them.

They toasted, and as his best friend took a long sip, Tom asked, "How are your grandparents doing? I still feel so bad about never mailing them a thank-you note for the wedding present they sent us. It was *way* too expensive!"

"Well, they're still pissed off they weren't invited. It's all they ever talk about."

"Wait, what?" Tom said, concerned. "It was a tiny ceremony. You know that. We barely invited *anyone*. Didn't you—?"

"Relax, relax," Kevin said, holding up his hands. "Totally kidding. You know they love you. They probably love you more than they love me. I mean, you practically lived at our house, growing up, and you never talked back to them like I did."

"True facts," Tom said, sipping at his beer. "How's single life treating you?"

"It was the best of times, it was the worst of times," Kevin muttered. "I mean, don't get me wrong. I'm having fun. A *lot* of fun. But still hoping 'the one' is out there somewhere. I'm getting tired of all the games and whatnot. I don't know. We'll see."

"And work?" Tom asked, raising his voice a bit as the music got even louder.

"Ahh, you know, same shit, different day," Kevin answered. "Bunch of bureaucratic bullshit, mostly. Dealing with a crazy man of a boss. Managing a team of slackers. Kids out of college, stoners, dumb-asses. The cream of the crop. I need better salespeople. I need *you*. You could crush it there, seriously. You would be a natural. I know you're sick of hearing it, but—"

"I'm sick of hearing it," Tom interrupted, shooting his best friend the sly grin that said he was joking but actually wasn't.

Kevin held up his hands in supplication once again. "Okay, okay, I'll stop. For tonight. But eventually I'm gonna wear you down and you're gonna come work for me. Why fight it?"

"You know me," Tom said as he stared at himself in the mirror behind the bar, past the bottles that partially obscured his face, "I love to fight."

———

Tom had an appointment to meet Chelsea and the house inspector out in New Jersey at 9 A.M. on a Friday morning, way earlier than he would have chosen. He'd closed the bar the night before . . . or earlier that morning, to be accurate. He was definitely dragging despite having chugged a giant plastic cup of iced coffee on the train out of the city. It was interesting to see the kinds of people leaving New York during rush hour, a mix of hipsters who had clearly been out all night and older people with luggage.

Jenny had tried but wasn't able to get out of work—a couple of other people were home sick—so Tom said he would handle the inspection on his own. He'd done a fair amount of repair work around his house as a kid. His dad, a businessman and a drunk, wasn't around—or sober—much of the time. As an only child, Tom had taken it upon himself to learn how to handle tools. Fixing things kept the house from falling apart and earned him some attention from his distracted mother, who liked to drink as much as, if not more than, his dad.

Buying this house and moving to New Jersey made him worry that he was replicating his parents' trajectory. It all felt hauntingly familiar.

Despite his exhaustion, Tom pushed these dark thoughts out of his mind and focused on his current task. The house inspector, a burly, hairy guy named Ray Dallesander, was already at the house when he arrived. Chelsea was there, too, on her phone. She waved but kept talking. Tom caught a slight whiff of alcohol on the other man's breath, poorly covered by the clashing scent of extremely minty mouthwash. Ray wore a giant green flannel shirt over paint-splotched jeans and huge, scuffed steel-tipped work boots. He shook Tom's hand vigorously, apparently trying to break all the bones in his fingers.

"Shall we?" Ray said, bad breath wafting out from beneath his graying mustache. In addition to alcohol and mint, Tom could also make out the scent of stale cigars. He fought not to physically recoil from the smell.

"Go ahead without me," Chelsea whispered, placing her hand over the phone for a second. "I'll be right in."

As the two men entered the house, Ray pulled his notebook— the first sheet already covered with chicken-scratch writing—out from under his arm and began to write. The moment he stepped inside, Tom's fingers trembled with excitement as he glanced through the dining room, toward the kitchen and the unseen basement door.

Ray wanted to start at the top of the house and work their way down, frustrating Tom, who desperately wanted to see the chrysalis again.

Up on the third floor, the inspector started by declaring that the secret stairway was stupid; he rolled his eyes as he peered down into the shadows. But he said that the wood felt sturdy enough as he walked up and down the staircase, not that Tom and Jenny would ever really need to use it. Unless Tom needed to sneak down to the kitchen to get some late-night booze, he added with a harsh laugh as he walked out of the room and made his way back down to the second floor.

Ray took his time going through each room and clearly loved the sound of his own voice. When he wasn't pointing out cracks in the wood or holes that might mean termites, the inspector told story after story about drunken shenanigans and mentioned probably a hundred different sports teams and players, about

1 percent of which Tom recognized. Tom's evident and total dis-interest in sports seemed to confuse the older man but did not discourage him; the stories continued, regardless.

Still, the inspector was impressed by the house, concluding that the previous owners had put some money or work or both into it.

As Ray launched into a fresh lament about one of New York's teams (baseball, basketball—Tom wasn't even sure), they reached the kitchen. Tom's stomach twisted when he stepped onto the linoleum.

The inspector glanced at the large gray stain on the floor but apparently decided it wasn't worth mentioning. After pointing out a few minor flaws, nothing Tom couldn't handle, Ray headed for the closed basement door.

"We don't need to go down there," Tom said from across the room, only then realizing that he had backed up against the far counter. "I need to clean it up first. It's a mess."

"Excuse me?" Ray said, bewilderment creasing his face. "The basement is probably the most important place to check. You've got your water heater, the furnace, plumbing that runs to the street . . . the guts of the whole—"

"I said, we're not going down there." Tom's raised voice sounded alien to his own ears. He slid open a drawer behind him, his hands moving almost on their own. His fingers curled around the handle of a knife.

Ray cocked his head, as if amused or sensing danger, but Tom said nothing more, and at last the older man shook his head, sighed, and walked out of the room, making more notes on his pad of paper.

"As long as you sign the paperwork at the end and your check clears, it's no skin off my back," he said. Followed by, "Fucking hippie fag," under his breath.

Tom let go of the knife, hearing it quietly clatter back into the drawer like an echo of a dream. He stared at his hand, tears filling his eyes.

What the hell was that? he thought.

When he lifted his head, the basement door seemed to be pulsating in and out. The sound of breathing rose in the room, soft but insistent. It was a sound that he recognized. And welcomed. The kitchen tunneled into darkness around him.

He took one step in the direction of the basement, his foot throwing off intense sparks of colors when it hit the floor. The high the chrysalis had given him before was reinserting itself into his consciousness but it was a pale reflection of the real thing. He needed to touch it again. Immediately.

Ray's voice boomed out of the other room, invading the darkness and stopping Tom in his tracks. "Let's go! I can't leave you in here, and I need to lock up! Some of us have to, you know, work for a living!"

The kitchen snapped back into focus, brightly sunlit. The breathing sound faded, replaced by birds chirping outside. Disoriented by the sensory assault, Tom tried to slow his own breathing, hearing his pulse race in his ears. The high was receding and his mind grasped for it, but it was no use. It faded away completely.

"I don't have all day!" Ray shouted from the porch, where Chelsea still talked on her phone, jolting Tom into motion.

Leaving the kitchen, he took one last look over his shoulder. The basement door stared back. Unmoving. Implacable.

Patient.

MONTH TWO

The house closing was awkward at best.

There were two lawyers in the room, neither one exactly pleasant. The lawyer for the owner in Europe was a pencil-thin woman in a harsh business suit. Her long gray hair flowed over her shoulders.

Chelsea hadn't been able to make the closing, which had kind of bummed Jenny out. While Tom "hadn't" been smoking a joint in the basement when they first saw the house, she'd spent some time talking to the real estate agent and started to kind of like her, despite the woman's uptight fussiness. She'd gotten the sense that maybe Chelsea didn't love Victoria, or maybe had fought with her during their sorority days, and that was enough for Jenny to reconsider her initial reaction to the woman. It helped that Chelsea's somewhat cold manner had thawed a bit as they chatted.

Jenny had even fantasized about Chelsea inviting them over for dinner once they moved to Jersey, she and Tom rolling their eyes at the insanity of having kids, enjoying a giant meal at a big table. Maybe even striking up a real friendship—her first New Jersey friend. But Chelsea hadn't been able to make it.

So they had to settle for a rude lawyer instead, a man Chelsea apparently worked with a lot, with a big bald head, a too-bushy beard, and a too-loud voice, when he deigned to speak at all. Two mean lawyers on one side of the table, Tom and Jenny on the other. And long stretches of silence as "their" lawyer stabbed his finger at documents, indicating where they should sign.

It doesn't matter, Jenny thought as she signed the last line on the last page. *The house is finally ours. It's* ours.

As they stood in front of the house . . . *their* house . . . Jenny shot Tom a glance from the corner of her eye. With the light streaming through his fingers and striping his face, it was hard to tell what he was feeling. Hell, she was having trouble figuring out how *she* was feeling.

They'd just gotten out of their rental truck, the biggest one they had been able to find after calling almost every place in Lower Manhattan. They had barely managed to fit all their crap into it. Who knew two people could cram so much stuff into a studio apartment?

Kevin, Victoria, and Lakshmi had offered to lend a hand with packing, which was a huge help. Kevin and Victoria always got along like gangbusters, which continually puzzled Tom and Jenny. Back when they were dating, they had joked that her sister and his best friend, two very different people, were probably going to hate each other on sight. But once introductions were made, it was clear that the two of them were destined to be fast friends.

When every last thing had been stuffed into the truck, shoved into the overflowing garbage area, or splayed out on the sidewalk for passersby to pick through, Jenny and Tom had treated their three helpers to soda and pizza in the empty apartment, their voices echoing bizarrely in the skeletal space, an empty insect shell.

"I'm going to miss this place," Lakshmi said as she picked at a slice of pizza. "You guys had some great parties here. Especially those early ones on the roof."

"Before the landlord realized what was going on and put a new alarm up there! Bastard!" Kevin said, laughing.

Even Victoria smiled at the memories. "It's certainly the end of an era," she said, a bittersweet tone in her voice.

"And now these two suckers are descending into the ninth circle of hell," Kevin said. "New Jerrrrrrsey . . . ," he added in a spooky voice, wiggling his fingers and waggling his eyebrows as if he were a kid telling a ghost story around a campfire.

"The most dreaded of states," Victoria added.

"Be nice, you two," Lakshmi admonished.

Kevin and Victoria laughed, but Tom and Jenny were quiet as they barely chewed and sipped, their stomachs sour with nerves, looking around the apartment that had been a part of their lives since before they were even married. Jenny was surprised to see a tear roll down Tom's cheek, though he wiped it away before anyone else could spot it. She fought to suppress her own tears. She never cried in front of her sister if she could help it.

"Well, I, for one, am very excited for you guys," Lakshmi continued. "I think it's really cool and really brave what you're doing. It's not easy to make a big change like this. I'm not sure I would be able to do it without melting into a puddle of anxiety."

"Thanks, Lakshmi," Jenny said quietly. "That means a lot to me. To us." Tom nodded but said nothing.

Kevin opened his mouth, seemingly about to unleash another joke at the couple's expense, but apparently thought better of it, and nodded instead. The four of them finished the rest of the meager meal in silence.

After locking up the apartment one last time and slipping the key under the door, they walked down the four flights of stairs—the only aspect of city living that Jenny wouldn't miss. On the sidewalk, the five of them hugged and made their farewells as if the Deckers were leaving for an Arctic expedition.

Driving away from the city felt like slowly ripping off a bandage, exposing raw skin beneath. They got lost a couple of times, even while using the GPS app on Jenny's phone, but eventually they turned onto the dead end that was Waldrop Street and pulled to a stop in front of their house.

Jenny had forgotten how big it was. Standing there, looking up at it, she wondered if they had made a huge mistake. Pushing the thought out of her mind, she wrapped her fingers into Tom's.

Her husband flinched, then looked down at her and smiled. "Welcome home," he said.

"Here's to this ginormous monster," Jenny said, holding up her paper cup of wine. After unloading the truck all by themselves, returning the vehicle to the rental chain, and getting a ride back to the house from a teenaged employee, they hadn't had the energy to unpack anything, even two wineglasses. And they weren't interested in inspecting and cleaning a couple of glasses from the already-stocked cabinets. At least not yet.

Tom stared at Jenny, gaze tracing her beautiful face, and then tapped his paper cup against hers.

"Can you believe this?" he asked. "The place is ours. It's actually ours."

"Completely surreal," she agreed. "But I'm happy. I'm completely exhausted but happy. You?"

"Yeah. It was weird to leave the city. Kind of felt like we were leaving forever. Which is obviously ridiculous."

"No!" Jenny said, leaning forward. "I felt exactly the same way."

Tom laughed. "We're so dramatic."

"Totally," she said, laughing, too.

"It was nice of them to help us," Tom said. "Especially Victoria. After everything else she's done for us."

"Wow. Was that difficult for you to admit, Tom Decker?"

"Maybe. And I'm sure she'll drive me insane in the very near future when she says something horrible to you or gives me advice I didn't ask for. But as of right now, I am feeling very appreciative of your pushy, generous sister."

"I'll drink to that," she said, proffering her cup again.

Tom tapped it a second time, smiling at his wife. "And yes, absolutely. Here's to our ginormous monster."

Jenny sat on the toilet, staring at the stick in her hand. In the corner of the room, the clothes dryer hummed quietly.

They'd only been in the house for a few days, but it was already starting to feel like home. Sort of. She had expected that to happen eventually, just not this quickly.

But what she was holding in her hand? She had not expected this. Ever. Even when she was a little kid and all the other girls were playing with dolls, she was busy having wipeout contests on her bike with the boys and the other tomboys. Though she'd heard that ticking clock lately, motherhood still wasn't something she had seriously considered.

Her stomach ached with anxiety but she was excited, too. And was that a hint of nausea already, or was she imagining things?

She didn't know how long she'd been sitting there. Five minutes? An hour? Her mind was racing. She was apprehensive about telling Tom. Yes, he was nervous about the idea of having kids but he would be thrilled by this news, right? Once the initial shock wore off.

Then she started to think about how this would affect her job and she felt sick again. Sean wouldn't be able to fire her, legally, but she knew he could be spiteful when his back was against the wall. She'd seen it before, when some of her coworkers' problems had made life inconvenient for him. He sure as hell wouldn't go to bat for her.

Jenny breathed deeply, pushing the dark thoughts away. There was no use worrying about it right now. As she stood up, placing the stick gently on the bathroom sink and pulling up her underwear and pants, she allowed herself a smile, felt the butterflies beginning to emerge in her gut.

This is one of the greatest days of your life, she told herself. *Enjoy it.*

In the kitchen, Tom was busy washing the dishes that had come with the house. They looked clean, but who knew how long they'd been sitting in those dusty cabinets or what the previous owners had done with them. For all he knew, they had tortured and murdered small children and bled their little corpses into the very cups he was rinsing at this exact moment, the fresh warm blood trickling down their trembling chins as they greedily drank—

Whoa, what the fuck?

Where the hell had those thoughts come from? Tom shook his head, clearing his mind of the disturbing imagery, feeling the presence of the basement door behind him. He had somehow forgotten about it in the last couple of weeks, with the frenzy of the house closing and packing and the move, but now the memories of touching the chrysalis came rushing back to him. *Had that all been real?* he wondered dizzily, even as he felt a longing to touch it again, a desire so sudden and deep that it literally hurt.

He fought the powerful urge, lost, and turned to stare at the closed door. Water dripped from his slowly clenching fingers.

Just as he started to head for the basement, Jenny called from the dining room, a mirror of the last time he'd headed toward the basement, in the presence of that slab of meat that called itself Ray.

"Tom! Come here!"

Disappointment flooded every pore of his body, but Jenny sounded weird. He had never heard that exact tone in her voice before, and it released him from the power of the closed wooden door. As he turned away from it, his mind cleared and he wondered why he'd been so intent on going down there in the first place. Even if everything he'd experienced in the basement had truly happened, which he kind of doubted at this point, that *thing* was disgusting and ungodly and he should destroy it as soon as possible, as he had intended to do in the first place.

"Tom!" Jenny called again.

"Coming!" he shouted back, wiping his hands on his pants and pushing the hair out of his eyes as he hurried into the dining room.

Jenny faced him across the giant wooden table, a coy smile spreading across her face as he appeared.

"Are you okay?" he asked. "You scared me, yelling like that."

She didn't say anything, just stood there with that enigmatic grin on her face. Tom felt himself growing frustrated. He was beyond tired, slowly starting to realize how much work this house was really going to be.

"Come on, Jenny, what?"

"I'm late," she finally said.

"You're . . . late? Are you supposed to be somewhere? I thought you had today off. I . . . What do you mean?" He shook his head.

"I'm late," she repeated. "I think I lost track of time, with everything going on, but I realized it yesterday. I stopped by the pharmacy on my way to the train station after work yesterday."

Understanding flirted on the edges of Tom's brain but didn't fully take hold. His mind went to the chrysalis, but he fought to focus on the moment. He got the feeling that something important was happening.

"Jenny . . . honey . . . tell me what's going on. Please."

Slowly, excruciatingly, she pulled her hand up from where it was hidden beneath the table and revealed the small stick. It took Tom a second to understand what he was looking at. His face screwed up in confusion, until a huge grin blossomed, his face turning red. He opened his mouth to speak, but nothing came out, just a series of ragged breaths.

"Congrats . . . *Daddy*," Jenny said. She rushed forward, the pregnancy test clattering to the floor, and wrapped her husband in her arms. They both burst into tears.

Blood ran down Jenny's arm, a thin rivulet making its way to her elbow before dropping to the grass.

"Shit," she muttered, staring at the thorn lodged deep in her finger.

She pulled it from her flesh and dropped it to the ground, then glanced at Tom, who was half hidden inside an unruly bush he was trying to trim into submission. The July sun was beating down, and his skin was slowly turning golden brown, a genetic gift Jenny had always envied. She'd put on layers of sunscreen, but her forearms were already pink. The only good thing about all this sun was that the bridge of freckles across her nose and cheeks had emerged, something Tom loved. She had nice memories of him rubbing his finger across them on sweltering summer nights in their tiny apartment. Which she still found herself missing now and then.

The lawn clearly hadn't been mowed since last summer, if then. In fact, the entire yard, front and back, rosebushes and all, was out of control. The previous owners obviously hadn't cared what their house looked like, inside or out.

Jenny was about to ask Tom if he'd seen a lawn mower in the basement when she noticed movement in the corner of her eye and turned to see a woman in a sundress approaching, accompanied by a little girl in a colorful T-shirt and shorts, maybe four years old. The girl held an aluminum foil–covered paper plate in her hands and could barely suppress a smile. The woman looked vaguely apologetic. Jenny grinned back at the girl and half waved at them with her uninjured hand.

"Hi," she said, feeling the sweat running down the sides of her face and hoping she didn't look too disheveled.

"Hi," the woman replied, stopping in front of the house. "Welcome to the neighborhood. I'm Andrea, and this is—"

"We made you cookies!" the little girl practically screamed, thrusting the plate forward.

"Paige, don't be rude! You haven't even been introduced yet."

The girl's face reddened; clearly embarrassed at being chastised in front of a stranger, she looked at the ground, arms sagging. "I'm Paige," she mumbled angrily.

"Nice to meet you, Paige," Jenny said, noticing that Andrea's face was wrinkling in annoyance and wanting to defuse the situation. "How old are you?"

The girl looked up, her expression brightening. "Six!" she shouted, thrusting the plate at Jenny again.

Six? Jenny thought. *I was way off. Ugh, I don't know* anything *about kids. I need to figure this shit out, and fast.*

"We made you cookies!" Paige said again, somehow getting louder each time she spoke.

"Awesome!" Jenny answered, attempting to match the girl's enthusiasm. "Thanks!" She took the plate from Paige and peeled back the tinfoil, even though she had puked her guts out about an hour ago and had absolutely no appetite. Her morning sickness was already bad and wasn't showing any signs of letting up.

The cookies were mostly charred to blackness, with small brown spots here and there, like a plate of tiny burn victims. "Oh," Jenny said without even meaning to.

"You obviously don't have to eat them," Andrea said, quietly. Her daughter's expectant expression said something very different.

"No, no . . . I want to," Jenny lied. Picking one up with her injured hand, she took a small bite, her teeth struggling to get through the dense cookie. "Mmm . . . ," she reluctantly hummed through a mouth full of ash. But the glee on the girl's face was worth the struggle.

"You're Jenny, right?" Andrea asked. Before she could reply, burnt cookie bits got caught in Jenny's throat and she coughed.

She nodded, but she must have looked confused because Andrea quickly followed up with, "News travels fast on a dead-end street," and a guilty smile.

"Yes," she said when her throat finally cleared, "I'm Jenny Decker, sorry, you caught me off guard. Honestly, this entire move has totally thrown me for a loop. I feel like I was living in Manhattan yesterday."

"No need to apologize!" Andrea said, putting her arm around Paige. "We can be a bit . . . overwhelming. And I totally get it. Frank—my husband—and I moved four times in five years. It was hell. I swear to God that I'm never moving again!"

"Oooh, you said the H-word, Mommy!" Paige shouted, looking happily scandalized.

"Do as I say, not as I do," Andrea said without missing a beat. "Anyway, Jenny, everyone in the neighborhood is so happy that you're here! It's all we've been talking about. It's never fun to have an empty house in a neighborhood, especially after what happened here."

Before Jenny could ask Andrea what she was talking about, Tom came up to them. His long hair was tied back in a ponytail, but wisps had come loose and he was sporting a pretty serious five-o'clock shadow. His T-shirt was wet with sweat, which also made the multiple dark tattoos glisten on his forearms. A pair of gardening shears dangled from a veiny fist.

"Hi!" Paige shouted.

"Paige, *volume*," Andrea reprimanded.

"Hi, I'm Tom Decker," he said, extending a slightly dirty hand.

Their new neighbor seemed to consider it for a second but then shook with the slightest of grimaces. "I'm Andrea Katz. And this is my daughter, Paige."

"Are you a rock star?" the six-year-old said loudly. Tom and Jenny laughed. Andrea looked chagrined.

"Not quite," Tom answered, grabbing a cookie. "Oooh, chocolate chip, my favorite," he said, and gobbled it down, seeming not to notice how it looked or tasted. Paige giggled.

"My dad is a businessman! He makes a lot of money!" the girl said; her mother blanched.

"Annnnnd that's our cue to leave you alone now," Andrea said, grabbing her daughter's arm and pulling her away. "But, welcome! We can't wait to get to know you!"

"Likewise!" Jenny said. Tom grabbed another cookie from the plate and popped it into his mouth as the mother and child crossed the street and vanished into their house on the other side of the cul-de-sac.

"How can you eat those?" Jenny asked quietly after their neighbors' door shut behind them.

"They're not so bad," he answered, pushing a strand of errant hair behind her ear. She did the same to him.

"I don't even know who you are, Mr. Rock Star. . . . ," she said, and snorted with laughter.

He laughed, too, and then looked at her stomach. "How are you feeling?"

"Pretty much like shit. Luckily, the taste of burnt cookie is distracting me from the overwhelming urge to vomit. Yay for me."

He rubbed his finger along the bridge of her nose, across the multitude of freckles there. "Well, you look great."

"Liar," she said, smiling anyway, then took a deep breath and looked around. "The yard is starting to look a little better. Small victories. But the lawn is ca-razy. Did you happen to notice a mower when you were down in the basement?"

Tom's expression went distant. "The . . . basement?" he asked dreamily, his voice breaking slightly. He moved the gardening shears from one hand to the other.

"Yeah, the basement," she repeated, looking at him quizzically. Maybe the awful taste of the cookie was starting to register in his brain. "Was there a lawn mower down there?"

He took another long moment to answer, then said, "I . . . don't know. I'll have to go look."

Inside, Tom drank glass after glass of water but couldn't seem to satiate his thirst. He watched through the window as Jenny continued to work in the yard, and then he walked through the house, room by room. He still couldn't believe it was all his . . . all theirs, he corrected himself.

Without intending to, he ended up on the third floor, in the small room, staring at the pictures and the strange, red scrawl that covered them. He studied them closely, his nose millimeters from the glass. Slowly, he started to understand what he was looking at.

After what felt like hours, he descended the secret stairs into the kitchen. Still inhumanly thirsty, he went to the sink, doing his best to avoid looking at the basement door, even though he was dying to visit the chrysalis again.

Instead, he drank more water, his stomach distending and beginning to ache, but was still thirsty. He knew there was only one way to fix the actual problem but fought the solution with every ounce of strength he had.

His eyes glazed over as he stared unseeing out the window, the hairs on the back of his neck feeling as if they were on fire.

They ate an early dinner on the porch swing, burgers, fries, and ice-cold cans of root beer, and watched as the sun set behind the houses up the street. Tom often worked Saturdays but had the night off for once. With their mismatched schedules, it wasn't often they could enjoy a leisurely dinner like this.

A few kids rode their bikes down the dead end and stopped to stare at the newcomers in silence before whispering to each other, laughing, and pedaling off, disappearing into the growing evening shadows. Tom and Jenny saw a shiny BMW pull into the cavernous garage of the house across the street, the door opening and closing with impeccable timing. Jenny assumed Andrea's husband, Frank, was behind the wheel, but wasn't able to make out the driver's face through the tinted windows.

Later, on the couch, Jenny fell asleep on Tom's shoulder while they watched reruns of an old sitcom on his laptop.

After the third episode ended, Tom looked at the time and was surprised to see that it was only nine o'clock. Jenny was snoring quietly. He carefully wriggled out from underneath his sleeping wife and propped a couch pillow under her head, then closed the laptop and placed it on the floor. Jenny mumbled something in her sleep and turned over to face the back of the couch. He pulled a blanket, the first one they'd ever bought as a couple, over her.

Tom knew his wife. She was knocked out, wouldn't wake up until morning. He, on the other hand, felt wide awake.

It was Saturday night, the weather was gorgeous, and he'd been meaning to check out what their new town had to offer after dark. Besides, he was dying for a smoke and figured the walk would be the perfect opportunity to indulge without polluting Jenny's lungs.

A few minutes later, Tom walked out into the night, letting the air and the darkness wash over him.

The dive bar was a hell of a lot rowdier than he'd expected. He had assumed that suburban bars would be like the ones he'd seen on TV and in movies . . . totally dead, even on a Saturday, with lame music and a handful of vaguely pissed-off locals, all male and a million years old.

But Nick's Bar & Grill was booming with classic rock and pulsing with adults of all ages. Tom shouldered his way to the bar and tried to catch the eye of one of the two bartenders, who were valiantly attempting to keep up with the frenzied crowd. Eventually, an old dude with a big white beard, long gray hair pulled back into a ponytail, and a leather biker jacket worn without any apparent irony cocked an eyebrow at him.

"Bourbon rocks!" Tom shouted over the din.

The man nodded and turned away to fill the order. The other bartender, a younger woman with short-cropped hair dyed green, gave Tom a surprised look, as if she'd seen a ghost, then quickly turned away.

The old bartender returned and placed a glass with a generous pour in front of Tom. "Passing through?" the man asked, sizing Tom up with his dark eyes.

"No, just moved in. Only been a Jerseyite for about a week or so."

"My condolences," the man said, nodding as if they shared a secret. "First one's on the house. That's how we get you hooked."

"Thanks, man," Tom said, and downed the drink in a single, long gulp, then fished a few dollars from his wallet and threw them down. He'd been a bartender long enough to know that you always tipped, even when the drinks were free. "How'd you know?"

The man walked away and returned with the bottle, filling the glass even higher than he had the first time. Tom noted the generosity of the pour. Here was a man after his own heart. People up and down the bar were trying to get the old dude's attention, but his gaze was locked on Tom.

"How'd I know what?" the bartender asked. "That you were an FNG? Take a look around."

Tom did. At first, he had no idea what he was supposed to be looking at, but it slowly dawned on him. He turned back to the old man and said, "The hair."

"And the tats. And the 'fuck you' look in your eyes. You just moved into Yuppieville, son. Let the osmosis begin!"

Tom laughed and sipped his drink. "No way. I'll never look like them."

By eleven thirty, Tom was the only one left in the place. The men in business suits quietly getting hammered, the couples enjoying date nights, and the groups of wild, drunken moms had all filed out, the streets quieting before going entirely silent. It was eerie how fast suburbia shut down, and how early it happened.

The old man kept the alcohol coming. Tom switched to beer after the first several glasses of bourbon and the bartender waived the charge for every third or fourth drink. Tom hadn't gotten much out of the guy except for his name, Malcolm. The female bartender had ignored him entirely.

Tom had been making regular trips outside to smoke, lighting each cigarette with his beloved Zippo. Each time he came back in, his seat was still empty, waiting for him even when the bar was packed. He wondered vaguely if Malcolm had something to do with that.

As Tom entered the empty bar after his latest smoke, he held up his hand as the old bartender poured him a fresh glass of beer. "Oh man, I appreciate it, but I think I'm done. I can't even see straight."

"Ahh, you can handle one more. I can tell."

Tom said, "Fine. Consider my arm twisted," even as he tried to blink away his dizziness. "But you have to join me. Everyone's gone and you won't get fired for having one. I speak from experience."

"I should hope not," the man said, "considering I own the place."

"Oh shit, you do?" Tom asked. "I figured some dude named Nick owned it. Unless you're lying about your name. Are you lying about your name, 'Malcolm'?" Tom slurred, making air quotes with his fingers.

The bartender laughed and then shouted over his shoulder. "Hannah! Come here!" The younger bartender stopped wiping down the bar, rolled her eyes, and walked over. "This is Tom," Malcolm continued. "Tom, this is Hannah."

She gave him a thin smile, said "Hi," then made her way through a curtain into the back area of the bar.

"Wow," Tom said. "Angry much?"

"Ha!" Malcolm barked, and clapped Tom on the shoulder. "That's what I keep saying! But don't take it personally. She has a chip on her shoulder, and I think you remind her of her brother."

"Oh yeah?"

"He died over in the desert a couple years ago. IED. His name was Nick."

"Wait. Nick? But. . . ."

"Yeah, my son. Nick. Hannah's brother. Don't you feel stupid now, FNG?" Malcolm said with a kind smile on his face.

"I . . . I'm sorry, man, I didn't know," Tom said, swallowing nervously.

"Tom. It's fine. You're a good guy, I can tell. Welcome to New Jersey."

"Thanks, Malcolm. Seriously. I needed this. And . . . wait . . . what the hell is an FNG?"

The bartender loosed another peal of laughter. "Fucking new guy, Tom. Fucking new guy."

Tom Decker stood in front of the closed basement door. It was pitch black outside, the moon completely hidden behind a wall of clouds, and totally silent inside the house. The taste of alcohol and cigarettes lingered in Tom's mouth. Tears streamed down his face.

He placed his hand against the closed door and giggled in agony as waves of heat and cold racked his body. He told himself to walk away, but the drunk voice in his head seemed far off, like a hitchhiker glimpsed in the rearview mirror, streaked in fading red light, then gone forever.

He had been fighting this moment and now was losing the battle. He knew it. But there was nothing he could do. His fingers trailed along the chipped wood, almost sensually, until they reached the doorknob, clenching around it the way a drowning man clings to a floating piece of detritus.

Turning his head, Tom roared vomit across the floor, laughing, tears streaming harder, snot and spittle falling from his chin.

When he was finished, he looked back at the door, which seemed to be growing.

The instant he opened it, he could hear the breathing noise again. Finally. He stepped forward into a darkness even blacker than the night outside, the most complete void he had ever experienced, and closed the door behind himself.

Jenny was trapped in a small room, calling for help, when the limbs of dismembered babies started falling on her from nowhere: arms, legs, an occasional head with torn-out eyes. At first terrifying and then simply overwhelming, they piled up on her. She searched desperately for a way out, but there were no doors or windows in the tiny room. The weight grew heavier and heavier, crushing Jenny facedown against the concrete floor. Little dead fingers found their way into her mouth, cracked nails pulled at her lips, rotting hands muffled her screams. She struggled to draw a breath against the suffocating pressure of the still-falling body parts.

She jerked upright on the couch, awake but confused, covered in sweat and gulping deep, panicked breaths.

Someone was sitting in the rocking chair across from the couch, head hung low, hands hanging off the sides and half-curled into fists, the chair moving back and forth ever so slightly.

Jenny immediately stood up, still disoriented but ready to fight.

The person didn't say anything and Jenny blinked rapidly, the echo of the nightmare still reverberating in her mind. She felt as if she could taste dirty fingers in her mouth and fought not to puke. Her vision cleared.

"Tom?" she whispered, cautiously moving closer. He reeked of booze and cigarettes and God knew what else. He wasn't wearing any shoes, and his feet were dirty. His T-shirt had a long tear along the chest, and his jeans were filthy, too, as if covered with mud. His eyes were black buttons in the darkness.

"What the fuck, Tom?"

He slowly stood up and faced her but seemed to be looking through her, staring at something in the distance, past the gaudy wallpaper behind her.

Jenny grabbed him by the shoulders and shook him roughly, terrified and starting to get pissed off. "Tom!"

He snapped out of it and shook his head, mouth hanging open as if his jaw had come unhinged. "Jenny?" he said, looking dazed.

"What the hell is going on? Are you okay? Are you drunk?"

His whole body sagged as he stumbled forward and sat down unceremoniously on the couch, holding his head in his hands. "Yes . . . I . . . I went out to this bar, Malcolm got me wasted. It's his fault. I . . . threw up in the kitchen but I cleaned it up. I . . . shit."

"You went out? Without me? You left me alone in this giant house? And who the fuck is Malcolm?"

"He offered me a job!" Tom shouted. "He owns the bar, Nick's. I don't have to commute into the city anymore!"

Jenny stood in front of him, arms crossed, fighting the white-hot rage she felt building inside her. "Tom. Listen to me. You need to go drink a huge glass of water and pound, like, forty aspirin. I'm going to bed. We can talk about this tomorrow, when you're . . . you know . . . making sense."

Without another word, she turned and walked away, breathing as slowly and deliberately as possible. It was pointless to start a fight with him now, as much as she wanted to.

———

Tom sat on the couch for several more minutes, or maybe it was hours, the slash of a smile still ripped into his face. He traced lines in the air with trembling fingers, laughing silently, his body in the room but his mind trapped in the basement, boxed in and infinite.

"I am *so* sorry."

Jenny was sitting on the porch swing eating lunch, a sandwich filled with meat, vegetables, and condiments that were individually appetizing but probably shouldn't have been put together between two slices of bread, when Tom shambled out of the house, his face a pale gray shadow.

She didn't respond to his apology right away, just took another bite and chewed methodically. It felt good not to be nauseated in the morning for once. Tom sat down on the porch floor, groaning with the effort. Clouds filled the Sunday sky. He played with his Zippo nervously.

"Seriously. Jen. I'm an idiot. It was early and you were conked out, so I figured I'd walk into town and—"

"Wait," she interrupted, "are you apologizing or are you making excuses?"

"Apologizing," he said quickly, licking his lips, opening and closing the Zippo. Jenny saw him swallow hard, probably trying not to throw up from the strong smell of her sandwich. "I'm sorry. Really."

She let that sit between them while she finished her lunch. Tom fidgeted, the metal lighter opening and closing frenetically.

"Can you put that away, please?" she said, and he nodded, slipping the Zippo into his pocket.

"Sorry," he repeated.

"You said something about a job offer?" Jenny asked, deciding to let the drunkenness of the previous night go for now.

"Yes!" he said, perking up. "Malcolm, this badass old dude who owns that dive bar in town—you're going to love him. Apparently, I look like his dead son and he needs another bartender. His pissed-off daughter is helping out, but their place is pretty new and it's doing really well, so he was just about to throw a HELP WANTED sign in the window. It's perfect. I can quit my job in the city, bartend in town . . . hell, I can walk to my job again. That'll give me more time to work on the house, and start really painting."

"And be a dad."

"Yeah, of course. Be a dad. I know that."

"I'm not sure you do, Tom," Jenny said, measuring her tone carefully. She had been thinking about this conversation all morning, while Tom slept off his bender on the couch. He hadn't even made it to bed, which she wasn't happy about. They had a rule about never sleeping apart, even if they were fighting. She inhaled slowly and looked him in the eyes. His extremely blood-shot eyes.

"It's time for us to grow up," she continued. "*Both* of us. I'm not pissed off about you going out and getting wasted . . . I mean, *I* was pretty hammered the night we first met, and we've been drunk together more times than I can count. But last night? Last night you scared me, and that's never happened before.

"Look . . . I get it. I know you're probably freaking out. We bought this gigantic house. We have a baby on the way. A baby, Tom.

"It's a huge responsibility. I don't think *I've* even processed it yet. But we both have to give up certain things—" Tom opened his mouth to say something, but Jenny held up a hand. "Please . . .

let me finish. I need to get this out. I'm not saying you have to give up your identity. You don't have to give up everything that makes you Tom Decker. I'm just saying that once this kid arrives, and even before that, really . . . starting pretty much right now . . . you can't show up at three in the morning like some kind of zombie.

"What if there's an emergency? What if you need to drive me to the hospital? And it's not only you, it's me, too. I can't have that occasional social cigarette anymore . . . can't drink at all, can't smoke weed for, like, a year and a half. Which is fine. I'm okay with that. Because it's time to grow up a little bit, whether we like it or not."

Tom waited a moment, as if making sure she was finished, then reached over and took her hand, smiled sadly, and said, "I know. I'll change. Last night was a mistake. The idea of being a dad and the move and everything else going on has been really stressful, and I just lost control a bit. I was trying to cut loose and I took it too far. I recognize that. It won't happen again. I promise."

Jenny knew he meant every word, and smiled back at him, a weight lifting from her chest. "I love you, Tom. I love you more than anything . . . except maybe the tiny dot in my stomach. I'm so excited to have a baby with you."

"I love you, too," Tom whispered, then leaned over and kissed her knee. "You're going to be an amazing mom."

"Damn straight," Jenny answered, squeezing his hand and letting go. "Speaking of which, there's a sandwich waiting for you in the kitchen, in some Tupperware on the table . . . if your hangover can handle it. Don't worry, it has about ninety percent fewer ingredients than the one I just inhaled."

Tom laughed and stood up. "Awesome. I'm actually starving."

"Once you've eaten, get your ass back out here. We've got a busy week ahead of us. We have our first doctor appointment, we should probably start looking for a used car, and we need to figure out which room is going to be the nursery. This house needs a ton of work. Plus, you apparently have a new job."

Jenny noticed Tom's eyes glaze over and she waved a hand at him.

"Hey. It's okay. Everything is fine. We're gonna make all of this work. Trust me."

"I lost my job, Tom." Jenny's voice was weak and distant through Tom's old cell phone. It sounded like she was crying, or had been and had tried to stop in order to talk to him. He was mowing the lawn, using the gas-powered lawn mower he'd bought at the home-goods store in the strip mall between their town and the next one. They'd bought a used car a few days earlier, the same day they'd gone to the doctor and seen the first sonogram. They both cried, looking at the ghostly image, tears flowing unabated until the doctor handed them each a box of tissues, and then they all laughed. Tom and Jenny couldn't believe the powerful emotions elicited by looking at a muddy, pixelated blob on a tiny screen.

Dr. Miller—a white-haired and somewhat stooped woman who had probably been through this hundreds, if not thousands, of times before—seemed to be genuinely excited for them. After the appointment, the Deckers sat in their car in the parking lot of the doctor's office for almost twenty minutes, passing the sonogram printout back and forth, marveling at the image of their unborn child. Talking quietly to each other about the future, they decided they wouldn't find out the sex of the baby. They wanted to be surprised when he or she came into the world. When they got home, they put the sonogram on the refrigerator.

Tom wasn't able to bring himself to return to the basement to look for a lawn mower—or for any other reason—and had decided it was probably a good investment to buy a new one anyway, even if their budget was tight. The lawn was big and would require serious work.

Now, listening to his wife fighting tears, Tom shut the machine off immediately, the harsh sound of the motor echoing in his ears.

"What?" he said.

"I got let go," she sobbed, no longer trying to hold back her misery. "We all did, even fucking Sean. They're closing the gym. Apparently, the bank is getting sued by a bunch of Holocaust families . . . something about Nazi gold? . . . so they're cutting all 'extraneous' costs. I'm *extraneous*, Tom!"

"It's okay, Jenny, it's going to be okay. Remember? You told me everything was going to be fine, and you were right. Where are you? I'll drive into the city and come get you. Just tell me—"

"No. I'll be home a little later. Victoria is on her way. I'm at a restaurant near the bank. Fuck! I can't even have a drink!" She took a deep, wavering breath. He could hear her trying to get control. "Fucking assholes. We're fucked, Tom. We don't have a full-time income anymore. And I guess I can get COBRA? But how long does that even last, and how good is the coverage? How are we supposed to pay for everything? How are we supposed to pay for *anything*?"

"We'll figure it out, Jenny," Tom said calmly, though he was feeling sick to his stomach. His mind was racing. He didn't have a college degree, having dropped out after his first year. He didn't have any marketable skills, really. Bartending—could they really pay the mortgage and the doctor bills and raise a family on that?

What had he expected was going to happen when he decided to move to New York City to be an artist?

She was right. They were fucked.

"Everything is going to be okay," he insisted. "We'll figure it out."

They sat at the big wooden table in the dining room, wine and Chinese food spread out between them. The combination was starting to become a bad-news tradition for them. *I never want Chinese again,* Jenny thought as she sipped at a can of seltzer and they went through their expenses. She noticed that Tom hadn't even finished his first glass of wine. She smiled sadly and looked at the papers in front of her.

They had no income whatsoever at this point, though Tom was supposed to start working at Nick's in a few days. He'd resigned from the bar in Alphabet City last week and was replaced within hours, by some struggling actor who needed the extra paycheck. Even with the new job in the offing, Tom had told Jenny, he battled regret as he worked his final shift at the best job he'd ever had, training the younger man, who he thought talked way too much.

Jenny fought her natural instinct to sink into depression. On learning the news, Victoria had outlined an entire plan for her sister, just as she did every time Jenny faced adversity. Her enthusiastic-yet-hard-nosed drill sergeant attitude was both annoying and amazing. Victoria knew people who had friends in the fitness industry and had already started emailing them. She was confident she could find a new gig for her sister in no time.

She also had a plan for Tom. Jenny didn't like it and knew he would hate it, but she realized immediately that Victoria was right.

"I don't know," Tom said, shoving a wonton into his mouth and washing it down with a gulp of wine. "We have a lot of expenses . . . especially the mortgage. And the car insurance isn't helping. Who knew a few fender benders and speeding tickets from back in the day would be such a headache? Not to mention the co-pay for all the doctor appointments and whatever COBRA doesn't cover. Maybe I can ask Malcolm for more hours . . . ?"

"You haven't even started yet," she said. "And even if you worked every night, it still wouldn't be enough. Not even close." Seeing that Tom had gone pale, she sighed. "I'm sorry if that sounds harsh . . . I'm just really stressing out."

"I know, I am, too. But I'm sure you'll find a new job soon . . . there are a million gyms in the city. And I can . . . I don't know . . . maybe I can do some handyman work around town? Maybe Chelsea can refer me to people . . . like she does with that jerk, Ray."

"Tom, who's going to hire a pregnant personal trainer? One of us needs to find a job that pays a full-time wage. And benefits, if possible."

"One of us?" he said.

Jenny hesitated, staring at him. "You," she said, quietly. "*You* need to. Victoria had an idea, and I think it's a good one."

Tom crossed his arms and swallowed, eyes narrowing. "If Victoria has an idea that involves me, there's no way it's a good one."

"Just hear me out, Tom. *Please.*"

He closed his eyes for a moment and then slowly opened them. "Fine. Go ahead. What's the idea?"

Jenny took a deep breath and started talking.

Exhausted, Tom sipped bitter coffee in a small café half a block south of Penn Station, staring through the dirty window that faced Seventh Avenue, barely seeing the people walking by. Men and women in business attire despite the oppressive heat, tourists clogging the sidewalks, guys in matching red shirts trying to talk them onto tour buses, jaywalkers weaving in and out of traffic.

He'd managed maybe four hours of sleep. When he had called Kevin at seven that morning, his best friend agreed to meet him two hours later in Manhattan, no questions asked. Tom could only imagine how rough he'd sounded.

Tom had fought the urge to visit the chrysalis that morning, though he wanted to more than ever. Feeling shaky without it, he'd stood in the kitchen for long minutes, until a glance at the sonogram on the refrigerator broke the spell. He walked out the front door without having gone downstairs, but now he couldn't stop thinking about it. He wondered how big it was, if it missed him.

Kevin was late, but Tom knew how unreliable New York City subways could be, especially during rush hour. Finally, his friend rushed in, dressed in black slacks, a crisp white work shirt, with a half-knotted paisley tie loosely circling his neck and a black suit jacket draped over one arm. Though it was already in the low nineties, with uncomfortable levels of humidity, Kevin looked unfazed by the heat, with not even a hint of sweat on his forehead. In contrast, Tom felt as if he were melting in his jeans and T-shirt. Buying a hot coffee probably hadn't been the smartest idea.

"One sec," Kevin said, and hustled to the counter, returning a minute later with an iced coffee. He took a huge sip of the drink, then sat down, setting the cup on a narrow ledge that ran along the window. "Sorry, needed caffeine immediately. Had a crazy night."

"Oh yeah?" Tom said, attempting to stay calm. He had no interest in talking about the real reason he was here. "Did you find 'the one'?"

"Not quite." Kevin laughed. "In fact, there were these two girls. They actually reminded me of those sisters we knew in high school. The ones with those giant brown eyes? They—"

"Wait, crap, no. Sorry. I'm here for you. Talk to me, Tom. What the hell is going on? You sounded like you were going to start crying on the phone."

"First off, thanks for coming. I know how busy you are," Tom said. Kevin was right—he did feel as though he might burst into tears at any moment. Every nerve in his body told him to run, that he was signing his own death sentence. "Are you sure it's okay that you get to work so late?"

"Okay? Please. I am *beloved* at that place. My boss thinks I am the second coming of the Messiah. I mean, yeah, he's a little troll man who has no soul, but he loves me. So, stop stalling. Tell me what we're doing here. I know it must be important to get you out of bed so early."

Tom tried to get the words out, but they wouldn't come at first. Kevin sat patiently.

"Jenny lost her job," Tom announced quietly, embarrassed, even though no one was paying attention to them.

"Shit!" Kevin almost shouted, then took another long pull of his iced coffee as he processed the information. "Shit," he repeated, more subdued, probably trying to stay calm so Tom wouldn't panic. "Is she okay? Are *you*?"

"I guess. I mean, we're both kind of freaking out. We just bought a house, and a car, and we need a lot of other stuff. And. . . ." Tom shook his head and glanced out the window. He imagined a crowd of people getting mowed down by a car and shook his head again. He didn't understand why such violent images kept appearing in his mind. His hands were shaking and he wanted so badly to touch the chrysalis.

"And what?" Kevin said, still sounding shocked.

Tom worked his jaw but didn't say anything.

"Come on, man, it's me. You can tell me anything."

He knew he shouldn't say it. Jenny had told him not to, and he had promised. But this was Kevin. His best friend. The person he had known the longest in his life, by far.

"She's pregnant," Tom whispered, looking Kevin in the eyes, regretting it immediately even though it was like lifting a huge weight off his shoulders. It was bad luck to tell people this kind of thing before the second trimester, or something like that. Jenny would kill him if she found out.

"She's . . . ? Fucking A! Congrats, man!" Kevin shouted, leaning over and hugging Tom, who couldn't help but smile despite his fear and anxiety. People in the café glanced over, then quickly returned to their own lives.

"Thanks, Kev. Seriously," he said as his friend disengaged, a big, dopey grin on his face. "I wasn't supposed to tell anyone. She's only a few weeks in."

"In the vault, my man, in the fucking *vault*. You know I would never rat you out. And now I know why you sounded so sick this morning!" Kevin said. "And why you wanted to meet up! I appreciate you wanting to tell me in person. I assume this is the part where you beg me to be the godfather," he laughed. "I don't know, I'll have to think about it, my schedule is very busy. But I do accept bribes. In fact—"

"There's something else," Tom interrupted.

"Oh shit. Twins?"

Tom closed his eyes and saw a faint image of the chrysalis outlined against the blood red on the inside of his eyelids, heard the thing's haggard, wet breathing. He wished he were walking down the basement stairs at this exact moment. Instead, he opened his eyes and chugged the rest of his coffee, his stomach churning as if he'd poured acid down his throat.

"I want to come work for you," he choked out.

Tom had never known Kevin to be speechless, not once in their two-decade relationship, but his best friend just sat there, staring, his mouth slightly open, for what felt like a long time.

Then, "Work for me? *Seriously?*"

"Yes, Kev, seriously. I need this . . . *we* need this. Me and Jenny. And the baby. It's time for me to grow up."

Kevin slapped Tom on the back, hard, making him wince. His best friend had a habit of being too rough, something that he had always been bothered by but continued to keep to himself.

"Yes!" Kevin yelled. "Hell yes! My man! We are going to have so much fun. It's gonna be like the old days, when we sold people candy bars we stole from the corner store. Remember how much trouble we used to get into? Remember that time we tried to steal all those dirty magazines? The three packs that were already wrapped in plastic, and my distraction was a complete disaster, and that old dude. . . ."

Tom suddenly felt sick to his stomach; it must have shown on his face because Kevin sobered instantly, putting his hand on his friend's shoulder.

"Tom. Listen to me. This is going to be *great*. Trust me. You can make so much money. The starting salary is really good and you'll have full benefits. You'll be an amazing salesman, I *know* it. You're a little shy at first, but people love you once you open up. They always have. And once the commissions start rolling in? Shit, you'll be making six figures, easy. *Easy*. Okay?"

Tom looked at his friend and faked a smile, but he felt as though the entire city was vanishing around him. Felt like an insect trapped in a dark hole, with dirt closing in, clogging his eyes and nostrils, filling his mouth, burying him alive.

"Okay," he answered from the darkness.

Kevin clapped his hands together, exuberant, staring at Tom. Then the smile on his face faded and he grimaced.

Refocusing on the moment, Tom realized that something was wrong. He started to panic. "What's the matter?"

Kevin stared at him for another moment, looking him up and down, nodding his head as if he were coming to a deep understanding of something profound and disturbing, and convincing himself to accept it.

"There's one problem," Kevin said at last, his expression offering a preemptive apology.

Tom stood in front of one of Springdale's multiple hair salons, his smudged, monstrous reflection staring back through hollow black eyes. The morning's humidity had vanished, transforming the summer day into something close to perfection. It was late afternoon, and the local youth camps had just let out. Sweaty, obnoxious kids were everywhere, their relentless chattering and shrieking hammering at Tom's brain.

He tried to focus, realizing he must look like a mentally disturbed homeless man, with his long greasy hair and tats peeking out from his decade-old indie rock concert T-shirt. He wanted a cigarette, bad, but he'd run out that morning and was afraid to spend any unnecessary money. Their bank account was on the brink of absolute collapse. He absentmindedly played with his Zippo as he stared at the muddy version of himself.

Children eddied around him on the picturesque street as he braced himself for what had to be done. Screwing up his courage, he dropped the lighter into his pocket, and strode forward. As he entered the quaint little storefront, a tinny bell announced his arrival. The three people inside—two hairstylists and a customer, all women who appeared to be in their midforties—stared at him. Tom wasn't sure what to say or do next. He'd never been in a place like this, except once or twice when he'd picked up Jenny before a night on the town.

The stylist not currently working on the customer approached Tom cautiously, the way a child steps toward an unfamiliar animal.

"Umm . . . hi," she said with a forced smile on her face. "Can I help you?"

Tom couldn't bring himself to say the words. He felt as if he were being dismantled, piece by piece. He didn't know if he could take this last step. He wanted to turn around and sprint the half mile home. He wanted the chrysalis. It was the *only* thing he wanted.

"Are you lost? Do you need something?" she said, fingers tightening on the scissors in her hand.

He thought about grabbing them and shoving them into her eye, then shook the image away and smiled back at her. "I . . . need a haircut," he was able to croak out.

"Oh . . . ," she said, a smile appearing on her face. "Of course. I actually just had a cancellation, so this is perfect. Perfect timing. Let me get your information, and then we can get started. My name is Daria."

Tom robotically recited his name and address as she tapped away at the computer. Then she ushered him to an empty chair by the sinks; when he sat, she tied an apron around his neck. The other two women continued their conversation, quietly. Tom was pretty sure they were talking about him but couldn't bring himself to care. He didn't even know who he was at this point. Everything seemed to be slipping away from him.

"I'm going to wash your hair first, and then we can give you a little trim," Daria said as she started washing Tom's hair. "I assume you just want a little off, clean it up a bit? You've got amazing hair."

"No," he answered, in a fog. "Chop it all off. I got a new job. I need to look like a corporate drone."

Daria laughed and patted his head in a motherly fashion. "Aha, understood. Well, congrats. And don't worry, hair grows back. But a new job can open up all kinds of doors. Who knows where it will lead you!"

Tom walked out of the salon a little over an hour later and crossed the street in a daze, making a beeline for Nick's. A car nearly hit him, but its blaring horn and yelling driver were a million miles away. He felt separated from his body, as if he were being carried forward by some unseen force.

Nick's was fairly empty, but that wouldn't last long with happy hour looming. Tom took a seat at the bar, the same one he'd occupied during his first visit. After Malcolm finished serving an older woman at the other end of the bar, taking her loose change tip with a scowl, he walked over.

"How are you doing, sir?" he said, throwing down a coaster. "What can I get . . . *Tom?*"

The two men stared at each other. "Ho-lee shit," Malcolm said, shaking his head slowly back and forth.

Tom's hand unconsciously went up to his newly shorn head as he studied himself in the mirror over the plentiful bottles of booze. Away from the harsh lights of the salon, in the shadows of the bar, the new haircut didn't look quite so ridiculous, but he still barely recognized himself. It didn't help that Daria had insisted on giving him a hot open razor shave, throwing it in for free, thrilled to be a part of Tom's extreme makeover. She even asked to take pictures, the typical before-and-after shots, to put on the salon's social media page, but Tom had declined—a little more forcefully than he'd meant to. If she had been offended, she didn't let on. Tom had given her a big tip. They couldn't afford it, but she had treated him kindly in a moment when he really needed it.

He stared at himself in the bar mirror, unable to look away. Even in the ratty T-shirt, he was beginning to look like a sellout, with his hair meticulously combed and parted and his cheeks and chin gleaming.

"Yeah . . . ," he responded, looking back at the older bartender.

The man's face had gone pale. "I'll . . . I'll be right back," Malcolm said, eyes watery, walking quickly into the back area. A few seconds later, Hannah came out, frowning. When her gaze came to rest on Tom, her mouth fell open and she stared at him without moving or saying a word.

"What?" Tom said.

Her face softened and she walked over. "Sorry," she said. "You just . . . look like . . ."

"I know," he responded. "Your dad told me the first time I was here. I look like your brother."

"Yeah, you do, and he had long hair when he was in high school, but when he left for the army . . . the last time me and my dad ever saw him . . ."

"Oh," Tom said. He could only imagine what it would be like to see someone who looked like a dead sibling. Or to have a sibling in the first place.

Hannah gifted him with a small smile, the first he'd ever seen from her, then grabbed a bottle of whiskey and two shot glasses. She filled both to the brim and slowly slid one over to Tom.

"Yeah . . . oh," she said, lifting her drink. Tom did the same. He and Hannah clinked glasses, then drained them and set them back down on the bar at the same time. The liquor burned as it went down his throat, but it immediately cleared his senses. He wondered if he was being overdramatic. He took a deep breath and looked Hannah in her mascara-laden eyes. As they stared at each other, her smile faded.

"Welcome to the family," she said, and poured another round.

"Thanks," he said as they drank again. He considered the shot glass, rolled it around in his hand, laughed without amusement. "It would be the first time I've had anything resembling an actual family in forever."

"Why's that?" she asked. "Wait. Let me guess. Did you piss them all off?"

"I'm an only child and my parents are dead," he said more seriously than he'd intended.

"Oh," she murmured, looking away, then back at him. "Sorry. I sometimes say stupid shit when I'm uncomfortable. It's not you, it's me. Aren't you glad to finally have an annoying little trans sister in your life?"

"You're . . . ? I had no idea. I'm sorry."

"What the hell are you apologizing for, dumb ass?"

"Sorry. I mean . . . not sorry. Just . . . ignore me. I'm having a really weird day. Month. Year."

"I guess that explains the Dudley Do-Right look you're rocking," she said, grabbing a cloth and wiping down the bar.

"Yeah, how do you think I feel? I got this new job that I don't actually want. Some stupid corporate-sales bullshit. And my wife is pregnant . . ." He realized too late that he was oversharing. "Shit, I'm not supposed to tell anyone that. I don't know why I said that."

"That's . . . Wow, congrats! Hold on."

Hannah stepped away and returned with a small bottle of champagne. The cork made a hollow noise when she popped it. She poured two glasses. "I won't tell anyone, Tom. But seriously, that's great. I mean, I never *ever* want kids and I think they're horrible little monsters, but I'm really happy for you."

Tom laughed and they clinked glasses for a second time. He sipped at the drink, the bubbles going up his nose and making his whole body relax for the first time in as long as he could remember.

"We're all monsters," he said as she threw back her drink in a single gulp.

"Ain't that the truth," she responded, smiling at him.

"What's the big celebration?" Malcolm said as he reappeared from the back. Any trace of his previous emotion was gone, replaced by his usual sardonic smile.

Tom glanced at Hannah, silently imploring her not to spill the beans. She winked at him and said, "Tom got a fancy corporate job!"

"Well, hell, congratulations!" Malcolm said, walking over and shaking Tom's hand. "Pour me a glass of that bubbly."

His daughter complied and Malcolm held up his glass, smiling at Tom. "Here's to new jobs, new haircuts, and tattoos that you can hide from your bosses but which will never go away."

Hannah reached over and lifted her father's shortsleeve, revealing a slightly faded tattoo on his shoulder that read FUCK THE MAN.

Tom laughed. "Now, *that* is pretty amazing."

"I was young, drunk, and on shore leave. I was pissed off at my commanding officer for some reason that I can't remember." Malcolm looked up as a few customers walked through the door, people dressed in suits and dresses. "So, does that mean I'm losing my new employee before he even starts?"

"Um . . . ," Tom said, feeling bad. "Yeah. I think so. I'm really sorry. With a new job, a new house, and . . . uhh . . . everything else, I don't think I can. I mean, if you're really in a pinch, I can probably—"

"Tom. It's fine," Malcolm said, leaning forward. "I'm happy for you. And I'm sure Hannah is, too."

"Hmph," she retorted as she moved farther down the bar to serve the new arrivals. But she threw a smile back at Tom as she did so.

"Seriously, Tom," Malcolm continued, "that's great. I'm happy for you. And for Jenny. You're a good guy. You deserve it. But you better keep coming in here! I get the feeling that we're gonna be great friends."

"Me, too, Malcolm," Tom agreed, nodding. "Me, too."

Jenny couldn't stop laughing.

Tom stood in front of her in the kitchen, embarrassed. Her first reaction to his new look had been shock, and she'd nearly dropped the glass of juice she was holding. After a moment, she burst into hysterics, surprising both of them.

"What the hell, Jenny?" he said, a surprising rage washing over him.

"I'm sorry!" she said, placing the glass on the counter and putting a hand over her mouth. "I don't know why I'm laughing. You actually look amazing!"

"'Actually'? Whatever," he said, and turned around, walking through the dining room and outside to the front porch, violent and bloody imagery bouncing around in his brain. He tried to force it out and mostly succeeded by the time he made it to the porch swing.

"Tom!" Jenny shouted, hurrying after him, no longer laughing. "Wait!"

He was sitting on the swing when she caught up with him, rocking gently, eyes gazing off into the sky.

"I'm sorry, honestly," she said again. "You really do look amazing. I've just never seen you like this. It's so . . . different. I don't know why I laughed. It must be the hormones or something, or the exhaustion of everything that's happening to us. I promise that I wasn't laughing at you. I was . . . in shock."

"It's fine," he said, his eyes focusing on her. "I'm just having a super-shitty day. And I look like an idiot."

"You do not look like an idiot. You look like a super-hot banker guy."

"Not helping."

He could tell from the look on her face that she was trying not to laugh. Catching on to the absurdity of the situation, he allowed a tiny smile to slip onto his unusually clean-shaven face.

"Super-hot rock-star banker guy?" she tried.

"Better," he admitted as she wrapped her hands around his arm.

"Good," she whispered. "I take it the meeting with Kevin went well?"

"Yeah," he said. "I suppose. I have a job now. I'm starting tomorrow. I already let Malcolm know that I can't work for him."

"Was he upset?"

"No. I don't think so. I think he's happy for me. It's weird . . . he already kind of feels like the father my dad never really was for me."

"That's . . . that's good, right?" Jenny asked gently.

"I guess so," he murmured. "I don't know."

"Well, I'm proud of you, Tom. And a new job is always kind of fun. Aren't you at least a little excited?"

Tom didn't answer; he couldn't speak. Thankfully, Jenny knew him well enough to know that he needed silence right then. She sat next to him and leaned into his shoulder.

Together they watched the shadows grow across their neighborhood as night descended on them and on the house that rose above them like some sort of insidious protector, like a giant mausoleum built for two.

At six o'clock the next morning, Tom stood in the kitchen, sweat dripping down his neck and along his back, flesh rippling with goose bumps.

The basement door stood wide open. When he'd gone to bed the night before, later than he should have, that door was closed. Or he thought it had been. Had he visited the chrysalis in the middle of the night and somehow forgotten about it? Had Jenny gone down there and moved the refrigerator and found what was rightfully his? The idea of her touching it filled him with a cold rage. He shook the anger away, looking out the kitchen window over the sink.

Hints of dawn were breaking on the horizon. Already warm, it promised to be a record-breaking kind of day, not a cloud in the sky. Tom was wearing the only suit he owned, the one he broke out for weddings and funerals. He was futilely attempting to tie his one and only necktie, which he had stupidly undone the last time he'd worn it, as he stared at the quiet suburban neighborhood on the other side of the glass, trying not to turn and look at the gaping basement doorway. Straining to hear the wet breathing.

Letting go of the tie, he rotated his body mechanically and stepped toward the basement, wanting to feel the chrysalis against his fingers. *Needing* it.

"Hey, sexy," Jenny intoned behind him.

"Jesus!" he said, starting and turning violently around.

She stood in the kitchen doorway, dressed in one of his T-shirts and a pair of light blue underwear, hair thrown back into a messy ponytail, rubbing one eye with a fist. "Shit, sorry," she said, moving toward him. "Didn't mean to scare you." She threw her arms around him and squeezed, putting her head into the crook of his shoulder. "Were you heading to the basement for something?" she asked, sounding confused.

"What are you doing up?" he responded, smoothing her hair down with trembling fingers.

"Mmm . . . that feels nice." She enjoyed the attention for a few moments, then disengaged, walking over to a nearby cabinet. "Ah, you know, just another lovely early-morning upchuck. And I wanted to see you before you caught the train. Make you some coffee."

"No, that's okay, I don't think I can handle any right now anyway. I feel like I'm gonna upchuck, too."

Jenny abandoned her coffee mission and walked back to Tom, putting her arms around his shoulder and smiling up at him. "You look so good, baby."

"Thanks. But I feel stupid. And I can't figure out this damn tie. I always prided myself on *not* knowing how to do one of these. Like the hipster idiot I am."

"Stop," she said. "Let me." She stepped behind him and tugged down on his shoulders. In response, he crouched slightly. Her arms appeared on either side of his neck and slowly looped the tie into a professional-looking knot. Tom stared into the darkness of the basement, a blackness that seemed to expand and contract as he watched, as if the shadows were coming to life. Coming for him.

"I used to watch my dad do this every morning," Jenny said dreamily. "With three women in the family—me, Victoria, and Mom—Dad's guy stuff was so alien . . . standing up to pee, the smell of his cologne, wearing a tie every day. Victoria and I thought it was cool. We'd sneak around and watch him when he wasn't paying attention. I really loved the way his fingers moved when he was tying his ties—he went so fast, they looked almost blurry.

"I was determined to figure out how he did it and used to practice on myself when I was home sick from school. There . . . ," she said, walking back around Tom and giving the tie a pat. "Were you . . . down in the basement this morning?" she tried again.

"Yeah, I was . . . looking for a briefcase . . . found an old one . . . probably full of spiders . . . ," he said, pulling his gaze away and looking down at the tie, which gently, perfectly hugged his neck. "Wow. Nice work."

"You are going to do great," she whispered emphatically, and kissed him on the mouth.

He kissed her back, trying to close his eyes, trying not to look at the basement doorway.

And failing.

The people who stood on the train platform at seven o'clock in the morning seemed to Tom like an entirely different species altogether. Chatting loudly, most holding iced coffees, they huddled in small groups. It was as if they had appeared in prearranged clusters, a post–high school nightmare come to life. Tom bit down on a yawn as he walked past them, attempting to make his way to the middle of the platform without jostling anyone. Holding the battered, mostly empty briefcase that he had found a day earlier, he felt like a fraud.

He thought about smoking a quick cigarette, but just as he remembered that he was all out, the train showed up and the perfectly placed groups of commuters boarded with well-oiled efficiency. The pinched-faced conductor nodded smugly at the men and joked with the women. Tom was the last one on, barely avoiding the closing door. The conductor smiled nastily at him.

Conversation inside the train car was even louder than on the platform. Tom managed to find an empty seat—a middle one, between two older women. Behind him sat two men in crisp business suits and a woman in a dark dress. They spoke loudly about a drunken night they'd recently had, in tones that Tom recognized from his bartending days as intended to be overheard, and they all laughed after almost every sentence. The guy directly behind Tom was a big, beefy fucker well over six feet tall, his dark hair combed and parted with military precision; his knee was shoved into the seat in front of him, and directly into Tom's back.

As the same conductor made his way along the aisle, Tom realized that he'd forgotten to buy a ticket, which surprised him. He had never forgotten while he was still bartending in the city.

"*Shit*," he whispered loudly. The woman to his right shifted uncomfortably.

The laughter behind him hit a climax as the conductor checked the group's tickets and chatted with them about things and people that all four of them seemed to know. Finally, the man in the uniform and hat stood over Tom and his seatmates. The two older women flashed digital tickets on their phones.

"I . . . uh . . . forgot to get one," Tom said, his voice breaking midsentence.

The man sighed and pulled out an oversized ticket book. "Where you going? Penn?" Tom nodded. The car seemed to have gone silent. "There's a five-dollar surcharge when you buy tickets on the train," the conductor said, violently punching holes in a long green sheet of paper. "That'll be . . . fifteen fifty."

Fifteen dollars. It seemed outrageous. He should probably swallow his pride at some point and just download the train app, or whatever it was. He tended to be a proud luddite, which was starting to feel like a dumb thing to take pride in. Tom swallowed his anger as the trio behind him burst into another obnoxious swell of laughter.

Tom reached into his pocket, his elbow accidentally jutting into the already-annoyed woman next to him, and withdrew his beat-up wallet. It had been a gift from his mother when he graduated high school—the last gift he'd ever received from either of his parents. It was falling apart and Jenny kept offering to buy him a new one, but he couldn't bring himself to part with it.

He flashed an apologetic smile to the woman on his right. Her lips peeled back, revealing black teeth filed to points. Blood began to ooze from her eyes. Tom blinked several times. No, her face was fine, totally normal, though annoyed. He must have been more exhausted than he realized.

"Sir!" the conductor said sharply. The people in the row behind them were still laughing, a horrible sound. How long had Tom been staring at the woman's mouth? *"Fifteen. Fifty,"* the conductor repeated as if talking to a child.

Tom handed over a twenty-dollar bill, the only cash he had on him. There went his lunch. They didn't have much money left at all. After that expensive haircut, all their credit cards were nearly maxed out, and they were still waiting on Jenny's last check from the Swiss bank. The conductor looked at the limp bill, then finished punching the piece of paper and handed it to Tom, along with four singles. He made a big production out of dispensing a pair of quarters from the coin changer attached to his belt. As he walked away, rolling his eyes, the knee shoved even harder into Tom's back.

Tom craned his neck around, giving the tall, muscle-bound asshole the evil eye.

"What?" the man said, matching Tom's hard gaze and raising a single manicured eyebrow. *"What?"* he repeated when Tom didn't answer, leaning forward as a malicious smirk crossed his giant face. Tom quickly turned back around. The people behind him laughed again, the knee digging in even deeper. Making eye contact with an older man across the aisle, Tom made a *Can you believe this guy?* face. The older man averted his eyes without responding, as if embarrassed on Tom's behalf.

Closing his eyes, Tom tried to ignore the seemingly endless, mocking laughter behind him and the growing pain in his back.

In his mind, he found himself in that dark hole again, the one that he had imagined when he first accepted the stupid job that he was now hurtling toward. He tried to claw out of the dirt that surrounded him, but its weight grew heavier, driving him farther and farther into the ground, his insect limbs shuddering uselessly before going completely still.

Jenny stood at the top of the basement stairs, surprised by how little light the overhead bulb threw off. She'd only been down there a couple of times but had never stayed long. The amount of junk was too overwhelming for her even to contemplate, not to mention the spiders and millipedes she saw furiously trying to escape from the light. She'd been fine with the idea of Tom getting at least some of the initial cleaning up out of the way.

But now that she had more free time on her hands, she was excited to poke around down there, see what kind of treasures she might find.

Tom always acted weird when they talked about the basement, and she thought maybe he was afraid to go down there, not that she could blame him. It was creepy, with the bad lighting and the shadowy mountains of stuff. She'd decided today to at least start making her way through the mess. Maybe once she got started, Tom would muster up the courage to pitch in.

Let's do this, she thought, and headed down the steps. As she reached the fifth stair, the wood gave way with a loud crack; her slipper-covered foot crashed through the resulting jagged hole. She fell, hard, feeling the sharp edges of the wood rip into her shin. She struggled to find something to grab on to, hands slapping the concrete wall to her left, trying to stay upright. Blood burst from her rent flesh, spilling onto the stairs and immediately sluicing down to the next step, and the next.

"*Ow!* Fuck!" she yelled, trying to pull her leg free without doing any more damage.

Below her, the basement waited in darkness as her blood dripped down, stair by stair, until it spattered on the dirty gray floor, reflecting Jenny's writhing figure and the dim, inky light from the naked overhead bulb that barely made it past her trapped body.

Kevin's boss, Pete Kroll, was a sweaty bulldog of a man, not an inch over five-six, who sported a buzz cut directly out of an inspirational sports movie. He wore a rumpled suit and a rumpled tie, and sat behind a giant faux-oak desk that was overflowing with papers, files, what must have been hundreds of fast-food and candy-bar wrappers, multiple crushed and leaky cans of diet soda, and several framed photos of him and a woman Tom assumed was his wife, whose hair was as tall as her husband's was short.

Pete stared at Tom for a full minute without saying anything. Tom shifted uneasily in his seat. Kevin, sitting inches away from him in a matching visitor's chair, was tapping playfully on his knees, apparently unconcerned with the silence. Tom wanted to run away, wanted to tear off his suit and race to the nearest bar, where he'd inhale an ice-cold bottle of beer.

"So," Pete said, rubbing his chin with a calloused hand as if he were considering the mysteries of the universe, "Kevin here says the two of you grew up together."

"That's right," Tom answered. "But don't hold that against me."

If the man was amused, he gave no indication of it. Instead, he snorted deeply, filling his mouth with phlegm, then spat into an unseen garbage can behind the desk. At least Tom hoped there was a garbage can back there. The sound of salespeople on phone calls echoed through the closed door behind Tom, its sole window frosted.

"Right. So. The job is simple. You sit out there and you call New York City businesses. Manhattan. All the boroughs. And beyond. Hoboken. Jersey City. Fort fucking Lee. Ask for the office manager. You tell said office manager that we can provide whatever they need. Business cards, toner, pens, letterhead, routers, 3-D printers, a pair of used panties, *whatever* they need. And we can provide it faster and cheaper than anyone else. You will be provided a list of other *A-list* New York City firms who have switched their business to us, a list that will make them come in their pants—as will our prices, our delivery speed, and our customer. Fucking. Service." Tom stared at the man, unsure if he was supposed to speak now. "That's *you*, numb nuts," Pete finished.

"Yes, of . . . of course," Tom stuttered.

Pete looked at Kevin, a dubious expression on his face, and then back at Tom. "Your hometown boyfriend here is one of the most natural salesmen I've ever seen. If you can do half the business he did in his first couple of months, before I promoted him to Executive Ass-Kicker, you and I will get along just fine."

"Tom is gonna fucking crush it," Kevin piped in, stopping his drumbeat and leaning toward his boss. "Dude has charisma oozing out of his pores. He had to beat the ladies away with a stick in high school."

"I don't give a fuck about high school," the man growled, staring Kevin down. "All I care about is whether or not he has a killer instinct." His gaze swiveled toward Tom. "So . . . Decker.

Tell me: Do you?" Tom swallowed, felt Kevin's eyes burning a hole into the side of his face, could practically hear his best friend's silent urging not to fuck this up. Pete leaned even closer, his chest hovering over the messy desk. "Well?"

"Yes," Tom lied. "I have a killer instinct."

Jenny sat at the dining room table, placing a series of adhesive bandages, from an old box she'd found in the bathroom, over the multiple cuts on her leg.

They hurt like hell but weren't too deep, thankfully, despite how much they'd bled at first. She wanted to avoid going to urgent care if possible. Tom was still at work and not answering his cell phone. She had no idea when his benefits started, or if they'd be retroactive if they didn't officially begin today. She didn't feel like taking a trip to the ER even with COBRA. In fact, she had no idea how much the stop-gap insurance covered. She started to panic. What if she had pregnancy complications before Tom's insurance kicked in?

The bandages were covered in blood, and the metallic smell was making her nauseated. Just what she needed.

There was a sudden knock on the front door. Startled, Jenny flinched, streaking her arm with blood. "Shit!" she shouted as the person at the door knocked a second time. *Give me a second!* Jenny thought as she limped painfully over to see who it was and what was so fucking urgent.

Gasping for breath against the pain, she opened the door to find her neighbor Andrea standing there, cradling a bottle of white wine against her stomach. Her daughter, Paige, was nowhere in sight, thankfully. *Some mom you're going to be,* she thought guiltily.

"Hi, Jenny! So sorry to pop in unannounced, but when you get five minutes alone, you have to take full advantage of . . . Oh my God, you're bleeding! Are you hurt?" Andrea charged into the house, setting the bottle of wine on the dining room table and inspecting Jenny's arm with the kind of focused intensity that seemed to be the purview of mothers with young children.

"I'm fine," Jenny said, pulling away slightly, not sure if she was appreciative or overwhelmed by Andrea's ministrations. "It's not my arm . . . I cut my leg walking down to the basement. One of the stairs caved in. The wood must have rotted or something."

Andrea quickly shifted her attention to Jenny's injured leg, prodding gently at the haphazard collection of blood-soaked bandages that were barely hanging on to the skin. "Sit. Sit down," she ordered as she led Jenny back to the table. "Do you want me to drive you to the hospital?"

"No, I'm fine. But thanks," Jenny said. "Tom will be home in a couple of hours. He just started a new job today, and he's super-excited. If it's still bleeding then, he can take me. And honestly, I don't think the cuts are that deep. But thanks again. Seriously."

"Okay . . . if you're sure," Andrea replied, sitting in the chair next to Jenny. "But I brought over a really expensive bottle of wine, and we're going to have a glass of it right now, and it is going to make you feel a lot better, trust me. We can use Tom's new job as an excuse! It's a celebration! We'll even save him a glass. Maybe half a glass." She laughed and winked.

"I . . . I shouldn't . . . ," Jenny said, her hand instinctively going to her stomach.

"Why not?" her neighbor protested. "It's five o'clock some-where. And you have clearly earned it today, my friend. I'll get the glasses, you stay here." Holding the bottle, she walked into the kitchen while Jenny silently wrestled with the idea of drinking wine during her first trimester.

Just a couple of sips, she decided.

"The wineglasses are to the right of the sink," she said. "Up top. The opener is in the drawer below that."

"Got 'em! No need for an opener, though," Andrea replied, returning with two glasses, a beatific smile on her face. "I can usually find whatever I'm looking for in a kitchen on the first try, even if I've never been in the house before. It's like some kind of housewife sixth sense!" She laughed at her own joke as she twisted the top off the bottle of wine. "I know, twist tops seem so junky, but apparently, they're all the rage now. I don't know. As long as it tastes good!"

Andrea poured generously, and the women toasted, the clink reverberating loudly in Jenny's ears, as if the immense guilt she was feeling wanted to be heard over and over and over again.

She took a sip. It was delicious.

"Oh my God, that's so good," she said.

"Right?" Andrea almost finished her glass in a single gulp.

"Tom and I usually only get the cheap stuff. We know next to nothing about wine."

"Me either. But Frank considers himself something of a connoisseur. *Snob* is more like it. He's been collecting bottles since college. Sort of a hobby, I guess you could say. So, our wine cellar is pretty ridiculous. You guys should come over sometime for dinner, and Frank and I can show you.

"Paige would love it if you came, too. I think she has a bit of a crush on Tom. The hair and tattoos and all that. Not many men look like that around here!"

Well, she hasn't seen him lately, Jenny almost said, and then bit down on her cheek, hard. She couldn't believe she'd thought that. What the hell was wrong with her? She liked the way Tom looked now.

"Once you're feeling settled," Andrea continued, "we'll have you over. We can drink a bunch of Frank's obnoxiously expensive wine, the boys can smoke cigars, and I'll catch you up on all the neighborhood gossip."

"Sounds . . . great," Jenny said, distracted. She took another sip. It didn't taste so good anymore.

"So . . . tell me all about yourself. You guys moved from Manhattan, right? It's the natural evolution of things. You guys just skipped a step. Usually it's Manhattan, then Brooklyn, and *then* suburbia."

Jenny smiled. "Yeah, we had this great place in Alphabet City, but they jacked the rent and we couldn't do it anymore. It all happened so fast . . . totally surreal. I never thought I'd have a house this big. I mean, I never thought I'd have a house *at all.*"

"That's funny. I always wanted a big house with lots of kids. I guess I'll have to settle for the big house! I come from a huge family, I'm one of seven, so I was kind of hoping to replicate that in my own life. But Frank has absolutely *no* interest in that. He thinks one kid is too many! How about you, do you come from a big family?"

"No," Jenny said. "Just me and my sister."

"Oh, a sister! That's so great. I have two sisters, and we are connected at the *hip*! Aren't sisters the absolute *best*?"

"Uhh . . . I guess. I mean, Victoria and I don't always get along. We have a . . . complicated relationship. And she's so busy. You know how it goes, high-powered career woman who's also married and belongs to all kinds of charitable organizations. She's got money coming out of her ears."

"Well, that's always nice. Do you at least get along with her husband? That's such a make-or-break thing, isn't it?"

"She's actually a lesbian."

"Oh," Andrea said. "That's . . . nice. Do you get along with her . . . wife?"

"Lakshmi? Yeah, she's great. The total opposite of my sister. Down to earth and really laid back. They're super-happy to-gether. Victoria needed someone to ground her a bit."

"How do your parents feel about . . . you know?"

"Having a gay daughter? Well . . . they're pretty conservative, to put it mildly, so it was a shock to them at first. I remember listening from the other room when she came out to them. She was home from college on winter break and I was still in high school. I was really impressed with how confident she was about it. I don't know if I could have done that, especially with my dad. He's . . . uhh . . . a bit rough around the edges. He and my sister didn't really talk for a while after that.

"But now? I think Victoria and my dad get along better than I do with either of our parents. It doesn't hurt that my sister is so fricking wealthy. My dad forgives almost anything when people are successful. It's some kind of weird litmus test for him. I don't know . . ."

"I hear you. Families are weird. One of my brothers is an ab-solute *mess*. He wants to be a painter. None of us have the heart to tell him that he's no good!"

Andrea laughed, and Jenny shifted uncomfortably.

"Most of his paintings just look like splotches," she continued. "And he's surprised when no one wants to buy them." Andrea took another large sip of wine. "Oh, and speaking of splotches, I noticed you weren't able to get the stain on the kitchen floor out completely. That must be awful. A constant reminder. If you want, I can put you in touch with my cleaning lady. She's to *die* for. I mean, she makes me look like—"

"Wait," Jenny interrupted, putting the glass back down onto the table. "What do you mean? Why is that stain 'awful'? I don't understand. A constant reminder of *what*?"

Andrea stared at her, the color draining from her face.

"You're . . . kind of freaking me out here, Andrea," Jenny said, getting frustrated with this woman she barely knew.

"Sorry! I'm so sorry," the other woman fumbled. "I . . . I assumed. That you knew. About the previous owners. What the wife did. To her husband. Your real estate agent didn't . . . *mention* this to you?"

"I have no idea what you're talking about. Please . . . just tell me."

Andrea took a deep breath, polished off her wine, then poured another glass, practically up to the brim. She sucked down half of it, took one more breath, and talked.

As Jenny listened, the two sips of wine turned to acid in her stomach.

MONTH THREE

The Deckers sat in their car outside Chelsea's large house, rain pounding loudly on the roof. The house was beautiful, the kind you'd expect an experienced real estate agent to own, and it made Jenny hate the woman even more. Chelsea's husband and kids had just left the house, which would make this easier. *Or at least a little less awful,* Jenny thought.

"You ready?" Tom asked, his voice steady.

Jenny didn't answer immediately. It had been over a week since Andrea told her the history of their house, how the previous owner, a seemingly sweet older woman, had hacked her husband to death one night with a carving knife. In their kitchen. Which explained the stain.

After showing a flustered and apologetic Andrea out of the house, Jenny had tried reaching Chelsea, but soon discovered that the woman was out of the country on vacation in Europe and wouldn't be back on the grid until she and her family returned. Furious, Jenny had called Tom, but hung up before he could answer.

It's still his first day, she'd reminded herself. *There's nothing you can do about it now anyway.*

She decided to stay calm and see what she could find out about the killing. The problem was that the story had barely been reported on. There'd been a multi-person shooting in Newark the same day, so the bizarre story of a retired archaeologist who stabbed her doting husband to death was shunted to the middle of the regional paper, sandwiched between the national news and the local high schools' sports scores. Mentioned as a morbid curiosity and then promptly forgotten.

When Tom got home, Jenny let him talk first, let him vent about how much he already hated his job. How terrible the cold calls to random businesses had gone. How much he hated the commute. How unsure he was about this entire new direction in his life. She assured him that it would get better and served him a glass of Andrea's expensive wine. Then Jenny told her husband about the bloody carnage that had occurred one room away.

Tom listened. And then Tom got *pissed.*

He'd agreed that there was nothing they could do until Chelsea got back.

And now, she was back. They'd called multiple times, but she never picked up. If they wanted to talk to her, it seemed, there was only one way. They had to do it in person. She hadn't left them much choice.

It was Saturday, and they hadn't really made a plan, just gotten into the car and driven over. It was dumb luck that the husband and kids had left. Tom admitted to her that he'd been having waking nightmares of getting into a fistfight with the guy.

They watched the house for a few more minutes, screwing up the courage to go knock on the door and confront the woman, when they saw Chelsea appear in one of the windows near the front door. She was laughing and talking on a cell phone that was cradled between her ear and shoulder as she grabbed her purse and an umbrella.

"Let's do this," Jenny said, exiting the car in a rush. Tom nodded, let out a nervous breath, and got out, too, following his wife through the rain and onto the porch. It hadn't been raining when they left their house, and they had neglected to bring coats or umbrellas—so they were instantly soaked, not that either of them cared.

Chelsea opened the front door of her house and stepped onto the porch, still talking animatedly on the phone. Oblivious to the two people approaching, she turned back to lock up, then pivoted again toward the street, coming face-to-face with two very wet and very angry former clients.

"Oh my God!" she shrieked, then said, "Britney, I have to call you right back. No. Everything's fine. Give me two minutes." Ending her call, she flashed Tom and Jenny a smile that might as well have been made out of molded plastic. Her forehead was smooth despite the smile, completely wrinkle-free. "Hi! I'm so sorry I haven't gotten back to you. I was—"

"Cut the shit, Chelsea," Jenny said. "You know exactly why we've been trying to reach you. Everything is *not* fine, and this is going to take a lot more than two minutes."

"My husband is inside, and he has a—"

"Look," Tom interrupted, "we don't want any trouble, but I think you owe us an explanation. At the very least."

Jenny crossed her arms across her chest and stared at the real estate agent.

"I suppose you found out about the . . . incident," Chelsea said.

"Incident?" Jenny shouted, stepping forward, her hands dropping to her sides and balling into fists.

Tom put a gentle but firm arm around his wife's shoulder, stopping her in place. "Yes, Chelsea," he said. "We found out everything. You should have told us when we first saw the house."

"Damn straight, you should have told us," Jenny said, her voice breaking as she struggled to maintain her composure. "You're lucky I haven't called the cops on you."

"I had no legal obligation to reveal anything about that house's unfortunate history," Chelsea retorted, her back straightening as her cool, professional demeanor reasserted itself. "You needed a house, I gave you options. And with about thirty seconds' notice, as a favor to your sister. It's not *my* fault if you two were being overly picky."

"*Overly picky?!*" Jenny shouted, getting loud again.

"Jen," Tom said.

"That's *right*," Chelsea continued. "'Picky' is a *nice* way to put it. Do you think I didn't see you both rolling your eyes at those first houses? I'm sorry that you have *limited* resources, but that is *your* problem, not mine. I showed you houses that were within your limited price range—nothing more, nothing less."

Tom could feel Jenny tensing in his grasp, so he squeezed gently, telling her silently not to cross a line. She didn't relax, but she kept quiet.

"You may not have been legally obligated to tell us anything," Tom said, "but you were morally obligated to mention it."

"That's a matter of opinion," Chelsea sniffed, shifting the purse and umbrella in her hands. "Now, if you don't mind, I'm late for an appointment."

Jenny shook off Tom's arm and stepped closer to Chelsea. She was only an inch or two taller than the woman but seemed to tower over her as she shoved a finger close to the Realtor's concerned eyes. "You're lucky I don't kick your ass," she hissed. "And I wonder if your husband knows about that little gangbang you participated in back in college . . ." Chelsea's face went pale, her ice-cold veneer instantly melting and falling away.

"What? I . . . ," she barely got out.

"That's right. When I told my sister about the fucking *murder* that happened in my fucking *kitchen,* she told me all about your little adventures in college. You just better hope that I'm a nicer person than you are, *Chelsea.*"

With that, Jenny turned and stomped down the porch steps and got into the driver's seat of the car, punching the engine and revving it.

Tom gave the terrified real estate agent a little smile and said, "Have a great day," and then headed out after his wife and into the growing storm.

Jenny stared out the café window, the steam from her decaf tea drifting lazily around her face. She looked sad to Tom, and who could blame her? It had been a difficult couple of months. Their tiny studio apartment in Alphabet City seemed like a million years ago.

"Well, *that* was intense," Tom said. "I don't think I've ever seen you like that before."

"I didn't mean to freak out. I was just hoping to scare her a little bit."

"Well, I think you managed to do that," Tom said, chuckling bitterly. "Gangbang. It's kind of hilarious when you look at her now. I can't imagine her having sex with one dude, let alone a bunch of 'em. But more power to her."

"Ugh. I feel terrible about saying that. Who even cares what she did in college? I lost control," Jenny said, sipping at her tea. They were both still wet from the intense August rainfall that continued to buffet the window next to them, and it was cool in the tiny coffeehouse across the street from Nick's. "It's been so crazy since Andrea told me about the . . . about what happened in the kitchen. A total blur."

"I hear you. Between work and the . . . you know . . . *murder* and trying to get the house fixed up . . . ready for the baby . . . *total* madness."

"I'm sorry if I've been distracted," she said quietly, looking back out the window, her eyes resting on Nick's blinking OPEN neon sign. "I'm so happy about being pregnant . . . but sometimes I wish we could go over there and cut loose. I still haven't even met Malcolm. Or his super-angry daughter."

"She seems to be getting a little less angry toward me," Tom said, rubbing the stubble on his face. He caught his reflection in the mirror. Between his messed-up rain hair, five-o'clock shadow, and damp gray T-shirt, he looked a little bit less like a corporate robot. He took a gulp of coffee and smiled at his mirror image. *At least* some *of me is still me,* he thought.

"Well, then," Jenny said, turning her eyes back to Tom, a wry smile creasing her face, "now I *really* can't wait to meet her."

Tom sighed. "I told you," he said. "She's like the little sister I never had. We'll get over there one of these days. Last time I saw Malcolm, he even said I could work a shift once a week, if I wanted. Or whenever was convenient for me . . . for *us.* Maybe it's something to consider once we get settled into the house a bit more. You know, when we're eighty."

Jenny laughed, and her smile widened. The sound washed over Tom. He loved her laugh.

"It's okay, right?" she said, leaning forward, her face getting serious. Tom realized that she was starting to show—her belly jutting against the low table a little—and another wave of emotion hit him, his eyes welling up unexpectedly. "That a horrible, horrible murder happened in our kitchen? It's okay, right, Tom?"

He took her hands in his, tried to keep the tears from rolling down his cheeks. "Yes. It's better than okay. I'm going to go *medieval* on that stain when we get home. I'm gonna scrub like no man has scrubbed before, and the next time you walk into that kitchen, you won't see it. And pretty soon, you won't even remember it."

"I like the sound of that," she said quietly.

"That house is ours," he whispered. "What happened before we got there is irrelevant. It never happened. The house, and everything in it, is *ours*."

A long black millipede crawled out of Jenny's left nostril and slithered into her mouth. Tom went rigid, letting go of her hands and inhaling a deep, shocked breath.

"Tom?"

What the hell? he thought, his mind flashing to the basement, picturing the chrysalis growing down there, glittering in the dark. Waiting for him.

"Sorry," he said, forcing a laugh. "I . . . got a chill. I don't know why they have the air-conditioning blasting in here when it's pouring outside."

"Right?" she said, taking his hands once more. "Say it again. What you were just saying about the house."

Tom stared at her eyes, trying with every fiber of his being to wipe what he'd seen from his mind. He could feel sweat beading along his forehead even though he was freezing. He knew the millipede hadn't been real, knew his hallucinations were getting worse the more he came into contact with the thing in the basement. But he wanted to touch the chrysalis again as soon as possible. He missed it so fucking much.

"It's ours," he said again. *Mine,* he thought.

The following Saturday found Tom in the basement for the first time in weeks. He had fought against the temptation for as long as he could, counting each day that he managed to stay away. He tried giving himself rewards each night that he avoided going down, like an extra beer. Ultimately, the fight was pointless. He had fought, and he had lost. Again.

He had no idea how long he'd been down there, clinging to the pulsating mass on the wall, the house melting away from him, piece by piece. He fell through an infinite star-scape, memories taking shape all around him, or perhaps future events presented for inspection, or was it all just made up? He had no idea and didn't remotely care.

He stretched his fingers and toes out into the void, realizing he didn't have fingers or toes and that there was no void, at the same time knowing that the void was everything and that he was the void.

When consciousness finally returned, he was lying on the basement floor, laughing softly, drool stretching from his mouth to the dust. He blinked, trying to figure out where he was, who he was, let alone what time it was, what day. He realized that a voice was echoing in the distance, coming closer and closer.

"*Tom?* Are you down there?"

Tom. He was Tom Decker. The voice was that of Jenny, his wife. She sounded annoyed. How long had she been calling for him? She probably wouldn't come down to the basement—she hated the place ever since she cut her leg when that stair broke. *Accidentally* broke, he reminded himself.

"Yeh . . . yeah, be right up," he choked out. With each visit to the chrysalis, he discovered that the physical signs that he'd touched its gelatinous casing, most notably the dilated and bloodshot eyes, lessened. And each time, the high seemed to be getting more intense, more mind-opening, and lasted longer.

He got up, wiping the drool from his face, and cast one last look at the chrysalis. It was definitely growing, its purple-black veins pulsing farther and farther out each day. He pushed the refrigerator back into place and went upstairs.

Jenny was standing near the basement doorway, waiting for him. "Didn't you hear me calling you?"

"I didn't, sorry. Trying to clear out some space for my art studio."

"I just got back and couldn't find you. I got worried."

Got back? he thought. *Where the hell has she been?* He glanced at the clock. It was two o'clock, and he surmised that since she hadn't asked why he wasn't at work, it had to be the weekend.

"It's gorgeous out," she continued. "You should have come with me. Especially since. . . ."

"Since what?" he asked, smiling even as the kitchen walls expanded and contracted around them, in time with his breathing. His skin always felt electric for an hour or so after he touched the chrysalis.

Jenny bit down on her lower lip and let out a nervous sigh. "There's an empty storefront on Preston Street, right up the road from the center of town. It's tiny, but it's super-cute and it's right by one of the public parking lots, so it would get a ton of foot traffic."

"Whoa," he interrupted, his head swimming. "What are you talking about?" He could smell her sweat. It smelled *delicious*. He fought an urge to rush forward and lick her face.

"I want—" She paused, then went on. "—I want to rent the storefront. Open a little studio, a small one, for personal training. Andrea already said she's interested in having me be her personal trainer, and I think I could get a handful of clients pretty easily. The people in this town obviously have a lot of disposable income."

"Yeah. I guess," Tom said. "But speaking of income . . . how would we pay for this? Start-ups cost money."

Jenny closed her mouth, sucking her lips in. She looked nervous. "Victoria offered to help out."

Tom stared at Jenny. He could tell she was trying to figure out how the news was hitting him, on top of everything else going on in their lives. He also wondered how he must look to her after rolling around on the dirty basement floor.

"But we already owe her so much money," he stated flatly.

"I know. I know we do. And that fact makes me incredibly uncomfortable. But this is a dream I didn't even realize I had. She's excited for me. Really excited. And they are *swimming* in money. She clued me in a little bit about their finances. It's pretty crazy, actually. But this would be a *loan*. Between your job and my studio, once it gets going, we can start writing her a check every month. Yes, it'll be another expense, but one that is totally worth it.

"Tom. I know I can do this."

He stared at her with what seemed to be an absolutely blank look on his face, and it was pretty obvious that she couldn't tell if he was thinking it through or figuring out how to say no or simply zoning out. It was no secret that he'd been acting a little strange lately.

"Tom?"

"I think it's a great idea," he said, stepping closer to her.

"You . . . do?"

"Yes," he said. "And I love you."

"I love you, too, Tom," she practically shouted, and kissed him hard on the mouth, trembling with excitement. He kissed her back, their tongues finding each other like two subterranean creatures meeting in a dark tunnel. He shook the image out of his mind and focused on what he was doing.

The intensity of the kiss increased and they lost their balance, Tom slamming into the counter with Jenny still clutched in his arms. She laughed, but he gasped and said, "Sorry . . . the baby . . ."

"It's fine, Tom. I want you. Right now."

They hadn't been intimate since the night Jenny got pregnant. With the stress of everything that had been going on, and the changes in their routines, plus her morning sickness—neither of them had particularly been in the mood.

As they fell to the floor, Jenny shimmied out of her shorts while Tom unzipped the fly of his jeans. He was inside her in a matter of seconds. His senses exploded, his body feeling as if it were merging with hers wherever their skin touched. He fucked her harder.

"Oh my God, *yes!*" she screamed, thrusting up onto him.

As Jenny closed her eyes at the beginning of her orgasm, Tom found his attention riveted by the remnants of the stain on the floor. He'd tried to scrub it away on more than one occasion but it was stubborn. When he touched it, the gray turned red, seeping off the floor and covering his skin, turning his fingers dark crimson. He put them in his mouth and tasted metal, dirt, and something so sweet that it hurt his teeth.

He and Jenny came at the same time, within minutes of that first frenetic kiss. Afterwards, Tom lay on top of her, breathing heavily. In his mind, they were in a forest, holding hands, and then they were in the Arctic, gliding across bone-white ice. He laughed, eyes closed.

"That was amazing," Jenny said.

Tom opened his eyes and looked into hers, trying once again to remember where he actually was. Slowly, it came back to him. "*You're* amazing," he responded. "And I'm really psyched for your studio."

Jenny pushed the hair off his forehead and rubbed her thumb along his stubble. "That means so much to me, Tom," she whispered, smiling. She took a deep breath, and her smile turned sinister. "Since you're handling all my good news so well today, I have one more tidbit for you. . . ."

"Uh-oh," he said, kissing her on the lips, then her cheeks, then forehead. "Sounds ominous." In his mind, they were flying through clouds. His stomach dropped, exhilarated.

"We're hosting our first dinner party next Friday. Victoria and Lakshmi. Kevin, of course. And my parents."

Tom's vision abruptly hyper-focused, and his mind returned fully to the kitchen. He blinked at his wife, fighting off a sense of profound disappointment.

"Your . . . parents?" he said.

"Surprised . . . ?" she responded, pulling him closer, kissing his neck.

Tom pictured Jenny's mother and father, pictured their aging, wrinkled faces, pictured smashing those faces in with a hammer.

Then he willed the images away and focused on the feeling of her lips on his neck.

Focused on the gaping entrance to the basement that stood only a few feet away from him, waiting for his next visit.

Kevin approached his best friend's cubicle, but Tom held up a finger, wordlessly asking for silence, trying to focus on the voice on the other end of the call he was wrapping up. He couldn't believe what he was hearing. Couldn't believe, either, how comfortable he already was wearing this stupid headset. Everyone in the office used one. Tom had tried to fight it on his first day, but his protestations lasted less than an hour.

He also couldn't believe how much he was enjoying being a salesman. At first, he'd hated it, hated the cold calls and the people hanging up on him. But ever since his last visit to the chrysalis, he was getting better at the job; people were listening to him now. He could practically feel his charm oozing through the phone. Especially on days that started with a visit to the basement. The high took him through the better part of the day.

"Yes, that's right, sir," Tom said, his eyes widening in excitement. "We can guarantee those numbers and that delivery date." He paused, listening. "Excellent. I'll email you the contract as soon as I hang up. Yes. Great. No, thank *you*."

Tom hung up and whipped the headset off, throwing it onto his messy desk and smiling broadly at Kevin. "Dude," he said.

"Do not tell me you just got the Corbitt account."

"Dude," Tom responded.

"Do *not* tell me you just got the Corbitt account!"

Tom stood up and whispered, "I just got the Corbitt account."

"Yes!" Kevin said, slapping his best friend on the shoulder before turning to face the two rows of salespeople, a ragtag collection of twentysomethings and middle-aged burnouts. "Did you hear that? My boy closed the motherfucking Corbitt account!"

There was some scattered applause and at least one eye-roll before everyone turned back to their own phones. Kevin shook his head, unsurprised.

"As soon as Kroll gets back from lunch, you're gonna tell him the big news," Kevin continued, "and I'm gonna take full credit for bringing you in. In the meantime, let's get my man a drink!"

"So, you ready for the shit show?"

"You mean talking to Kroll?" Tom responded, biting hungrily into his medium-rare burger, ketchup smearing across his cheek. "Nah, it's nice to finally have some good news for him." He wiped his face with a napkin and took a long sip from the glass of beer in front of him.

"Good news? *Great* news!" Kevin shouted, causing people to look over. The restaurant was only half full, the lunch crowd already starting to disperse. "But I'm not talking about Kroll, you idiot. I'm talking about tonight. The dinner party. Your goddamn in-laws!"

Tom laughed. He studied a french fry before shoving it into his mouth. "Not so much nervous as dreading it," he said, chewing. "Her family is such a pain in the ass. There's her mom's passive-aggressive bullshit, and her dad's aggressive-aggressive bullshit. Not to mention Victoria. For the life of me, I can't figure her out. I mean, she is obviously incredibly successful, and she's smart as hell. But I think she's pretty much hated me from day one."

"Nah . . . ," Kevin said before polishing off his beer. "You're being paranoid. I love Victoria. She tells it like it is."

"I guess."

"Yeah, she's tough, but she's not evil, man. She's just always looking out for her sister, and I'm telling you, I have to respect that. I do the same shit with my brothers. They probably hate me sometimes, but guess who they call when they're in a bind? If you guessed Kevin Jenkins, then you guessed correctly, my friend."

"I know, I know. And she has lent us so much money for the house and now for Jenny's studio. I don't know how we're going to—"

"Wait, Jenny's what?"

"Oh man, I've been so busy with Corbitt that I forgot to tell you. Jenny's going to open a fitness studio. You know, a small thing, catering to housewives and whatnot, but she is *so* excited."

"That is *great*, man! Shit, that is the best. And it makes total sense. She is so good with people. Wow. I can't wait to congratulate her tonight."

"Well, be subtle about it. I don't think she wants her parents to know yet. Especially her dad. If that guy knew how much money we're borrowing from Victoria, he would never let me hear the end of it. Ever. He already thinks I'm a massive loser."

"You *were* a massive loser. But now you're working for me." Kevin laughed.

"Ha ha," Tom deadpanned.

"But seriously, man," Kevin continued, "you should *own* this party tonight. After closing Corbitt? . . . Shit, you're an animal . . . a fucking beast."

"Yeah," Tom said, laughing, taking another bite of under-cooked meat. "That's me. A beast."

———

Tom felt like he was going to vomit.

Apparently, Andrea had "accidentally" told another neighbor about the get-together, who told another, and word of the party at the Murder House spread like wildfire on Waldrop Street.

Jenny broke the news to Tom as soon as he and Kevin arrived. Jenny seemed excited, surprisingly, even though the plans had changed, something she normally found unsettling. She preferred it when things went according to a pre-planned schedule, which was happening practically never lately.

They would still have dinner with Jenny's parents, Victoria and Lakshmi, and Kevin. Andrea, her husband, and the other neighbors would arrive later, after dinner and after the older couple had left for their nearby hotel. Then the real festivities could begin.

Tom dreaded the whole evening. He hated crowds, always had, even back in high school and college, despite his reputation of being good-natured and social. Despite his ability to talk easily to people, it wasn't something he actually enjoyed, and he often found himself in a corner at parties, not knowing what to say to anyone, convinced he was being judged by everyone present, skin crawling with discomfort. Jenny had often questioned his decision to be a bartender considering his disdain for crowds, but Tom felt safe behind the bar, effectively walled off from the horde, in control.

Kevin, on the other hand, was beyond excited. He thrived on big events, especially a room full of strangers. He didn't just have the gift of gab—it was as if he had invented it. He was also a talented cook, and happily began helping Jenny prepare the food while Tom finished cleaning up the house.

Jenny's parents, Russell and Tabetha, arrived with Victoria and Lakshmi, having picked the younger couple up at the nearby train station. Russell looked tan and fit, his salt-and-pepper hair combed and parted perfectly. He took his appearance very seriously. Tabetha wore a dress and a bit too much makeup and seemed genuinely happy to see everyone. Tom said hello awkwardly, giving his mother-in-law a kiss on the cheek and struggling through an awkward handshake with Russell that felt more like a tug-of-war. For Tom's father-in-law, everything was a competition. Everyone marveled at Tom's new look, and even Russell nodded in seeming appreciation.

Kevin hugged everyone, whether they were expecting it or not. Russell's face blanched at the greeting, but he suffered through it.

Eager to impress her judgmental family, Jenny had gone all out on the meal, with Kevin's help. The spread included a glazed ham, mashed potatoes, a huge green salad, string beans with sliced almonds, dinner rolls with garlic butter, and three desserts. Tom had worked hard all week to get the ground floor in shape, as well as the spare bedrooms upstairs, but that also meant he'd been forced to shove a seemingly endless array of objects into his and Jenny's bedroom and many of the closets. He'd even taken some things down into the basement, which barely had any room left to begin with. He told Jenny that he'd been so busy working on the rest of the house, he hadn't had much time to get rid of what was down there. Once things settled down a bit, he'd said, they would have more time to take care of various work around the house. Jenny had laughed at that. She asked him when he expected things to settle down.

But the house, or at least the parts of the house that would be seen by the people who didn't live there, looked great. It was the first time that Tom and Jenny didn't feel embarrassed to have visitors there.

"So, Tom," Russell said as they all took seats at the dining room table, the as-yet untouched food, wine, and candles looking like a still life from another century. "Jen tells us you have a new job. Something in . . . sales, was it?" There was a slight note of contempt behind the word "sales." Russell stared at Tom, waiting for an answer.

"That's right," Tom said as pleasantly as possible. "In fact, I'm working with Kevin now."

"How nice," Tabetha said, pouring herself a huge glass of red wine, which her husband eyed suspiciously. "Working with your best friend must be a real treat."

"It is," Tom confirmed, smiling at his mother-in-law.

"Well, it can be a disaster if you aren't careful," Russell said, piling an obscene amount of food onto his plate. "Remember . . . I owned my own company for thirty years. I've seen people turn on each other, seen it get ugly. Broken contracts, lawsuits, you name it. I hope you two have thought this through very carefully. Yes, sir, it could get very, very ugly . . . ," he finished, pointing a forkful of meat at Tom and Kevin.

"Well, I guess we're lucky, then," Kevin said, flashing his megawatt smile. "Since Tom is *already* so ugly."

Victoria burst out laughing, quickly covering her mouth. Everyone else joined in except Russell, who just shook his head and shoved the oversized piece of flesh into his mouth.

"Your sister told us about your little workout studio!" Tabetha said to her younger daughter. "How exciting!"

Tom noticed Jenny's eyes go wide, then move to Victoria, shooting her sister a withering gaze. Victoria simply shrugged and smiled.

Russell made a sound in the back of his throat. He was always more than happy to openly criticize Tom, but he would usually keep quiet about what he considered his daughters' poor choices. Later, he would bad-mouth them to his wife behind closed doors, who then passed the remarks on to Jenny or Victoria. After that, they would all be angry with each other.

"And how are you paying for all of this?" Russell asked, unable to stay silent, raising an eyebrow at Jenny. "The studio, the new house. There's no way Tom's new job is paying off that fast, and I can't imagine that *gym* gave you much of a severance."

A moment of silence blanketed the room until Victoria said, "I'm helping them out."

"Victoria—" Russell started to say, but his older daughter cut him off.

"Dad. Do *not* start. How I spend my money is none of your business. No one gave you grief when you bought that midlife crisis mobile."

"Hear! Hear!" Tabetha intoned, raising her wineglass in salute.

"Watch yourself, young lady," Russell growled, though he was half-smiling at his more successful daughter. These days, it seemed as though she could get away with anything.

"Besides, Jenny is going to do great," Victoria said, holding up her own wineglass. "I'm really proud of the way she's bounced back after losing her job. Not everyone could do that. To Jenny!"

The sisters often softened toward each other in the presence of their parents, and Tom always loved to see it. Maybe Kevin was right. Maybe he'd been too judgmental regarding Victoria.

"And to Tom!" Kevin interjected, clinking Victoria's glass. "He closed a huge deal today. *Huge!*"

"You did?" Jenny said. "You didn't tell me that!"

"Well," Tom said sheepishly, "things have been so crazy. I . . . I meant to."

"That is so great," Jenny said, staring at her husband, a big smile on her face. "I knew you could do it, honey. I *knew* it."

"Congratulations," Russell said, nodding. "That sounds . . . impressive." It was the first compliment Tom could ever remember receiving from his father-in-law.

"May Tom outsell every sales associate we have," Kevin finished. "Except me, of course!"

The table laughed at Kevin's joke. He winked at Tom, and everyone clinked glasses and drank. Drops of red wine splashed onto the white tablecloth and spread into bizarre shapes. One appeared to Tom like a skull. He didn't like the way it seemed to be looking at him. He realized he was getting shaky, that he wanted the chrysalis. Needed it.

Instead, he rubbed and rubbed at the little crimson skull with his thumb as the dinner guests talked and laughed, trying to alter its shape, to blot it from existence, but no matter how hard he tried, he couldn't get the stain to stop staring at him.

The house was packed.

Word of the party had somehow reached people from all over the neighborhood, including the main street and another dead end that ran parallel to Waldrop, and a couple dozen bored suburbanites had started showing up around ten o'clock and semi-apologetically inviting themselves in, holding up bottles of alcohol as proof of their good intentions.

The rest of the meal with Jenny's family had gone well, and thankfully, Russell and Tabetha didn't outstay their welcome.

Russell said goodbye to Tom in a way he never had before, with something almost resembling grudging respect.

Tom and Jenny planned on announcing the pregnancy to her family at breakfast the next morning—good news somehow often devolved into massive fights with her family, and this way, Russell and Tabetha would have to leave soon after the announcement and head back to Upstate New York. Regardless of his wife's tumultuous relationship with her parents and her sister, Tom still found himself battling jealousy. He sometimes wished he had *any* family left to fight with.

Jenny was in a great mood, welcoming their unexpected guests with enthusiasm. She told Tom to relax when he questioned the notion of a bunch of strangers invading their home. How often did they throw parties like this anymore? Tom would have guessed that she was drunk if he hadn't known better.

It was a good thing Russell and Tabetha had left right after dinner. The suburbanites were ready to get crazy. One of the newly arrived neighbors was apparently a DJ and he'd reconfigured the ancient stereo system in the living room, which was now blasting trance metal at a deafening volume. Tom and Jenny had pulled up the horrible black-and-red rug a few weeks earlier, revealing a beautiful natural wood floor that was currently slick and sticky with spilled beer and wine.

Tom was dying inside. The high of the dinner had faded, and all he could think about was the chrysalis. He felt as if he were falling down an endless black hole, depression setting in like a fever. At one point, he found himself in a corner of the living room, sipping a sweaty bottle of beer, surrounded by shadowy, chattering figures that sounded like insects.

"What the hell are you doing over here, man?" Kevin asked as he approached from nowhere. He was clearly drunk, a dark-haired woman who wore bright red lipstick draped across his shoulders, eyes glowing.

"Hey," Tom said, feeling his gut tighten. He knew his best friend was about to call him out. "I'm just . . . taking it all in."

"Bullshit," Kevin slurred. "I know you. I've known you your whole. Damn. Life. You're standing here, hating yourself, hating every person in here. Except me, of course. No one hates me." The woman on his shoulder laughed and buried her head into his shirt, lipstick getting everywhere. "Tomorrow, when we're nursing massive hangovers, you're gonna wish you'd talked to more people. That you had at least fucking tried. Go ahead. Tell me I'm wrong."

"You're wr—"

"Nope!" Kevin shouted, holding up his hand in Tom's face and laughing. The woman was laughing, too, her teeth stained scarlet. "Stop being a wuss! Go find your wife and have some fun!" he commanded, then turned and stumbled off into the crowd, the dark-haired woman smiling sadly at Tom before following Kevin.

Tom stared after them, then polished off the rest of his beer and headed for the kitchen to get another. If he wasn't allowing himself to visit the chrysalis, he might as well get as drunk as possible. But he'd had a lot to drink already and barely felt it, which only increased his depression and annoyance.

The kitchen was even crazier. People clearly wanted to get a look at the stain, or what was left of it. They gawked as if it were an exhibit in some fucked-up museum; a few people were even trying to take selfies with it in the background. Tom attempted to get to the refrigerator, but every time he took a step, the horde of people would eddy and shove him in the other direction, toward the basement. The door seemed to grow larger than ever as the masses of clothing and flesh, hair and ragged fingernails pushed him closer and closer to it.

At last he was pressed up against the wood. He had tried so hard to avoid it today. But finally, he wrapped his fingers around the doorknob and felt himself relax.

Tom Decker slipped into the basement at 11:43 P.M. No one saw him open or close the door. No one noticed that he was gone for just under twenty minutes. For Tom, though, it felt as if he were absent for much, much longer.

The party was booming.

Jenny wasn't sure what time it was. Though she hadn't had a single alcoholic drink, her adrenaline was pumping and she felt amazing.

The guy shouting into her ear was tall and really good looking, with a sick body underneath his pink collared shirt—sleeves rolled up to his elbows, khaki shorts, and designer flip-flops. She wasn't exactly sure what Hottie McPinkshirt was saying— someone had switched the music over to Top 40 hits, and an impromptu dance party had broken out all over the house—but she gathered that he was recently divorced, lived at the top of the street, near the main drag that fed into their dead end, had a young son whom he saw every other weekend, and his name was Chad Forsythe. Of course it was.

". . . and that's what happens when you invest without doing your due diligence!" Chad said, laughing at a joke she must have missed. She nodded and smiled, slyly checking out his body yet again, and then felt a hand wrap around her wrist.

"Jen!" Victoria shouted, flashing a pleasantly genuine smile.

Jenny could tell that her sister was drunk, but it looked like *Fun Drunk Victoria* had shown up, rather than *Pissed Off at the World Drunk Victoria*.

"What's up. I'm Chad, the neighbor," he said, pushing his chiseled chin forward.

"What's up," Victoria deadpanned back at him. "I'm Victoria. The dyke sister."

The man's mouth fell half-open at the blunt statement. Jenny bit back a laugh, wrapping her arm into her sister's. "Have you seen Tom?" she shouted.

"Not for a while," Victoria responded, surveying the party. Chad took the hint and turned around. Discovering another group of random neighbors, he jumped forward and launched full steam into a new conversation without a moment's hesitation. "Last I saw," Victoria continued, "he was standing in a corner, moping. You know. The usual."

"Ugh," Jenny said. "I was hoping that big deal he closed at work meant he was going to cut loose a little bit. He seemed to be having fun at dinner, once Dad got a couple drinks into him and settled down."

"He did," Victoria agreed. "And as much as I hate to admit it, his new look works for him. Plus, he seems to be really enjoying the job. I mean, making that deal already? Dad was right. It's impressive."

Jenny knew Victoria must be really drunk if she was complimenting Tom so freely, but her sister wasn't wrong: Tom had never been so at ease around her family. Maybe it was because Kevin was there—he always made social situations a bit more bearable. She didn't know if it was the house or the baby or the haircut, or just the job infusing Tom with some confidence, but she liked it.

"How about Lakshmi? I don't think I've seen her once since dinner!" Jenny said.

"Me neither!" Victoria shouted back, draining her glass. "Come on, let's go find them! Sister mission!"

Jenny nodded, mock serious, and pulled Victoria along, both sisters laughing uncontrollably, as if they were eight and ten again and Jenny was leading Victoria toward a pile of presents on Christmas morning.

Victoria spied Lakshmi talking to a fortysomething-year-old man and grabbed her wife by the arm.

"Thank you," Lakshmi said, and the three of them burst into hysterics, forming a tight circle, effectively shutting the rest of the party out. "Are you having fun, Jenny?"

"*Yes!*" she answered, still laughing. "Though I don't know who any of these people are!"

"At least you get to meet all your neighbors at once!" Lakshmi said, smiling.

"You want me to kick their asses to the curb?" Victoria asked dramatically, rolling up a shirtsleeve. "Just say the word, sis."

"No!" Jenny said, breathless with enjoyment. These kinds of moments with her sister were so rare, so special. "I love this! This is like those parties on the roof in Alphabet City where random people from the building would show up. Remember that? Remember that old drunk guy who thought you were the ghost of his dead wife?"

Victoria guffawed. "Ugh! Don't remind me! His breath smelled like old, rotten fish."

"Eww," Jenny and Lakshmi said simultaneously.

"I'm really happy for you," Lakshmi said, putting her arm around Jenny.

"What . . . what do you mean?" Jenny answered, nervous that her sister-in-law had found out about the pregnancy. She knew she was being ridiculously secretive, but she wasn't ready to tell anyone yet. Maybe she would have enough courage in the morning, as she and Tom had planned, when her parents came over for breakfast.

"Just . . . all of this. The house . . . the fitness studio. I know how hard it is to start a new life, a new business, how stressful it can be. But I think you're going to do such a great job. I realize I'm younger than you, so this may sound ridiculous . . . but I'm proud of you."

"You're right, that does sound ridiculous," Victoria said, kissing her wife's cheek.

"Quiet, you," Lakshmi responded.

"Thanks," Jenny said, putting her arm around her sister-in-law, then around Victoria. Victoria put her own arms around her sister and her wife, too. The party raged on around them, but they were completely separate from it for a moment. "I would love to get some advice from you about starting a new business, Lakshmi. We should get lunch sometime, maybe the next time I'm in the city."

"I would love that, too. And we can gossip about Victoria behind her back."

"Hardy har," Victoria said, smiling.

"How's Tom handling everything?" Lakshmi asked Jenny.

"Really well, I think," Jenny responded, looking around but failing to spot him. "I mean, he spends a lot of time in the basement . . . He's turning it into an art studio, which is really important to him. I stay out of his way—it's a mess down there. But I'm *so* glad he's doing well with the new job . . . It's something that I was actually really nervous about."

"Me, too," Victoria said, not unkindly.

"I just hope he's able to keep up with his art. I would hate for him to lose that part of himself."

"Let's go find that goofy bastard," Victoria said, and Jenny smiled at her sister. It was no secret that Victoria had questioned Tom's "worthiness," but something seemed to be changing, and Jenny welcomed it.

The three of them broke formation, a laughing chain of humanity, and made their way to the kitchen, where the lights were still on. At that moment, Jenny felt a deep connection to her sister and Lakshmi, and to Tom, and wished that she were with him. To her delight, they found him in the kitchen.

". . . had no choice!" Tom was saying to a crowd of strangers, one arm draped around Kevin's shoulder, his eyes wide and sparkling, a huge smile on his face. Jenny had never seen him like this, had never seen him even vaguely like this, at a party. "I had to pour my chocolate milk on his head!"

Everyone roared as Tom held an empty beer bottle over his best friend's head, mimicking the event from decades earlier. It was a story Jenny had heard Tom tell a million times before, but never like this. It was surreal. The crowd's reaction seemed impossible, but she couldn't take her eyes off Tom either. Charisma seemed to be coming off him in palpable waves.

A single drop of beer from the bottle hit Kevin's head, and he pushed away from Tom, mock angry. "That was your first mistake, Decker," he growled. "And your last." He turned to the crowd. "After school, he knew what was coming, so he took off immediately, but I was on his heels, my hair still sticky, ready to exact some motherfucking vengeance." The crowd surged forward, hanging on every word, the music continuing to blast in the other room but seeming to fall away entirely as the two men spoke.

"I cut through a golf course," Tom said quietly, as if relaying the plot of a spy movie. "A shortcut I thought only I knew about—"

"Nope!" Kevin said, holding his hand up in his best friend's face. "Wrong!" Tom burst out laughing, as did everyone else. Tears filled Jenny's eyes, and a huge smile erupted across her face. She loved seeing Tom like this, whether he was drunk or not. "I caught up with him in his own backyard, right as he was running up the porch steps."

"I was sooooo close to safety," Tom lamented.

"I lunged at him and grabbed him by one foot, and dragged him face-first down the stairs!"

In chorus, Tom and Kevin made the sound of a nine-year-old kid's face bouncing along a set of wooden stairs. The party guests exploded into laughter at the horrifying story, chugging more alcohol and closing ranks around them.

"We've been friends ever since!" Tom shouted.

"And my boy just closed the Corbitt account!" Kevin added, and the crowd roared again, though none of them knew, or cared, what the Corbitt account was.

"And me and Jenny are gonna have a baby!" Tom yelled, and everyone immediately went silent. Victoria's hand tightened around Jenny's as if they were at sea and her younger sister was drowning.

"What?" Victoria whispered.

All eyes fell on Jenny as the crowd parted, creating a path between Tom and his wife, the barely visible bloodstain on the floor lying halfway between them. Jenny's mouth hung open in naked shock, and then, to her surprise, a feeling of excitement and happiness consumed her.

"It's true!" she yelled, pulling free of Victoria and walking toward Tom. He rushed forward, meeting her on top of the dim outline of spilled blood. They kissed passionately, and the surrounding, insanely drunk group of friends, family, and strangers promptly lost their shit.

The house was quiet.

The party had raged for another hour and a half after the surprise announcement of Jenny's pregnancy, as if the good news were an infection that touched everyone in attendance. Every last drop of alcohol in the house was found and consumed, even some old and suspicious-looking bottles that must have been left by the previous couple. *Murder booze*, some of the guests started calling it.

But eventually, one by one, two by two, and in small groups, the neighbors vanished, most not even saying goodbye, until only Tom, Jenny, Kevin, Victoria, and Lakshmi were left, surveying the piles of garbage and toppled furniture. The homeowners simultaneously said, "Tomorrow," shooed everyone off to bed, and soon settled in themselves.

Jenny fell asleep almost instantly, but Tom lay wide awake beside her, his mind and blood racing. The shadows on the ceiling slithered as if alive, reaching down and surrounding him, comforting him. They lifted him and carried him down one flight of stairs, and then another, and through a maze of junk that was getting easier and easier to traverse, until he was standing in front of the pulsating chrysalis.

He stared at it, marveled at how big it was becoming, almost as big as that little girl across the street, Paige. Marveled at how beautiful it looked, reflecting the string of lights he had recently purchased and begun to place along the path.

After a few minutes of silence, Tom Decker threw his arms around the chrysalis, gently placing his cheek against its sticky, oozing surface, and wept tears of unabashed joy.

MONTH FOUR

"Oh my God," Victoria whispered.

She and Jenny were standing in the small space that would eventually become a thriving private fitness studio. Or at least that's what Jenny hoped. Currently, it was an empty space with a lot of dust bunnies rolling around on the floor.

"It is *so* cute," Victoria continued. "Great call, Jen. And the location . . . for the price? Amazing."

"Really?" Jenny said, feeling better about it already. Ever since the party a few weeks earlier, she had talked to or seen Victoria every day, something that had never happened before during their twenty-seven-year relationship, not even when they were kids, living in the same house. Victoria was a master of the silent treatment. "But it's so bare."

"Which makes it even easier to imagine the possibilities! I mean, put some mirrors along one of the walls, get some equipment in here, and it's going to be perfect."

"Yeah," Jenny said, nodding, putting her hand on her pregnant belly, "you're right. This is really exciting."

"Shall we go sign some paperwork?" Victoria said, and Jenny nodded enthusiastically. The building's owner, an old woman who'd lived in the town her whole life, had been kind enough to give Jenny a key to the studio before everything was official—a sign of great things to come, she hoped.

As they left, Victoria said, "Speaking of real estate, did I tell you that I finally got Chelsea on the phone?"

"What?" Jenny nearly shouted. "No!"

"Yep," Victoria said, rolling down the sleeves of her shirt. A cool September wind was blowing through Springdale and there was heavy rain in the forecast, but for now, it was shockingly bright despite the growing chill. "I called from a coworker's cell phone, since she's been ignoring me since you confronted her. I reamed her out for a good two minutes before she hung up on me. Of course, I called right back, but it went straight to voice mail, so I left a message with a 'fucking bitch' or two thrown in there for her to chew on. I'm tempted to call her husband next."

Jenny laughed as they began walking the few blocks to the quaint little law office where they'd be signing the paperwork.

"You do *not* have to do that. But—oh, man, I wish I could have been there to hear what you said."

"I wouldn't want to contaminate your virgin ears with my salty language," Victoria said, smiling.

"Yeah, right," Jenny responded, absentmindedly putting her hand on her stomach again, which her sister noticed.

"How are you feeling?"

"Ahh, you know, the usual second-trimester stuff. I think I feel him—her?—moving around a little bit, but I'm not sure. Maybe it's gas."

"Knowing you, it's probably gas," Victoria said.

"Very funny. The best part is that I'm not really nauseous or throwing up every day anymore. That was the *worst*."

"I'm sure. That's why I never plan on getting pregnant."

"Never say never," Jenny admonished.

"Never," her sister replied quickly. "There, I just said it. So, that's it? No other symptoms? Doesn't sound so bad."

"Well, I didn't mention the heartburn, the shortness of breath, constantly having to pee, the constipation—"

"All right, all right," Victoria interrupted. "I get it."

"Hey, you brought it up."

"Fair."

They walked in silence for a few seconds.

"I've been meaning to ask . . . why didn't you tell me sooner?"

"What?" Jenny asked.

"That you were pregnant. Why didn't you tell me sooner?"

"Oh. I . . . I don't know. I thought that was the rule. You don't tell anyone until you get past those first three months. That way, if anything . . . if something bad happens, you don't have to . . . *un*tell people."

"Yes, that's the general rule of thumb. But I'm not 'people,' Jenny. I'm your sister. I hope you feel that you can tell me stuff like that."

"Yeah, I . . . I do. I mean . . ."

"I realize we fight too much. I'm sometimes harsher on you than I mean to be. But I love you." Victoria stopped walking and faced her sister, who also came to an abrupt halt. "You know that, right?"

"Of course."

"Yeah?"

"Yes, Victoria. I know."

"Good, because you're my sister. You're my best friend. I would do anything for you."

"Vic, you have made that *abundantly* clear. In fact, if we're being honest, I still feel incredibly bad about—"

Victoria raised a hand to Jenny's face, silencing her. "Ah ah ah. If you're going to bring up the money, stop right there. It is my pleasure to help. And besides, when your gym becomes a world-wide franchise and Tom is the top . . . whatever salesman in New York City, I'll be the one coming to you for loans. And you'd better not say no to your poor older sister!"

"Ha," Jenny said as they started walking again. "Never."

"Oh! I almost forgot to mention!" Victoria blurted. "I'm black-listing Chelsea in the sorority and with every alumnus I can get through to."

"Victoria!" Jenny said through laughter. "It's fine. I was pissed off, yes, but I'm more or less okay with it now. That awful stain is pretty much gone, and Tom and I are talking about having the entire kitchen totally redone once he closes a few more big deals and I get the studio up and running."

"If you really get hard up for cash," Victoria said, putting on her huge sunglasses, "you can start charging admission for people to come see the murder floor in your haunted house."

Victoria laughed at her morbid joke but Jenny didn't, her stomach twisting at the thought. She pictured an old man bleeding to death in her kitchen, taking his last ragged breaths as he stared up at the woman to whom he'd been married for decades. Jenny's eyes welled with unexpected tears. *Stupid hormones,* she thought.

They walked the rest of the way in silence, Victoria turning her face up to bask in the sun while Jenny stared down at the gray, cracked sidewalk.

———

Tom followed the pitiful squealing into a part of the basement he had never seen before. It felt odd being down here without immediately visiting the chrysalis—which was the reason he had come downstairs in the first place—but the quiet mewling in the dark had piqued his curiosity.

As he shoved his way through seemingly endless piles of the previous owners' belongings, which he had been meaning to get rid of for months, he remembered his original plan for the basement: an art studio. He felt his body flush with regret. When was the last time he had painted? When was the last time he had even *thought* about painting?

He reached the source of the cries . . . a small squirrel crouched on the floor in the far corner, near the hot-water heater and the furnace.

So that's where this stuff is, Tom thought, remembering Ray, the house inspector who had called him a fag. It seemed as if that had happened a million years ago, but it still made Tom's blood boil. He put the memory out of his mind and focused on the animal on the floor in front of him.

The squirrel, which was shivering, didn't retreat even though a human was looming over it. Tom squatted down for a closer look. The poor little thing's back legs were twisted at strange angles, and a number of large, deep cuts were visible along its abdomen. Another animal must have gotten hold of it, Tom figured, a neighborhood cat or something. Seeking any refuge it could find, somehow the squirrel had ended up down here.

"Shhhhh," Tom intoned, trying to comfort the creature. He looked around for something to wrap it in, realizing from the extent of its injuries that the animal probably wouldn't survive, no matter what he did. Still . . . maybe if he fed it and let it recuperate? He had to at least try.

Not immediately seeing anything amidst the piles of stuff that would fit the bill, he pulled off his T-shirt and gently swathed the wounded squirrel in it. It lay trembling in his hands, chest heaving. Looking closer, Tom saw that it was young and kind of cute.

"It's okay, buddy," he said quietly, carefully heading back toward the stairs. He felt a strange surge of affection for the little creature, its wrapped body nestled against his naked chest. *I guess this is what being a dad feels like,* he laughed to himself.

Before he reached the steps, the chrysalis's now-familiar breathing reached him, somehow sounding more urgent than usual, more feverish. The squirrel stirred in Tom's arms as he abruptly changed direction and made his way through the maze to the pulsating mass stuck to the wall. He'd gotten sloppy about returning the ancient refrigerator to its original spot after his visits, but then again, no one else ever came down here.

He stared at it, head cocked, wondering why it seemed agitated. The squirrel writhed in his grasp, eyes bugging out of its head; he could feel it clawing ineffectually at the fabric in which it was wrapped. Curious to see if the chrysalis would react, Tom held the animal nearer to it. The mass started pulsing faster, and the raspy breathing sound increased.

Without really thinking about it, Tom moved the squirrel even closer to the chrysalis until, at last, its furry little face touched the gooey surface. The mucus flowed up and onto the terrified animal. The squirrel unloaded a horrible shriek and locked its gaze on Tom as the man loosened his grip. Within seconds, the little creature's entire body was stuck to the chrysalis, and the thing began to envelop it. Tom's heart pounded in his ears as he watched, his now-empty T-shirt dangling from his fingers. His gaze was riveted on the spectacle before him as more and more of the squirrel vanished inside the dark mass, until it was completely gone.

The whole thing had happened in total silence after the squirrel's initial shriek of terror. Tom stared at the surface of the thing where the squirrel had been, but there was no indication whatsoever of the death struggle that had just occurred.

Tom slowly put his shirt back on as a rank odor filled his nostrils. Unable to resist, he placed his own hand on the same spot on the chrysalis, half-expecting it to vanish within as well. Instead, the mass shuddered contentedly against his palm. After a few confusing moments where Tom felt nothing, the usual high began to assert itself in his brain.

He closed his eyes, falling up into an unyielding, unending light that consumed him completely.

A bunch of the salespeople were going out for drinks after work; they practically begged Tom to join them. Kevin threw in a few choice insults to goad the newbie into accepting, but Tom declined politely. He was exhausted, and he loved getting home as early as possible these days. Jenny was really starting to show, and they were pretty sure they had felt a first kick a couple of nights ago.

Regardless, Tom had no real interest in hanging out with a bunch of virtual strangers, even if his best friend was there. He saw plenty of Kevin these days.

If Jenny fell asleep early, which was happening more and more frequently, he could go to Nick's and hang out with Malcolm and Hannah. His home away from home.

Or, if he was feeling particularly brave, he could continue working on the nursery, which he'd finally gotten up the nerve to tackle a few days earlier. Shopping for a crib had been bad, but actually putting one together was the devil's work. And he'd heard horror stories about installing a car seat.

Let's not get ahead of ourselves, Tom thought, smiling and looking around the packed commuter train, which had just departed from Penn Station, shooting noisily through the underground tunnel beneath the Hudson River. He didn't usually make the 5:06, but it wasn't surprising that the train was standing room only, even in a car without working air-conditioning. People were sweaty and cranky, but Tom was happy—he'd snagged one of the last empty seats.

As the train exited the tunnel into New Jersey with what felt like a sonic boom, Tom felt strangely detached, as if he were watching his fellow passengers on a movie screen or taking in their painted likenesses at a museum. Even the colors of the train car itself seemed off to him. This kind of thing was happening to him more often these days. An unfortunate side effect of visiting the chrysalis, but totally worth the high he was getting most days.

Everyone looked pretty tired, ready for the weekend, cavernous circles carved beneath their eyes. Summer had ended and autumn was taking over, and people's melancholy faces seemed to reflect the season.

As Tom continued to scan the train car, his gaze fell on the tall man who'd shoved his knees into Tom's back on the first day of his job. He had seen the man several times since then but did his best to avoid him. The guy was loud and imposing, and seemed to know almost everyone on any given train or platform, although he was usually the one doing most, if not all, of the talking.

The big man was in rare form today, clutching a giant can of beer partially wrapped in a paper bag and hovering over a pretty, seated woman who was in her early twenties at most. He was talking at the woman, who was clearly trying to ignore him, staring at her phone, her eyes glazed with what seemed to be fear. The loud talker's crotch was practically in her face. Tom could see a thin spray of beer spittle shooting out of the man's mouth every time he spoke.

Without realizing what he was doing, Tom stood up and began walking toward them. The aisle was fairly crowded, but he maneuvered himself around annoyed commuters, gaze locked on the tall man. The guy was half leaning down now, clearly enjoying his one-sided conversation. The young woman was definitely terrified, shoulders hunched, leaning away from him. Everyone else in the car was avoiding looking at them, wanting nothing to do with it.

". . . gorgeous," the tall man was saying as Tom drew within earshot. "You don't want some kid . . . you need a real man. I'll show you how it's done. Over and over again. You know what I mean? Yeah, of course you do." The woman didn't respond, just shifted uncomfortably in her seat.

"Hey!" Tom shouted, voice alien to his own ears. The entire car went silent. The harasser's head swiveled toward Tom; the guy's eyes were red and confused, but focused enough to be dangerous. An animal caught in the act of killing, drunk on bloodlust. "Leave her alone."

"What did you say to me?" the man slurred.

"Leave her. The fuck. Alone," Tom repeated, more quietly.

The young woman glanced up at him, then quickly looked away. Energy crackled in the train car, the kind of electricity that builds moments before a physical altercation.

"Wait," the other man said, a smile blooming on his giant,

puffy face. "Wait . . . you're that loser who's always standing alone on the Springdale platform." He stepped toward Tom, thrusting his chest out, his free hand curling into a fist. He'd probably been striking this same bully pose since high school, maybe even earlier.

Up close, Tom saw that the guy was bigger than he'd thought, but he didn't give a shit. His blood was pounding in his ears. His skin was tingling. He was excited.

"Yeah . . . ," the tall guy said. "Always standing by yourself, staring at people like a fucking retard. Is that what you are? A little fucking retard?"

"Walk away," Tom responded, his voice barely above a whisper but clear in the silence that had fallen over the car.

The man licked his lips, took a deep gulp of his beer, chuckled, and then swung a meaty fist toward Tom's face. Tom saw it coming, like a grainy slow-motion video, and leaned back slightly, allowing the drunk man's hairy fingers to pass within millimeters of his nose.

Off-balance, the man gaped wordlessly, shocked that his much smaller adversary had been able to react so fast. Tom pulled his own arm back, then unleashed and planted his fist on the man's cheek. It was easily the most powerful punch Tom had ever thrown. The feeling of the skin of his knuckles splitting open with the impact was nearly orgasmic. The tall drunk staggered back and slammed into the bathroom door, denting it, his eyes rolling back as he slid, semiconscious, onto his ass on the floor of the car. Somehow, he held on to his beer, which spilled all over his pants at the impact. Tom stood stock-still, breathing evenly, as a smattering of applause broke out.

"About damn time," someone murmured.

Thank you, the young woman mouthed. Tom nodded in response and walked casually back to his seat, which miraculously was still empty. He plopped down and stared ahead, his mind blank. When the conductor appeared, Tom flashed the monthly digital pass on his phone without looking up.

He continued to stare at the seat in front of him while people in the car buzzed about what had just happened, while the conductor discovered the drunk passed out on the floor and called for the cops to meet the train in Newark, while the young woman he'd helped shot him a grateful smile when she got off. Lost in a dull, pleasant fog, Tom saw and heard none of it.

They clinked their glasses of expensive red wine and took tentative sips, smiling at each other, eyes sparkling.

"Oh man, that is delicious," Jenny said, putting down her glass. She grabbed a roll from the bread basket and slathered it with way too much truffle butter.

"Are you sure it's okay for you to be drinking?" Tom asked, savoring the flavor of the wine. In a good mood, he had splurged for a fifty-dollar bottle, something he'd never done before. He'd topped out at about twenty dollars until now. But why not? He felt the pain radiating up from his busted knuckles and he loved it. A celebration was in order.

"Well, Dr. Miller said that I shouldn't but I've researched it and found totally conflicting reports. I think a glass of wine now and then is fine, as long as I don't go overboard. Trust me, I'd love to pound this entire thing and then polish off the rest of the bottle . . . but one glass with the ginormous dinner I'm about to inhale? I think the baby will be fine."

Tom took another gulp and watched Jenny as she attacked the piece of bread, her entire body going slack with pleasure at the taste of the fancy butter. This was the first time they'd been out to a nice restaurant since . . . hell, he couldn't remember when. Maybe back when they were first dating and he was trying to impress her, even though he couldn't really afford to do so. He had pushed his credit cards to the brink of extinction during those early days.

Jenny looked absolutely beautiful. She didn't need makeup, but when she did wear it, she looked different and exotic to him. The splash of freckles across her nose and cheeks sparkled in the candlelight. She had curled her hair slightly and wore it down. He realized it had gotten longer recently.

He wanted her right now.

Having to wait through an entire dinner, maybe dessert and coffee, and the twenty-minute trip all the way home . . . he wasn't sure he could stand it. The new dress she was wearing that allowed for her baby bump only made her hotter.

He drained his glass and refilled it, a few bloodred drops spilling onto his fingers. He licked off the errant wine and smiled at his wife, who watched him with an amused expression on her face.

"All right, fine," he said. "One glass. But if our kid comes out with three eyes, I'm blaming *you*."

"Fair en—Jesus, Tom, what happened to your hand?" The bruises and cuts on Tom's knuckles had caught the light as he brought his fingers to his mouth. A few nearby diners looked over, annoyed, at Jenny's sudden outburst.

They'd read in a review that this was the kind of place where people expected near silence from fellow patrons. They'd both cracked up at that while they were getting ready, shouting at each other from room to room, pretending to order ridiculous dishes from a faraway waiter.

"I . . . uh . . . scraped it trying to move some stuff around in the basement. It's still pretty crazy down there."

"Let me see," she insisted, and Tom held out his hand. She took it gently, running her fingers over the wounds. "Ouch . . . you should put some antibiotic on this."

"Yeah, you're probably right," he said. "Things have just been so hectic. I feel like I don't even have time to breathe."

"Right?" she said. "It's like . . . I wake up, blink a few times, and then it's time to go back to bed. I don't know how you're doing it. You've been coming to bed so late—you're getting, what? Four or five hours of sleep a night? I can only imagine how much coffee you're drinking at work."

"I actually haven't had that much lately. Kind of gave it up," he said, still surprised by the fact. But he was getting his morning jolt down in the basement these days.

Jenny stared at him, obviously incredulous. "You're insane. If I were getting four hours of sleep a night, I'd be showering in coffee. And the fact that you gave up cigarettes cold turkey? I'm proud of you, Mr. Decker." She took another small sip of wine. "This tastes incredible. You may have to get a restraining order between me and this bottle."

Tom laughed and freed his hand from Jenny's, grabbing a dinner roll. He glanced at the kitchen. Their food was taking forever.

"How's the studio coming along?" he asked.

"Great!" she said. "I can't wait for you to see it. I should be able to open sometime in the next couple of weeks. The floor needed some work but it's all fixed now. One of Victoria's friends owed her a favor and somehow got it all done for free! And I ordered a couple of those giant green exercise balls that you think are ridiculous, and a bunch of weights. Everything's secondhand but basically brand new, and nothing was too crazy expensive.

I mean, I'll probably be training bored housewives and out-of-shape, middle-aged businessmen. I don't think anyone is going to question the age of my equipment. Unless it's totally falling apart! Which it won't be. I'm thinking about calling it Spring Forward Fitness. Because we live in Springdale. What do you think?"

"I like it," Tom said, smiling. "Maybe you can whip me into shape . . ."

"Ha! Fat chance . . . Ooh, here comes the food!"

The waiter, an older man with slicked-back white hair, had arrived with two huge plates. But the Deckers' excitement diminished when he set them down. There was a tiny amount of food in the middle of each massive platter: delicious-looking, but barely more than an appetizer portion at most restaurants. Jenny had ordered the fish; Tom selected beef tips in some kind of red sauce, simply saying "bloody" when the waiter asked how he wanted the meat cooked. The waiter hadn't seemed amused, but the steak looked undercooked to perfection regardless.

"Fresh pepper?" the server asked.

Tom shook his head and Jenny said, "No, thank you, but can you bring a lot more bread, and some relish? And mustard? And mayonnaise?"

Both Tom and the waiter cocked their heads at her, and she offered them a sheepish grin. "What can I say? I have weird cravings. Pregnant lady prerogative."

The waiter mumbled, "Let me see what I can do," and skulked away with a vague air of having been insulted.

Jenny looked at Tom and wrinkled her nose in unintentional disgust. "Don't wait for me," she said. "You don't want all that blood to dry up."

"The blood is the best part," he said, shoving a forkful of meat into his watering mouth.

———

The bathroom was fancy as hell and smelled like an upscale floral shop, with soft piano music playing from unseen speakers.

Jenny had just peed—she felt like she was peeing every five minutes these days—and was washing her hands and staring at herself in the mirror. Even though the pregnancy sometimes made her feel as if she were an alien living in her own body, she felt good tonight. Great, in fact. She wasn't a huge fan of makeup, but she liked the way it looked in the bathroom's light. For a second, she thought she saw something crawling on the wall behind her and turned quickly, but there was nothing there. She laughed at herself and turned back to the mirror. Apparently, she still had cockroach PTSD from living in the city. But she *had* been seeing weird things lately. She figured it must be the pregnancy, but none of the books she'd read mentioned anything about hallucinations.

She sighed and grabbed a cloth hand towel from the nearby basket, drying her hands. After tossing the towel into an already-full disposal basket, she looked into the mirror one last time. Smiling, she ran her fingers through her hair. The way Tom had been looking at her all night made her feel gorgeous and sexy.

As she exited the small unisex bathroom, one of several in a hallway at the back of the restaurant, she was surprised to find her husband waiting for her, a serious look on his face.

"Tom? Is everything okay?"

By way of an answer, he moved forward and gently pushed her back into the bathroom, stepped in after her, then shut and locked the door behind him.

"What . . . what are you doing?" Jenny asked.

Tom didn't say anything, and for a second, his wife was filled with fear as she stared into his eyes, eyes she suddenly didn't recognize. Was this another hallucination? She backed up against the sink as he moved slowly toward her. He kissed her mouth softly and whispered, "You are so fucking beautiful," into her ear.

A wave of excitement washed across Jenny's body as Tom gently lifted her up and onto the sink and pulled down her underwear, staring into her eyes the entire time. They had drunkenly joked over the years that they should fuck in a public place someday, but they'd never even come close to actually doing it before.

"What if someone hears us?" she gasped.

"Don't scream, then," he whispered, even quieter, and then he was inside her, moving slowly and unbelievably gently. She closed her eyes. Buzzing from the wine and the gourmet food and the feeling of being fucked by the love of her life as smugly serious people dined a few feet away, Jenny leaned her head back against the mirror, shock and pleasure overwhelming her.

"Oh my God, Tom . . . ," she whispered as he put his arms on the wall behind her and pushed harder. She bit down on her lower lip, afraid that she actually *might* scream.

It was the slowest, most quiet sex they had ever had. And very possibly the best.

MONTH FIVE

The first month of her fledgling workout studio was going even better than Jenny had hoped. There was only one other place to exercise anywhere near their smallish town, and it was one of those mega-franchises that was the size of a cruise ship and cost an average person a month's salary for an annual membership. Its huge indoor pool was a big drawing point, admittedly, but ever since some kid had experienced a phenomenal bout of diarrhea in there—info that quickly went viral—membership had allegedly dropped at a drastic rate.

For now, Jenny was doing "pay as you go," instead of making people sign contracts, and customers seemed to love it. Word of mouth was high, and the local free weekly newspaper had even run a front-page feature on the studio, including a photo of a beaming Jenny inside the newly refurbished space. She had asked that they shoot her only from the shoulders up, and thankfully they had complied. She wasn't hiding her pregnancy, not that she really could at this point, but she wasn't exactly broadcasting it to potential clients either.

So far, no one seemed to mind having a pregnant personal

trainer. A few women, moms themselves, had admitted that it actually made them feel a bit more comfortable when working out. Regardless of the reasons, Jenny's little studio was a hit in the making.

Of course, Victoria had warned her that most start-ups launched in a big way, then tended to fizzle. The key was to keep the momentum going.

Good old Vic, Jenny thought as she cleaned up the studio after having finished with her last client of the day. She used to consider her sister a buzzkill, but Victoria had been full of shockingly good advice when it came to her new business venture. It was nice to have someone watching her back so closely, even if the advice was sometimes a bit too harsh.

As she walked over to the front window to turn over the OPEN/CLOSED sign, she was surprised to see someone in the doorway, the late-day autumn sunlight streaming in behind him. It took her a second to recognize Chad, the good-looking, divorced neighbor she had last seen at her house the night of the big party. Today he was wearing casual work clothes: a white dress shirt with several buttons undone at the top of his hairless chest, and formfitting khaki pants. And a very expensive-looking pair of black dress shoes.

"Hey, Jenny," he said. "Sorry, I didn't mean to startle you."

"No," she laughed, pushing a couple of errant strands of hair behind an ear. "It's fine. I just wasn't expecting anyone else today. You looking for a personal trainer?"

"Hmm," he said, his face taking on a faux thoughtful expression. "I came in to say congratulations on the big opening. I never thought I'd be getting an aggressive sales pitch."

"Aggressive?" Jenny responded, meeting his expression with

mock outrage. "That was nothing. If you want aggressive, I can show you aggressive."

Shit, she thought, *am I flirting?*

Chad put up his hands. "All right, all right, you win. I know better than to mess with a small business owner. But seriously, Jen, congrats. The place looks amazing, much better than the comic book store that was here before. I mean, I'm not sure if you ever came in here back then, but that guy who owned it was a real creeper."

He laughed and Jenny said, "You done with work for the day? What do you have, bankers' hours?"

"I wish. I had to cut out early to pick up my son and take him to a doctor's appointment. He has this mild cough that won't seem to go away. My ex is away on a business trip, unfortunately. It's not easy to keep our separate schedules straight, let alone make sure our kid is on time for all of his appointments and practices."

"It's nice that you're still on good terms with her."

"Yeah . . . it was just one of those things. Dated in high school, got married too young, realized we barely knew each other." An immediate silence filled the room. Jenny studied her sneakers until Chad chuckled nervously. "Sorry about that. It's been a long week. I'm looking forward to getting huge ice cream sundaes with him after the doctor."

"That sounds fun," Jenny said, smiling up at him. "Don't let me hold you up."

"Oh, you're not. I have a few minutes to kill before he gets out of school, and I saw that article on you a couple days ago. Very impressive. I just wanted to say hi. Haven't seen you since that rager you threw a couple months ago."

"Ha. Yeah, that was crazy. It's a good thing our house was already a mess!"

"It wasn't a mess at all. You . . . it looked really nice," he said.

It got quiet again as they stared at each other. Jenny could feel sweat rolling down the back of her neck and along her spine, giving her goose bumps.

"Well, anyway," he continued, "I'll get out of your hair. Good luck with this place. Not that you need it."

"I'll take all the luck I can get."

"Fair enough. And who knows?" he said, stepping outside. "Maybe I *will* need a personal trainer. The holidays are coming up, and I have a major dessert addiction. I do love my sweets, Jen."

He flashed a closed-mouth smile at her as he closed the door.

After a minute, Jenny let out a long sigh and laughed to herself. Chad's energy was so relaxing, so calming. Totally different from Tom's, who had such a short temper lately. She assumed it was the stress of the new job, the work still needing to be done around the house, and the impending baby. Still, sometimes she felt as though she didn't even know him, and sometimes his anger scared even her.

She shook these thoughts out of her mind, then flipped the sign with a bit more force than she had intended.

Tom was nervous as hell. In all the time he and Jenny had been together, he'd never spent any time alone with Victoria. Had actively avoided it for the most part, in fact. It wasn't a secret that his sister-in-law had never really approved of him, and it felt obvious to Tom that she thought Jenny could have done better, which made this lunch invitation all the more puzzling.

It didn't help that the kitchen faucet had broken that morning while Tom was getting a drink of water, still trying to satiate a thirst that never seemed to go away. A violent stream of liquid sprayed out from its base and soaked the counter, the floor, and anything else within range. By the time Tom had shut off the valve under the sink, mopped up the puddles all over the kitchen, realized there was a huge greasy stain on his shirt, and changed into a new outfit, he hadn't had time to visit the chrysalis, something that had become a morning ritual. And most nights now, too.

He'd missed his usual train, and Kroll barked at him about being late, making a point of mentioning Tom's flattening sales numbers over the last couple of weeks. That was true—Tom found himself becoming more and more irritable with people who said no to his cold calls, which made it harder for him to convert them to customers. His charm offensive had become less and less effective, just like the diminishing high he got from the chrysalis. Kevin had told him to tone it down. It was a small office, and people talked. The last thing either of them wanted was for Tom to permanently get on Kroll's bad side so early in his tenure. Especially after such a great start to his sales career.

The only good thing about missing the train was that Tom had seen the tall, mouthy businessman for the first time since their altercation the previous month.

Noticing the man on the platform waiting for the 7:41, Tom surmised that he must have stopped taking the 7:06 after Tom had knocked him senseless—he hadn't even noticed the guy's absence. When the man saw Tom walking up the concrete steps onto the train platform, he visibly stiffened and turned away.

Tom felt no real satisfaction at the sight, which surprised him. Once he thought about it, though, he realized he was feeling less and less in general these days, unless he was booming off the chrysalis. And even then, he had to spend more time touching the dark mass just to maintain his previous levels of intoxication. Sometimes he barely got high at all.

And since today he hadn't been able to visit the basement, he was in a terrible mood, uncomfortable in his own skin, itchy all over.

Worse, Victoria was late. Which was particularly annoying because she prided herself on always being on time and gave other people shit when they weren't, especially Jenny. And especially when Jenny was late with Tom.

She's probably doing this just to fuck with me, he thought, staring at the menu. He didn't even like sushi. Another classic Victoria move, picking a restaurant without bothering to ask what the other person wanted.

The image of his hand shoving a chopstick through Victoria's throat and out the back of her neck flashed through Tom's mind.

Shit, he thought. He hadn't had one of those bizarre, violent, blood-drenched thoughts in a while. He'd figured they were related to all the stress of the last several months: the house, the baby, the job. . . . They'd stopped—or so he'd thought—once life had become more stable.

But maybe things *weren't* more stable? Everything did kind of feel as if it were crumbling around him. . . .

"Tom!" Victoria shouted as she rushed in, sunglasses wrapped around her face even though it was cool and cloudy outside. "I know, I'm super late. I got caught in this horrible meeting, and then of course I was gifted with the worst cabdriver in Manhattan."

"No problem," he answered, half-standing as she air-kissed his cheek and sat down across from him, flipping her sunglasses to the top of her head. Tom had to admit to himself that the frantic, windswept look was working for Victoria; it made her look more like Jenny than usual. It was always surprising to see traces of his wife in Victoria's face. Most of the time, he didn't think they looked alike whatsoever, but every now and then, he caught Victoria flashing Jenny's smile or laughing Jenny's laugh.

"I was trying to decipher the menu," he said, looking back down.

"This place has the best sushi on the Upper West. You like sushi, right?"

Tom didn't answer, just stared blankly at the Japanese words in front of him. Victoria waved a waiter over and ordered without looking at the menu, without asking Tom if he was ready.

"And you?" the waiter said to him.

"Umm . . . ," Tom responded, the menu going blurry. A white-hot rage was building inside him. The feeling was terrifying. Because it made no sense. And because it felt so good.

"You should get the steak teriyaki bento box," Victoria said. "I remember you saying at the party how much you're enjoying rare meat these days."

"Fine," he answered, handing the menu over to the smiling server, who bowed slightly and walked away.

Victoria took her chopsticks out of their paper wrapper and began rubbing them together, small pieces of wood flaking away and landing on the table. Tom watched the splinters curiously, as if they were tiny limbs being shorn off a stick figure.

"So," Victoria said, "how's work?"

"Ehh, work is work," he answered robotically, something his father had always said to his mom—an answer Tom hated as a child. He pictured his father's decomposing face and forced the image away.

"Yeah, I hear you," Victoria said, smiling. "I think my inbox is actively trying to murder me. And possibly my homophobic coworkers, too."

"I guess I'm lucky to be working with my best friend," Tom mused.

"That's true. Kevin is a *great* guy. I hope you guys can make it work," Victoria answered, then said nothing, staring at her chopsticks, searching for imperfection.

God, Tom thought, *she's just like her father. This is going to be even worse than I thought. She's probably here to ream me out about something I didn't even realize I did.*

"So," he ventured, "it was a pleasant surprise. Hearing from you, I mean. The lunch invite."

"Well, you've really changed," she responded.

"Who knew a fifty-dollar haircut and shave could have such an impact?" Tom said, ignoring her barb. Many times over the years, Tom had seen how Victoria operated, especially one-on-one. He'd seen her aim verbal assaults at Jenny repeatedly, had even been the indirect recipient of her spite at times, but he'd never been alone with her before.

"I don't only mean your hair, though it is an improvement. I don't think I realized what nice eyes you've had all these years. No, it's something else. Almost everything about you seems different. If I didn't know better, I would think someone who looked exactly like you had swooped in and replaced you," she said.

"That's right," Tom said, drinking some water. "I'm an evil clone. Here to make a fair-to-middling paycheck and spend my hours fixing a beat-up old house."

"I'm serious, Tom," Victoria said, staring him in the eyes. "I'm trying to compliment you, in my own awkward, strained way.

I'm . . . I'm impressed. And trust me, it pains me to say that. I've always been wary of you."

"I've noticed."

She flashed a toothy smile. "What can I say? Jenny is my baby sister. Sure, we bicker a lot and she drives me crazy, and I'm sure I do the same to her. But I love her more than anyone else in this world."

"So do I," Tom said in almost a whisper.

"I wasn't always sure about that," Victoria replied. "You seemed very caught up in your own world. The bartending, the endless drinking, the attempts at being an artist. . . . I was worried. About Jenny, about both of you. I have to admit that I assumed you were one of her phases. She's had a lot of them, so I was genuinely shocked when she told me you two were getting married. I didn't get it."

Tom opened his mouth to speak but she powered on.

"I didn't get it," she repeated with a shake of her head, "but when I saw you two at the wedding—it wasn't the first dance or the cake-cutting bullshit or anything, it was just a simple moment when nothing else was really going on—when I saw the way she was looking at you, and the way you looked back, I realized that you were really, truly in love with each other, and that made me happy. Even if I was still nervous."

"Thank you?"

"I'm not trying to be rude, Tom, I just . . . I want to be honest with you. Then, at that really nice dinner you guys hosted and at the after-party . . . I realized that you had changed. *Are* changing, growing into the man I always wanted Jenny to find. A huge weight seemed to lift off my shoulders. So, I wanted to buy you lunch and say thank you and that I'm sorry for assuming the worst all this time."

Tom's jaw nearly dropped open. He had never heard Victoria apologize, knew that Jenny hated the fact that her sister refused to say the word "sorry." This was big. Huge. He stifled a surprised smile. "Thank you," he said instead. "Seriously."

"You're welcome," she answered as the waiter approached, holding a tray covered with plates of food. Then Victoria leaned forward, her voice lowering, smiling again. "But if you hurt her, Tom, I swear to fucking God that I will kill you."

"This place is way nicer than I expected," Jenny said as she and Tom entered Nick's. "The way you described it, I was expecting a dive bar straight out of Alphabet City. But this is totally charming."

Despite what his wife was saying, Tom could tell that she was nervous. He'd told her how friendly he'd become with Malcolm and Hannah, even going so far as to describe them as "the father and sister I never had." Jenny had seemed surprised to hear that, which made sense. Tom was very guarded with his friendships, really wasn't close to anyone other than his wife and Kevin. He had so many unresolved issues with his parents, even all these years after their deaths. It was nice that he had this makeshift family now, and Jenny had expressed multiple times how excited she was to meet them.

They sidled up to the bar, which was mostly empty at this time of day, between lunch and dinner on a Sunday. Jenny was careful not to squish her growing stomach. It had been quite a while since she'd sat at a bar.

As if sensing their arrival, Malcolm came out of the back. His eyes lit up when he saw Tom and Jenny. "FNG!" he shouted, moving forward. "And Mrs. FNG!"

Jenny shook the older man's hand and said, "FNG?"

"Don't ask," Tom said, smiling. "Malcolm has a potty mouth."

"How dare you!" the bartender said, also smiling. "It stands for Fun Nice Guy, as everyone knows." Tom laughed. "Can I get you two something to drink? The first round is on me."

"That's very kind of you, Malcolm," Jenny said, "and it is *so* nice to meet you. I would love a ginger ale. But we're happy to pay for our drinks."

"Pssh," he said, still smiling. "And for the Fun Nice Guy?"

"I'd love a beer. The usual."

"No double pour of bourbon? Huh. First time for everything," Malcolm said, winking at Jenny and walking away to make their drinks.

Jenny raised an eyebrow at her husband. "Exactly how much bourbon do you drink here, Mr. Decker?"

"Don't listen to him. He's just messing with us."

"Mmmm-hm," she responded.

A pair of arms wrapped around Tom and Jenny's shoulders, causing both of them to flinch from the sudden contact. They turned to see a young woman with a chagrined look on her face. "Oops, sorry, I was trying to surprise you," she said, blushing slightly.

"It's . . . fine, you just caught us off guard," Tom said. "I'm really happy to introduce you to Jenny. Jenny, this is Hannah, Malcolm's daughter."

"Apologies again for scaring you," Hannah said. "Especially since . . . you know . . ." She waved a hand toward Jenny's stomach.

Jenny laughed. "Don't worry about it," she said. "I think this baby is pretty tough. And it's *great* to finally meet you. Tom has told me so much about you and your dad."

"Uh-oh," Hannah said.

"I was nice," Tom retorted.

Malcolm returned with the drinks and said, "Hannah, did I just see you try to scare a pregnant lady? What is wrong with you?"

"I didn't—" Hannah started, but Jenny put a hand up, silencing everyone.

"This pregnant lady could kick all of your asses, so let's move on, people."

Malcolm let out a deep laugh, and Hannah used the opportunity to escape. She put on a black apron and went to serve a small group of customers at the other end of the bar.

"I've passed by your studio a couple times," Malcolm said, putting his hands on the wooden bar top. "It's looking really nice in there."

"Thanks," she responded. "You should come in sometime for a free session."

Malcolm laughed and patted his respectable belly. "I don't know about that. I've worked hard on this bad boy. And I don't even have a baby in here as an excuse."

"Well, the offer stands, if you ever change your mind," Jenny said, smiling. "Or maybe you and Hannah can come over for dinner at our house sometime. I mean, I know how busy you are with the bar, but if you ever both have a night off."

"That sounds fantastic. I'll check the schedule and let you know," he responded. "So . . . what's a beautiful young woman like you doing with a rapscallion like Tom Decker?"

Tom felt irrational anger boiling up and fought to tamp it down. An image of smashing the old man's face in flashed in his mind, and he shook it away. *What the hell was that?* Malcolm had become like a father to him. The man was simply joking around with Jenny, a sign of affection after months of building a close relationship with her husband over many drinks. Tom breathed deeply and felt some of the tension leak away. He longed for the chrysalis and then remembered that he had just visited it that morning. He hated that the highs from his contact with it were getting shorter and shorter. He wondered if it would stop working altogether. What would he do then?

"*Someone* had to try to civilize this monster," Jenny joked, and Malcolm laughed yet again, his eyes twinkling. It was obvious that he already liked her.

He leaned in even closer. "It's funny . . . ," he said, leaning toward Jenny.

"What's that?" Jenny asked, leaning in, too. Tom imagined their lips meeting and then cursed at himself, looking away and finding his haunted reflection in the mirror. Why had he even come here? He should be home, down in the basement. No . . . home, working on the nursery, which still wasn't done. Putting up Halloween decorations. Finding more animals to feed to the chrysalis. So much to do. Too much. He fought back tears of frustration and rage.

"Well, the FNG here looks like my son . . . ," Malcolm was saying.

"I'm so sorry about what happened to him," Jenny said quietly.

"It's okay . . . I mean . . . thank you, but it's okay." Hannah had wandered over and stared at her dad, clearly curious about where he was going with this. "So, anyway, like I said . . . the FNG looks like Nick, and the weird part is . . . you look a bit like my wife, God rest her soul."

"Really?" Jenny said.

Hannah looked at her more closely. "Yeah . . . ," she said, "I guess I can kind of see that."

"I mean, it's not as strong a resemblance as Tom and Nick . . .

but she had freckles on her nose, too," Malcolm said. He reached into his pocket and pulled out a wallet, then extracted a beat-up old photo, displaying it for Jenny to see. Sure enough, the woman in the faded photo bore more than a passing resemblance to her.

"Huh," Jenny said, and looked over at Tom. He was staring at himself in the mirror behind the bar, seemingly lost in his own world. She nudged him with her elbow. "You hear that, rapscallion? I look a little bit like Hannah's mom."

I guess that means you're fucking your own son, Tom almost said out loud but stopped, forcing himself to snap out of whatever daze he was trapped in.

"I guess that means she must have been very, very beautiful," he said instead, looking at the photo and pushing a strand of hair behind Jenny's ear.

Malcolm smiled and put an arm around his daughter. "That she was," the older man said. "That she was."

MONTH

SIX

"I want to throw another party," Jenny said, glancing at her husband in the driver's seat.

It was snowing. They were driving home from Manhattan, stuck in holiday traffic after celebrating Thanksgiving at Victoria and Lakshmi's beautiful two-bedroom apartment. Tabetha and Russell had opted for a cruise this year, promising that Christmas in Upstate New York would be a lavish affair. Despite that, Victoria had gone all out, as usual. Even though there were only four of them, she'd served enough food to feed multiple families. They had barely made a dent in the main course after all the incredible appetizers, and the table had been cluttered with mostly unopened wine bottles. Tom poured only a single glass of white and he had barely touched it. Jenny drank glass after glass of water. She was so thirsty lately.

During dinner, she found herself watching Tom as he sipped at his wine and hardly touched his food. He was drinking less and less alcohol lately, at least around Jenny. She vaguely wondered if this was his way of silently telling her that he was worried he was becoming an alcoholic, then brushed the notion away. Tom had always gone through phases of heavy and light drinking, depending on what was going on in his life. Never quite this extreme, maybe, but he'd never had this much going on before either. After all, they'd had that big conversation months ago on the porch about both of them growing up a little. She should have been glad he was taking that to heart, if that's what this was. Still, part of her was increasingly worried by his behavior. It was often like living with a stranger.

He was also in a full-on funk at work, and Jenny knew that had to be putting a strain on his friendship with Kevin, even if Tom would barely admit either thing. Pete Kroll was riding Tom mercilessly, and with good reason: Tom simply wasn't delivering on his early promise.

Jenny was getting really worried about him. He always looked exhausted, and his temper was getting shorter by the day. They were three months away from bringing their baby into the world, and Jenny had hoped this fact would energize her husband, not drag him further down. Kevin had called her a week earlier, asking if everything was okay at home, and she had responded, "Of course." But even as she said it, she knew she was lying.

"Hmm?" Tom murmured from the driver's seat, white-knuckling the steering wheel as he stared into the brake lights of the minivan in front of them. It was a few minutes after midnight and they had come to a complete stop on the highway. Tom's face looked hollowed out and demonic in the dark red light. Jenny wasn't sure if she was hallucinating again or not.

"We should have another party," she repeated. The last one had been while Tom was on a roll, and he had been kind of going downhill ever since; maybe repeating the party would get him going again. "An early holiday party, maybe even next weekend, before everyone gets crazy with Christmas and whatnot. Andrea mentioned that it's her and Frank's last free weekend until the new year. Of course, it doesn't have to be as insane as last time—"

"I don't know," Tom interrupted as they started moving again.

"It would be nice to do it before I get too much bigger. I may not want to see anyone in a few more weeks."

Jenny stared at his profile. He'd been so quiet at dinner, which surprised her. Victoria said that they'd had a very nice time at lunch a couple weeks earlier, though he seemed a little distracted. Tonight, it had been like that get-together never happened: Tom was distant and practically monosyllabic.

At one point, Victoria had pulled her aside and told her to stay over because it was snowing; Tom was specifically *not* included in the invite. But Jenny had begged off even though part of her was eager to spend a night with her sister, away from her husband, just to clear her head a bit.

The cause of the congestion became clear—a bad accident in the right lane that had clearly just happened. Jenny involuntarily looked over as they passed and wished she hadn't. There were no visible corpses or injured people, thankfully, but one of the two wrecked cars had a huge, bloody, raw-edged hole in its front windshield, like some kind of violent mechanical birth gone horribly wrong. Her mind started to conjure horrible imagery of what had happened, and she wished the thoughts away.

"Tom?" she said, looking at his stone-like face.

"What?" he snapped.

"The party?"

After a long moment, he said, "I'll think about it."

It was almost one thirty in the morning by the time they made it home. There had been a disturbing number of accidents along the way, most likely due to the unfortunate combination of icy snow and tipsy holiday drivers. Jenny had successfully willed herself not to look at another one. She and Tom barely spoke after his angry retort. She'd dozed off for a while, until her forehead lolled against the cold window, shocking her awake.

It was still snowing; the short, precarious walk from the car to the front door left them covered with flakes. Even the porch swing had a layer of white on it.

Inside, Jenny took off her boots and snowy jacket, then gingerly backed up and sat down at the dining room table. Even simple acts like sitting had become much more difficult than normal. Tom headed for the kitchen, wordless, boots and coat still on, snow melting off him and falling to the floor, creating a series of tiny puddles.

"Tom . . . ?"

He stopped dead in his tracks in the kitchen doorway, without looking at her.

"Yeah?"

"About the party—I'd like to start inviting people tomorrow. Today. It's Black Friday, so I thought I'd do a cute little invite, make the party a 'black and white' theme, like—"

"I said I'd think about it!" he yelled angrily, then stalked into the kitchen and out of sight.

The intensity of his voice, its sheer volume, sent an almost literal shock through her body. He had never spoken to her like that, not even during their most heated arguments.

The house was silent except for intermittent creaking probably brought on by the recent bitter cold. Jenny looked around. The space was painfully dark. She'd flicked the switch when they entered, turning on the light above the dining room table, but two of the three bulbs had burned out weeks ago. Another thing that Tom had promised multiple times to fix, like that goddamn basement stair, which was still a shattered mess. If anything, it looked worse than ever.

He hasn't even finished the nursery, she thought.

"Tom?" she called into the darkness at the back of the house.

There was a long silence. Then:

"I'm going downstairs to paint a little. You must be exhausted. Go to bed. I'll be up in a little bit."

She heard the basement door creak open and shut, muffled footsteps on the stairs. Then nothing.

Jenny remained stock-still, looking at the kitchen doorframe and the shadows beyond, then at the door, farther along the same wall, that led upstairs. She *was* exhausted, but part of her wanted to follow Tom down to the basement. She would step defiantly over that jagged hole that had drawn blood from her and give him the holy hell he deserved for treating her like that. Who the fuck did he think he was? Did he have any idea what she was going through? The constant ligament pain in her lower abdomen, her aching feet, her huge mood swings, the massive bouts of insecurity, fear, and depression. Not to mention running her own brand-new business, which was doing quite well but which she was already worried about—how long could she keep working?

And yet . . . what would she really gain from storming down there and yelling at Tom, interrupting his painting to point out how strange he'd been acting? If he already wasn't listening to her, what good would that do? Maybe she had pushed a little too hard, too fast on the whole party thing. She was just excited about the prospect of one last big gathering before she hunkered down for the apparently very bad winter that was bearing down on them. By the time the holidays were over, she'd probably be in no mood for entertaining. And once the baby was born? Who knew how long it would take before they reemerged into daylight.

"Tomorrow," she murmured before getting up and making her way to bed.

"They're *all* unique. Every single one of them."

Jenny bolted awake, sitting up faster than she should have, her abdomen clenching in pain as a result and her head swimming.

In the dim light coming from the bathroom down the hall— she'd left the light on so Tom wouldn't kill himself coming up the stairs—she could see her husband standing over her, still wearing his coat. One arm was stretched out over the bed, and he appeared to be holding something in his hand. She risked a glance at the clock. It was a few minutes after 4 A.M.

"Tom? What the fuck?"

The last time he woke her up like this, months ago, he'd been wasted, so she'd understood, kind of, and forgiven him. Tonight, he didn't smell like alcohol, and his speech wasn't slurred.

As her eyes acclimated to the light, she realized that Tom was holding a clump of snow in his bare hand.

"Every single flake is fucking unique, Jenny. How many times has it snowed on this planet? How many snowflakes does that equal? Billions and billions and billions. And each snowflake is unique. How is that even possible? Do you know what that means?"

"Tom, you're scaring me."

"It *is* scary. It means the infinite is possible. Not only possible, but happening. Every day. Everywhere."

Jenny noticed that the bottom of the snowball was darkening. She squinted at it. Red. "Tom! You're bleeding!"

"Did you know," he whispered, leaning in closer, "that every single person's blood is unique, too, like their fingerprints? Which means we're infinite, too, Jenny. We are *infinite*."

Bloody ice water dripped onto the bed from the melting snow. Jenny shot to her feet, moving faster than seemed possible, and grabbed Tom's arm. She towed him, unresisting, out of the bedroom, down the hall, and into the bathroom. She angrily flipped on the light before positioning his injured hand over the sink, letting the crimson splash against the porcelain. Turning on the water, she washed away the snow and revealed a deep, bloody gash in his dirty palm.

"Jesus!" she said. "Tom, pull yourself together! I don't know what the fuck is going on with you, if it's the job, or the idea of being a dad, or owning this giant fucking house . . . but I can't take it anymore. Do you hear me? Enough!"

Tom stared as if he didn't recognize her, then blinked several times. His eyes refocused and immediately welled with tears. "I'm sorry. Jenny. Oh my God. I'm sorry."

Her heart ached. He looked so lost and confused, like a little boy who had wandered away from home during a storm, with his hair matted against his forehead and tears in his eyes. His skin was incredibly pale in the bright bathroom lights, and there were huge circles under his painfully bloodshot eyes. She realized that he hadn't had a haircut since his makeover, months earlier. Shaggy and unkempt, his dirty mop fell into his eyes. How had she not noticed that until now?

"I don't want to hear that you're sorry," she said, pushing aside her pangs of sympathy. "Your skin is ice cold. I want you to get into the shower, warm up, and clean yourself off. Put a bandage on that hand. I want you to come to bed and get a good night's sleep—at least eight hours, and hopefully more like ten. We have nothing on our schedule tomorrow, so you can get up whenever you want.

"After you wake up, you and I are going to eat a giant breakfast. Lots of eggs. Huge glasses of milk. Then you're going to look me in the eye and apologize for yelling at me earlier. And we're going to have a long talk. And this shit is not going to happen ever again or you and I are going to have a very serious problem in the near future, baby or no baby."

Tom stared at her, his eyebrows beetling. He looked scared.

"Understood?" she asked.

"Yes," he barely choked out.

"Fine. Good night, then," she said, then left the bathroom, shutting the door behind her.

Tom stood in the bathroom for an indeterminate amount of time, stuck in place, cradling his injured hand. If someone had asked him where he was, what day it was, what had just happened . . . he would have been unable to answer.

The crowd of people pulsed around Tom, shoving him up against his living room wall. The party was out of control. They'd invited very few people, like last time, but once again, word had apparently spread, possibly fueled by stories of their last bacchanal, and by ten o'clock, the ground floor was jammed with strangers. Music was blasting from somewhere, most of the lights were out, and someone had brought a strobe, so all Tom could make out were flashes of faces, of sweaty bodies pressed up against each other.

He was miserable and on the brink of tears.

Ever since Thanksgiving night, when he'd scared the shit out of Jenny with that bloody snowball, he'd steered completely clear of the basement. Cold turkey. The next morning, a truly remorseful Tom had promised to change, and key to that change was avoiding the chrysalis, which he knew was ruining his marriage and his life.

The last time he'd gone for any length of time without visiting the basement, he longed for the chrysalis as if it were an absent lover. This time was worse. He was physically aching, having trouble eating, and couldn't concentrate. Thinking he'd caught a cold, Jenny had suggested canceling the party, but Tom insisted that they proceed. She'd put so much time and energy into it, had made it happen on such short notice. He focused on making sure his behavior was as normal as possible during the days leading up to the party even though he was collapsing in on himself.

Kevin hadn't been able to make it. He was dating a new girl, Felicity, and things had quickly become serious. He seemed convinced that she was "the one." It was probably just as well, since Kevin and Tom weren't talking very much. They weren't fighting; Tom was focused on his job, working hard to get his numbers up. That meant he wasn't in a joking mood most of the time, and that was Kevin's default setting.

Victoria and Lakshmi were there, somewhere, but Tom had barely seen them. He gathered that Victoria was still pissed off about Thanksgiving, but he couldn't find it in himself to give a shit. He was having enough trouble focusing his eyes and trying to keep food down.

He attempted to walk forward, to find a path through the mob of partiers, but a group of wolves with bloody faces pushed him back against the wall. No, not wolves. People, mostly women, dancing, their hair wild and flowing, wearing bright red lipstick, having fun, unaware that Tom was there at all. Their hands were all over him.

"Get the fuck off me!" he screamed.

The crowd in front of him burst out laughing, shifting slightly away from him without interrupting their conversations or their dancing. Pushing off the wall, Tom tried to shove his way through the throng of shadowy bodies. Garbage and spilled drinks covered the floor, making it hard to maneuver. Furniture had been moved and knocked over. It was absolute chaos.

He needed to get to the basement. He needed to get his hands on the chrysalis. *Now.*

Eyes and mouths surrounded him, gaping, gawking, and yammering as he pushed frantically past people who were barely clothed, people who were kissing each other and running fingers down naked skin. The music seemed to get louder with each step he took; the strobe light flashed frenetically. He felt as if he were suffocating. Every cell in his body was begging for the chrysalis. *Please,* he thought. PLEASE.

The half-naked crowd suddenly parted and went silent.

A woman walked toward him along a narrow path between bodies, the partygoers shuddering collectively as she passed them. A black dress covered her body, even flowing over her unseen feet, and long black gloves ran to just above her elbows. She had long, dark hair; her face was concealed by a thick black veil. In her hands she held an iron goblet, carved to show tiny naked figures in the metal, writhing in paralyzed agony. The music was still playing, but to Tom's ears it was tinny and distant, like the memory of a nightmare. The strobe light throbbed in time to the beat.

As the woman approached, shadows overwhelmed the people around and behind her. Their mouths widened in ecstatic pain, their bodies undulating silently, and they vanished completely, as if the darkness were eating them alive.

When she took her last step and stopped in front of him, Tom's world had been reduced to a small circle of pulsating light surrounded by absolute darkness and a thin strain of high-pitched music that sounded like a single unending wail from some ancient, dying creature. "Drink," the woman whispered through the veil, offering him the goblet. He could feel the heat radiating off her.

Tom looked into the cup: red wine, thick and viscous. No . . . it was blood, he realized, and the heat was coming from the liquid, not the woman. As he stared, he saw the blood tremble and realized there was something swimming in it, just below the surface. Several somethings. Long insects with multiple eyes and legs, unlike anything he had ever seen before. The veiled woman raised the goblet closer and closer to his face.

"Drink . . . ," she commanded again. The smell of the blood hit him, metallic, pungent, gut-churning.

Without thinking, Tom batted the cup away, using his right hand, which still bore the scab from the last time he'd visited the chrysalis, on Thanksgiving. He'd woken up on the basement floor that night, thrashing wildly, and cut his hand on the rake that he'd intended to use to destroy the dark mass on the wall, back on the first day that they saw the house.

"No!" he shouted as the blood flew across the circle of light that surrounded him and the woman in black. Some splashed into his eyes, and the room went completely dark. He reeled backwards, hearing the goblet break into pieces as it hit the floor.

Oddly, it sounded like glass shattering rather than metal. He clawed at his eyes, trying to regain his vision. Shocked murmurs reached his ears, along with the sounds of shuffling feet and soft classical music. Tom blinked as his sight cleared and he looked around.

There were no throngs of half-naked people, no orgy-like dancing, no woman in black. He was in his own living room, staring at a dozen or so of his and Jenny's friends and neighbors. The guests were dressed in sports jackets and trousers or cocktail dresses, all in black and white, just as Jenny had specified in her invitation, and they were staring at him in horror. Jenny stood right in front of him, barely a foot away, clutching one hand with the other, a look of pain on her face. An arterial spray of wine was spreading on the floor and wall. He had clearly knocked a proffered drink right out of her hand—broken glass littered the ground. Tears were rolling down Jenny's cheeks.

Tom knew he had crossed the final line. Victoria stepped forward and wrapped her arm around Jenny's shoulders. None of the other guests said a word, moved, or seemed to be breathing.

"I . . . ," he managed to say, but nothing else.

"*Get. Out,*" Victoria said through clenched teeth.

Nick's was packed.

Maybe because it was Saturday or because the holidays were looming or because the weather had warmed up a bit, to a balmy mid-forties, or maybe it was all these factors combined. The crowd was a bit younger than usual, local twentysomethings staying in town for once rather than traveling into Manhattan. As Tom staggered in, he felt like an ancient animal climbing up from the primordial muck.

He moved toward the bar, trying to avoid touching anyone. He could still feel the naked, sweaty bodies he had been forced to touch earlier that night, even though that hadn't actually happened. Had it?

There was some new guy tending bar. Long hair. Tats. For a second, Tom thought he was looking at himself. Was he somehow back in Alphabet City? Was this his chance to do everything over? No, that was insane.

"What's up, man?" the bartender said, throwing a coaster down in front of Tom.

"Bourbon, double, straight," Tom croaked.

"Coming right up," his doppelgänger said before walking away to fill the order. The multitudinous voices in the bar were deafening. Tom looked around, but the faces were indistinct. He tried to focus his eyes as he searched the room but couldn't locate Malcolm or Hannah. He hadn't been there since his visit with Jenny. Things had just been so crazy. He missed talking to Malcolm, missed having someone in his life who didn't judge his mood swings, his paranoid thoughts.

Had he really just slapped a glass out of Jenny's hand? It didn't seem possible. Tom cradled his head in his palms. He missed the chrysalis so fucking much.

"Here you go," the bartender said. Tom looked up and found himself staring into a glassful of amber liquid. It filled his vision and then, within seconds, his empty stomach. But his brain hardly noticed it. "Keep them coming," he demanded.

"Your funeral," the obnoxious, long-haired hipster responded.

Tom could feel the crowd behind him but wondered, were they really there? Was he? Or was he in the basement? As he drank his second, then third glass of bourbon, he realized that he was sobbing, tears and snot rolling down his face. Which was especially confusing because he felt nothing inside.

"Hey, FNG, what the hell is going on with you?" Malcolm was standing behind the bar, in front of Tom, arms outstretched on either side of him, a familiar pose, a concerned smile on his face.

Tom wiped a sleeve across his face, tried to smile back, failed. "Malcolm, maybe . . . better to leave me alone." Tom was surprised at the sound of his voice. Clear, no slur whatsoever. It was as though he'd been drinking water.

"Fuck that. Hold on, I'm coming around."

Malcolm appeared next to Tom seconds later, then led him to a two-person table at the back of the bar. The crowd parted for the bar owner and the haggard man he was dragging after him as if they recognized that a rescue operation was under way. Malcolm nodded at the two guys currently occupying the table, and they understood his silent command, vacating the area for the establishment's well-liked owner.

"I forgot my drink at the bar," Tom mumbled as he dropped into the uncomfortable wooden chair.

"Don't worry, it's not going anywhere," Malcolm responded, pushing a bowl of peanuts toward Tom. "Here. Eat."

"I'm not hungry."

"I don't give a fuck. *Eat.*"

Staring at the older man, Tom grabbed a handful of the nuts and shoved them into his mouth. Though they tasted like sawdust, he chewed dutifully. He had to swallow several times before the disgusting paste went down.

"Happy?" he asked.

"Over the moon," Malcolm answered gravely, returning Tom's hard stare.

"I told you, just leave me alone. I'm . . . not right in the head anymore."

"Bullshit. To all of that. If you wanted to be alone, you

wouldn't have come to my bar. You know what I think? I think you came here for help. We haven't been friends all that long, but you're almost like a son to me. No matter what kind of a shitty day or month you're having, I *know* you. There's nothing wrong with your head. You're struggling with some heavy shit—big house, new job, kid on the way. Maybe a bit too much alcohol. Trust me, I get it. I've been there."

Tom swiped the wooden bowl of peanuts off the table, sending it clattering onto the floor. Several of the bar's patrons looked over.

"You don't know anything about me!" he shouted, leaping to his feet. "Leave me alone, you old fuck!"

Malcolm stood, too—slowly, looking sad. He held up his hands in a placating gesture. "I know you don't mean that, Tom. Come on. I think the diner's still open. Let's go get some greasy food and talk. This place can live without me for a couple hours."

Stepping forward, Tom violently grabbed Malcolm's shirt in a fist and shoved him, hard, against the wall. "I am not your dead fucking son."

The older man looked surprised, then visibly deflated. Tom didn't care. He felt the anger radiating off his body, could feel it infecting the entire bar. He reveled in it.

He heard angry shouting and wondered vaguely if it was all in his head until a bunch of arms grabbed him and someone shouted in his ear, "Get the hell off Malcolm!"

Tom fought against the arms, but there were a lot of them. Blazing-hot rage continued to bubble inside him, and he fought harder, an unnatural strength swelling through his body. More people rushed forward, smashing Tom against the wall.

Blood burst from his nose and he laughed, feeling a blast of emotion for the first time in months, a kind of twisted happiness, loving every second even though he still wasn't sure if it was actually happening. Was it possible that he was still at the party? Maybe he was in the basement, pressed up against the chrysalis. Maybe he'd wake up on the floor with Jenny calling softly from the kitchen, imploring him to come to bed.

No. This was definitely real. He was pressed up against the same wall that he'd just pinned Malcolm to, people shouting at him to calm down. The old man was nowhere in sight.

Blood poured from Tom's nose into his open mouth and he realized that he was still laughing.

"Is that all you got?" he shouted.

"You want more, motherfucker?" a man yelled into the side of his face. "Let's drag this asshole outside!"

Tom felt power running through his veins, and shoved himself backwards. His attackers stumbled back, but this time Tom threw out his elbows, again and again, faster than he would have imagined possible, and smashed several unseen faces. He took pleasure in their screams.

Released by his opponents, he spun to face them, grinning widely beneath the blood coating his face. One of his attackers had fallen; Tom loomed over her. The woman looked up at him, blood streaming from her nose, her face a red-streaked mirror of Tom's own, minus the smile.

It was Hannah. His sister. Wait. No. He was an only child.

"I'm going to fucking *kill* you," she snarled.

Tom abruptly felt the fight go out of his body. His vision seemed to clear, and the noise of the room rushed back to him as he fought to control himself.

"Hannah? I . . . I didn't mean . . . I'm sor—"

He didn't get a chance to finish. Fist after fist struck him everywhere—cheeks, stomach, back, ribs. He raised his hands to protect himself, but there were too many of them. He couldn't see their faces, could barely see the bloody, cracked knuckles coming at him from every direction as his world was once again swallowed by darkness.

There was no pain, not really, but his body was failing to respond to his brain's commands. Something in his fractured mind was making him smile, which was apparently driving his attackers into a frenzy. Tom collapsed to one knee, feeling something crack there at the impact. Still he felt nothing. People were bellowing, pounding on him; the entire place was whipping itself into an animalistic fury.

As if in a dream or hallucination, he was lifted and carried on a forest of human limbs like a latter-day savior. The comforting darkness shrouded his mind completely as Tom laughed maniacally. Blood ran from his nose, dripped from his ears, streamed from a nasty cut on his lower lip.

He was dumped unceremoniously into a pile of snow; the intense cold, after the heat and violence of the bar, was a shock to his malfunctioning system. Someone kicked him in the gut one last time for good measure. Then they abandoned him, disappearing back into the bar on a cacophony of shouting and vicious laughter.

Tom barely heard any of it. New flakes fell from the sky, coating his exposed skin in a thin, freezing sheen. He raised a trembling hand to the dark, cloud-covered sky, blinking several times as his vision returned, and watched snowflakes land on his raw, pink fingers.

"Unique . . . ," he whispered. Blood and tears started to freeze on his face as he sank into unconsciousness.

Sometime later, Tom stood shivering in the doorway of his completely dark house. He could barely feel his fingers or toes. How long had he been lying out in the snow? How had he gotten home? What time was it? What *day* was it?

"Jenny!" he shouted, but there was no response other than the creaking of the old house and the occasional clank of the radiators. Otherwise, the house was utterly and painfully silent.

He made his way through the dining room and living room. Signs of the abandoned cocktail party were everywhere, like a stage play suspended in the middle of a scene, with the characters hiding offstage, ready to step out in faceless masks and shredded, bloody clothes, and stab Tom with sharpened knives.

Shaking his head, Tom forced the images away. He went to the door that led upstairs, opened it, and shouted his wife's name again. No response. As far as he could tell from the bottom of the stairs, it was pitch black up there—no sign of the bathroom light she always left on for him. He called her name again but knew in his gut that she wasn't there.

He needed to focus. His wife was missing.

Closing his eyes, Tom tried to separate the real memories from the imagined ones.

They'd been throwing a small party, and something had happened. He knew that much. He also had a vague memory of getting his ass kicked at Nick's. But why?

What the hell was going on?

In the kitchen, he turned on the lights; one bulb popped quietly and went dead. Two things immediately caught his attention: a note on the counter and the door to the basement, which stood open, beckoning to him. His palms were immediately slick with sweat, heart thumping with excitement. He was alone in the house with the chrysalis. Finally.

He stepped toward the basement, then, with a huge effort, stopped himself and turned to the note.

What the fuck is wrong with you? he thought.

Tom forced himself to grab the small piece of paper.

> *Tom, I've gone to stay with Victoria for a while. I don't
> know what's going on with you . . . if you're on drugs or
> terrified of our new life and having some sort of break-
> down or trying to get rid of me without coming out and
> saying it . . . but I can't be with you right now.*
>
> *I'm afraid of you. But I also love you and I know you
> are a good man. I just don't know where that man is right
> now. I'll call you in a couple of days. Maybe some mar-
> riage counseling might even be a good idea.*
>
> *Love, Jenny*

Tears were running down Tom's face, but he felt almost nothing
other than an overwhelming desire to go down to the basement.

An intense pain shot through his gut, and he turned to look at
the refrigerator. The one up here, the one that worked, that wasn't
hiding the only thing he wanted right now. When was the last
time he had actually eaten something? He couldn't remember.

But he didn't have an appetite. Even the thought of food made
him feel nauseated.

He crumpled the note into a ball and dropped it to the stained
kitchen floor, all the while staring at the basement door. The
darkness beyond was so complete, so inviting. An inadvertent
giggle leaked out of his mouth and he surged forward.

He pulled the refrigerator away from the wall.

A sigh of relief escaped him when he saw the chrysalis. It was
larger than ever, its dark veins glistening in the multiple colors

from the string of Christmas lights. The overhead fluorescents had burned out weeks earlier, which was fine. Tom welcomed the warmth of the shadows down here.

He could hear the ice-cold snowflakes tapping against the paint-covered windows, an almost gleeful sound, a drum roll to his reintroduction to the dark, growing mass clinging to the wall.

Gently, Tom placed both hands on the pus-covered thing. It didn't shiver against his touch, as usual. *That's odd,* he thought, but closed his eyes, waiting for the rush.

Waiting.

After a minute, Tom opened his eyes. There was no burst of pleasure. Instead, his mind was becoming clearer, horrible memories of the party and Nick's filtering into his consciousness.

"No . . . ," he said, pushing his hands harder against the chrysalis. Nothing happened. Maybe it was . . . *mad* at him? Angry that he hadn't fed it any animals in more than a week? "Come on. . . ."

The breathing sound continued to fill the basement, but it was softer and thinner than before.

"Please . . . ," he implored. Still, nothing.

Frustrated, he pulled his hands away, eyes brimming with tears. Images flooded his mind: his corpse hanging from a noose, the rope tied around the basement rafters; his hand wrapped around the handle of a kitchen knife, slicing open his wrists, then up along the veins; his body, bleeding to death on top of the still-present bloodstain on the kitchen floor.

"No!" he insisted, clenching his fists but feeling his will to live leaking away.

A small glob of gelatinous goo ran down his wrist and onto his forearm. Without a thought, he leaned forward and licked it off his skin. The taste exploded on his tongue, simultaneously horrible and amazing, like dog shit caked in powdered sugar. He gagged but managed to swallow.

A painful warmth spread out from his stomach, inching through the rest of his body. When it hit his brain, stars exploded into his vision. He staggered away from the chrysalis, crashing into a pile of water-stained boxes and rolling to the floor, his shoulder slamming into the ground. Between the impact and his earlier beating, he should have been in agony. Instead, his body was racked with waves of euphoria. Rolling onto his back, Tom inhaled deeply, smiling, each breath kick-starting a new vision of the infinite. Nearby, the chrysalis expanded slightly. The breathing grew louder as Tom writhed on the dirty basement floor, awash in ecstasy.

MONTH SEVEN

Tom woke with a start and blinked several times, clearing grit from his eyes, then slowly sat up, swallowing nausea. He tried to remember what day it was but couldn't. *It's December*, he thought. He'd been living alone for weeks. But was it a weekday? Weekend? He had no idea. He was in the basement; that he knew.

He looked down at himself. He was wearing a rumpled, dirty suit and one shoe. No help there—he might have gone to work that day, or simply not taken off the suit he'd worn a day earlier. Or *days* earlier.

Slowly, he stood up, fighting to retain his balance. He stumbled over to the chrysalis and stared at it for a few moments. Saying goodbye to it in the mornings had become increasingly difficult. He considered scooping some of its mucus into his mouth, but he knew he'd overdone it the night before, could still feel the effects reverberating through his mind and body.

He pushed the refrigerator back into place, hiding the dark mass once again.

In the kitchen, in the blinding light of morning, Tom staggered to the counter and grabbed his phone, checking the date:

December 18th. He'd lost a full week to the basement, surviving on what the chrysalis gave him.

Had he been down there the whole time, in the same suit? He had no idea.

Outside, birds were chirping and the sun was shining. Tom remembered vaguely that the Northeast was going through an unseasonably warm phase. Putting his phone down, Tom squinted into the light. All the snow was gone. Naked tree limbs danced gently in a breeze that he could practically see, the day awash in surreal colors that throbbed in rhythm with his heartbeat, which increased as the colors started cycling faster.

Gripped by abdominal cramps, Tom violently vomited what looked like black tar into the kitchen sink. His stomach heaved over and over again, an impossible amount of opaque, viscous liquid pouring from his aching throat. A horrible odor wafted up as it began to overwhelm the drain and fill the bottom of the sink.

When the spasms stopped, he remained hunched over, his face hovering next to the gleaming metal faucet, trying to catch his breath. Dappled sunlight played against the back of his neck, causing sweat to break out there. At last he managed to straighten up long enough to grab his phone, turn around, and slide down along the cabinet, away from the sunlight and the sludge he had just purged from his body.

He focused his eyes and started scrolling through his phone.

It was 6:20 A.M. on a Monday. He had several dozen unread emails and a handful of missed calls, voice mails, texts. Tapping the button for voice messages, Tom put the phone against his ear, resting his head back against the wood and staring blankly at the open basement door. His stretched-out feet barely touched the faint bloodstain in the center of the kitchen floor.

The first message was from five days earlier. It was Jenny.

"Hi, Tom. Um. How are you? I've called before but figured I'd actually leave a message this time. I don't really know what to say. Other than I love you and I'm not giving up on us. I saw Dr. Miller last week and pretty much cried the entire time because you weren't there. I told her you had to work and that I was just emotional because of the hormones. But it sucked to be there without you, to see our beautiful little baby by myself. And don't even get me started on the birthing classes." She laughed bitterly. "Those suck to do alone, too."

Tom looked over at the refrigerator, but the sonogram they'd so lovingly placed there was gone. Had she taken it? Had it fallen off at some point during her absence? He had no idea and hated that he didn't know.

"I . . . miss you," Jenny's voice continued. "A lot. I'm not saying that I'm going to automatically forgive everything you've done, but I really want us to talk. It's been a few weeks since the party, and I'm not so upset anymore, though Victoria is and says I should be. Anyway, I'm still teaching at my studio in Springdale, but I'm living in the city. With Vic. For now. Who ever thought I'd be doing a reverse commute?" She laughed; it sounded bitter.

"Just feel free to come by the studio sometime. I mean, give me a little notice. But maybe we can go grab a coffee and talk. It's weird to be so close to you every day and not talk to you or see you. Yeah. Okay, so . . . bye. Take care of yourself, Tom."

The next couple of calls were spam and he deleted them. The last message was from Kevin, three days earlier.

"Tom, it's Kev. I hope you had a good week off. I know how much you needed it. And I'm sorry to call today, I realize it's Friday and technically you're still on vacation, but I thought you'd want to know that the deal you somehow managed to close last week before you left, the Bessecker account?

"Based on the numbers you gave us and the projections we ran, it's going to pay off big-time. Kroll is freaking the fuck out. Dude is in love with you right now. We just need to verify some of the details that you left out. Let's grab a drink on Monday? Or we can even talk at the office holiday party next week. I know things have been . . . um . . . complicated lately. I can only imagine what you're going through, with Jenny and what not. . . .

"I'm actually supposed to. . . . Anyway, let's . . . ah, I'll talk to you on Monday. Cool? I feel like we haven't had a real conversation in weeks, man. Later."

Tom deleted the message and stared at the time. Almost six thirty. He could easily shower, change into a clean suit, and grab his train, make a grand reentrance in the office. He couldn't remember any details about the Bessecker account, but that wasn't unusual anymore: his memory had developed huge, gaping holes. He vacillated wildly between feeling completely in control and having the sense that he was an absolute stranger in his own skin, viewing not only events but also his actions through a distant and distorted prism. He knew that he was tilting toward chaos but had a hard time caring.

He dragged himself to his feet and stood still for several long minutes, paralyzed by indecision. Finally, he placed the phone back on the counter, tightened and straightened his tie, and took a deep breath. He looked at the front door, which seemed impossibly far away through the rest of the kitchen and the dining room. Then he walked down the basement stairs without hesitation, closing the door behind him, easily avoiding the broken step without even bothering to turn on the old, dangling, naked lightbulb.

———

"Thanks for coming, Kev."

Jenny hugged Kevin and held on for what felt like dear life. If he was uncomfortable, he gave no sign of it, wrapping his arms around her firmly and waiting until she was ready to disengage.

At last, she did, displaying an embarrassed smile. "Sorry," she muttered.

"Are you kidding me? I *love* hugs. I come from a family of huggers. None of that half-assed, pat-on-the-back stuff."

Jenny laughed as the maître d' beckoned them forward.

Kevin had suggested Indian, and Jenny jumped at the suggestion. Tom had once gotten sick after eating that cuisine, food poisoning he claimed, and had categorically refused to ever try it again.

It smelled amazing in the restaurant. Jenny hadn't been eating well lately, even though she knew it wasn't good for her or the baby. Victoria kept making incredible meals or bringing home super-expensive takeout in an attempt to seduce Jenny into eating more. She always took a few bites to appease her sister, but the food sat like a rock in her stomach. She actually felt more nauseated lately than she had during her first trimester. And the hallucinations were getting worse.

A young waiter filled their water glasses. Kevin handed Jenny a menu and said, "What do you usually get at Indian restaurants?"

Jenny stared at the front of the menu, which had the place's name and logo emblazoned on it. She was too overwhelmed even to open it, felt her eyes glazing over. "I'm . . . not sure."

Glancing up, she could read the sympathy on Kevin's face. She knew that he had never seen her like this before.

"Do you . . . want me to order for us? I come here all the time."

"Yes, please," she answered. "I'm so distracted lately."

Kevin smiled and handed his menu to the waiter, saying, "We're ready to order." The young man scrambled to get his pen and notebook while fumbling to tuck the menu under his arm. Jenny smiled at the kid's nervousness and saw Kevin smile as well.

"Okay," the waiter said, staring at Kevin with anticipation, pen at the ready.

"We'll take an order of samosas, one chicken tikka masala, and one saag paneer. Plus, naan. Lots of naan. Let the naan flow free."

"And a beer, please," Jenny almost whispered, sheepishly, handing over her menu.

Kevin raised an eyebrow at her, then smiled and said, "Make that two. That awesome Indian beer you have. Please."

The waiter nodded and walked away, toward the kitchen.

"I read that it's okay," Jenny blurted. "The beer, I mean. As long as I don't overdo it. In case you were wondering."

"I wasn't judging you," Kevin said, holding up his hands, palms out. "I'm glad I had an excuse to order one myself."

Jenny smiled. "Thanks for meeting me during your lunch hour. For everything."

"You're welcome, but I haven't really done anything. I'm just worried about you. How are you feeling?"

"Oh, you know, great, except for the horrible heartburn, the intense back pain . . . and let's not forget the hemorrhoids."

Kevin's forehead wrinkled in surprise.

"Oh my God, Kevin, I'm so sorry. That took TMI to a whole new level. Ugh, I'm so tired, I don't even know what I'm saying sometimes."

"Jenny, it's all good. I'm the oldest of four kids and am helping take care of my elderly grandparents. I think I've pretty much seen it all. You caught me off guard, that's all." He took a sip of water, and then a flash of realization washed over his face. "Oh shit, wait. Heartburn? Indian food is probably the worst thing for that. Why don't we go somewhere else?"

Jenny smiled again and reached into her purse. "No, we're good. I've got some of those heartburn pills you take before a meal." She laughed, unwrapped one, and popped it into her mouth. "Look at me. Am I a proactive mom-to-be or what?"

Silence hung over the table; tears suddenly filled Jenny's eyes. Kevin offered her a napkin, but she shook her head and wiped the moisture away with a sleeve.

Her face hardened. "I promised myself I wouldn't cry today. Been doing that too much lately."

"How's the gym going?" Kevin asked quickly, clearly uncomfortable.

Jenny knew that he was one of four boys and always struggled when talking, *really* talking, to women, often masking his own discomfort with charm and confidence.

"*Great*," Jenny almost shouted, then blushed slightly. "It's . . . just amazing. I figured the further along I got in the pregnancy, the less likely that anyone would want to be trained by me, but it's totally been the opposite. Word of mouth has been out of control. Mostly women, moms who can't stand the meatheads at that mega-gym, but also a few men. It's been such a good distraction from . . . everything else."

They both fell silent again, dancing around the one thing they really wanted to talk about. Jenny opened her mouth to broach the subject, but the waiter reappeared, awkwardly carrying a tray. He slid a plate of samosas loudly onto the table, followed by two sweating bottles of beer plus glasses. Jenny thought it was cute how nervous the kid was. It reminded her of being young, when the most ridiculous things seemed insurmountable. She laughed to herself, wishing she still had only those kinds of problems. Thinking of her teen self, she smiled.

"Would you like me to pour the beer for you?" the server asked.

"Nah," Jenny and Kevin said with the same inflection at the same time. They laughed and clinked their bottles together as the waiter hurried away.

"To your baby," Kevin said.

"To . . . my baby," Jenny echoed quietly.

The beer was ice cold and absolutely delicious. She had to stop herself from chugging the entire thing. Instead, she forked a samosa.

"These look ridiculously good."

Kevin said, "I could practically live off them," and put one on his own plate.

Continuing to stall, Jenny said, "How's it going with . . . Felicity, was it?"

"She finally told me that she prefers Liss," he said with a chuckle. "She said she didn't tell me earlier, because I went on and on during our first date about how cool I thought her name was. It's actually been . . . um . . . weirdly great. Kind of suspiciously good. I think this might be the longest relationship I've ever been in."

"That's a good thing, right?" Jenny said, biting into the samosa, which tasted as fantastic as it smelled.

"It's a *really* good thing. I haven't had the best track record with women. I'm waiting for Mr. Hyde to come out and ruin everything." He bit a samosa in half. "Damn, these things are better every time I come here."

They chewed in silence for a minute.

"So . . . ," Kevin said.

"Yeah," Jenny answered, knowing time was up. She couldn't avoid the real reason they were here anymore. "How's he doing?"

"Umm . . . ," Kevin said, clearly struggling. "He's doing really well at work. Shockingly well, actually, considering . . ."

"Considering what?"

"I mean . . . obviously, considering what's going on with you guys. It's still hard to process what you told me about how he acted at your party. He's clearly been super-stressed. But it's more than that. It's like he only has two modes now: on and off. He's either on the phone, closing deals with these brand-new companies, or he's a fricking zombie. He doesn't talk to me anymore, or to anyone, really. On the phone, he's super-aggressive with potential clients. I think he's pissing some of them off, but he's also somehow logging big deals. He doesn't even come in every day, but his sales are so fantastic that no one cares. And he's super-secretive now—won't share the details of his deals with anyone, not even me. Maybe he thinks I'm going to try to steal his clients? I don't know."

"Is he . . . in danger of being fired?"

"Not at all. Kroll doesn't give a shit about his behavior or his crazy hours. All he cares about is the bottom line. Dude only asks one question: 'How much?' That is literally all he cares about, and with the deals that Tom's been logging in to the system, well . . . That's the good news, I guess?"

"Jesus . . . ," Jenny muttered.

"I know. I don't like Kroll, I mean, he's an asshole, but seeing his personality in light of what's going on with Tom? The guy could give less than a shit that one of his best employees might be having a nervous breakdown." He took another bite and chewed for a few moments. "Have you . . . have you talked to Tom lately?"

Jenny bit down on her lip, staring at the second samosa that she'd deposited onto her plate. Her appetite had vanished.

"Not since the party at our house. I left him a message, but he hasn't gotten back to me. It's been so tempting to just walk over there and talk to him, see if he's doing okay, but I can't bring myself to do it. I'm still so angry and confused. I don't know what's wrong with him. I think it must be drugs or something. It's the only explanation that makes sense."

"I've thought the same thing, but the way he's acting . . . the 'symptoms' don't really fit anything. Maybe coke, but the mood swings seem too abrupt, and he's never in the bathroom. I mean . . . literally never. I've tried talking to him, but he either ignores me or acts like he doesn't know me. It's really frustrating."

"Tell me about it," Jenny murmured.

"I'm sorry," Kevin said.

"Sorry? Kev, you have *nothing* to apologize for."

"I'm his best friend! I've known him almost his whole life. I should have seen this coming. I shouldn't have pushed him into this job, I should have listened more when he told me you guys were having a kid, made sure he was okay. . . .

"I don't know. I just feel like I totally failed him."

"Neither of us failed him," Jenny said. "There's something else going on. I don't know what it is, but the Tom who knocked that glass of wine out of my hand, the one who's ignoring you—that's not the Tom you grew up with or the one I fell in love with."

"Yeah. I guess you're right. I don't know what to do."

"Is he in the office today?" Jenny asked nervously. If he was, that meant he was nearby. She missed him so much.

Kevin hesitated and then said, "Yeah. He came in right before I left to meet you."

"Would you try to talk to him again? Maybe today? And let me know how it goes? If he's willing, I could have lunch with him tomorrow in Springdale. Or coffee. It doesn't have to be a big deal. I just want to talk to him. I don't want to lose him . . . lose us."

"Yes," Kevin said, his face hardening and his eyes getting watery. "Absolutely. I don't know why I've been such a pussy about talking to him about all of this. Uh, sorry."

Jenny laughed. "It's okay, Kev. I've heard worse. Remember, I used to work for asshole investment bankers."

Kevin smiled as the waiter appeared and began placing dishes down in front of them. "Our holiday party is this afternoon. I'll talk to him then, whether he likes it or not."

Jenny leaned forward and gave him an awkward hug, especially with her stomach jutting into the table and the young waiter recoiling, as if human contact were something he had never witnessed before.

"Thank you," she whispered, leaning her forehead against his. "I appreciate it so much. And I love you, Kev."

"I love you, too, Jenny. And I love Tom. I'm gonna fix things between you."

The holiday party a year earlier, Kevin's first, had been a drab affair. A half-assed attempt at lights, a few bottles of wine, a collection of awkward employees eager to get the hell out of there.

This year was different. When Kevin returned to the office after his long lunch with Jenny, he found the lights dimmed and music pumping. A DJ had a light show going, with red, green, and yellow lights streaming into the shadows. There were way more people there than Kevin had expected. He didn't even know half of them, though some seemed vaguely familiar.

The office looked and felt different; the bass line and the frenetic lights hammered at his brain after the quiet of the restaurant. Talking to Jenny had been nice, almost like hanging out with Tom before everything went sour. He missed his best friend a lot.

Speaking of which, where *was* Tom?

And had Kroll paid for all this? "Holiday spirit" didn't really fit in with his MO.

As if summoned by the thought, his boss appeared in front of Kevin, holding two glasses. "Kevin Jenkins!" he shouted, proffering one of them.

"Hey, Pete. This is . . . wow. Much different than last year."

"Right?" Kroll said, smiling drunkenly. Kevin had never seen the man have a single drink, let alone enough to get intoxicated. What the hell was going on? "The company across the hall was having their party tonight, too, so they offered to combine them and bring all their stuff over. Including their booze! They're some hipster sneaker company or something. They jumped at the chance! Jumped! Get it? They're a *sneaker* company!"

Kevin nodded. Yeah, he got it.

"I know it's the season, but . . . what's the occasion? You seem pretty . . . uh . . . happy," he said, trying the drink Kroll had handed him. It was some kind of fruity, sugary vodka concoction. Disgusting. He struggled to keep even the first sip down.

"What's the occasion?" Kroll repeated, slapping Kevin on the back. He put one arm around his taller employee and stretched out the other as if he were showing off a display at a car dealership. Half his drink sloshed onto the floor at the gesture. "Look around you, Jenkins! Sales are up . . . way up! We are going to have the best year of this company's existence. And it's all because of you!"

"Me?"

"Well . . . not you, exactly. Because of Decker. But you brought him in. He's a beast. Pisses off more people than he charms. But he won't take no for an answer, and the deals he's closing—they're *big*.

"Your boy, Decker," he said, poking a pointy finger into Kevin's chest, "your boy has turned into the biggest asshole I've ever met. But assholes run companies. And assholes love other assholes." Kroll burst into a sputtering explosion of laughter. Fighting the urge to punch his boss, Kevin swallowed more of the sugary alcohol. It was horrible, but he needed it. He didn't know how much more of this happy, drunk Kroll he could take.

"I can't wait for the contracts to start rolling in! They're taking *forever*. But Decker said they're on the way! Then we can really celebrate. Come on!" Kroll said, wrapping his arm around Kevin again.

The office seemed to have grown impossibly large—something about the music and lights, the rearranged desks and discordant laughter elongated the shadows and created a maze. Kevin wished Liss were there. She had told him that she was going to show up at some point, but at that moment he longed for her, strangely afraid he would never see her again. He had finally found *the one*, and now he was trapped with a sweaty arm on his back, being led into the back of a dark office. Every instinct told him that this was a mistake.

No, that was ridiculous. He shook his head, trying to clear it.

He'd had too much to drink at lunch, and then the horrible concoction that Kroll had given him. He felt shaky. Like when he was young and one or more of his siblings would go missing in a public place and he always felt it was his fault, knew he would be blamed.

Kroll led him away from the party.

"Where are we going?" Kevin said, unsure whether his boss heard him over the din until the man laughed.

"We're off to see the asshole!" he sang.

Unnerved, Kevin wanted to shake Kroll's arm off his shoulder and leave. Wanted to find Liss, wherever she was, and take her home and never come back to this place.

A distorted figure came into view in the shadowed near distance. A desk had been moved into the farthest corner of the office, into the darkness. Someone was hunched over it, phone cradled between ear and shoulder, the cord slithering down into the shadows like a parasitic tentacle. Dull light from the computer monitor on the desk washed over the figure, making it look otherworldly, neither dead nor alive.

It was Tom. Or Tom's shadow. It was hard to tell the difference.

"There's my asshole!" Kroll shouted.

The figure didn't move.

"Tom?" Kevin croaked out.

The music and the party fell away behind him. Childhood memories flooded Kevin's mind. Tom was a year older than him, but they never talked about that, even though it had always bothered Kevin that Tom was a grade ahead of him at school. When Tom moved on to "cooler" social cliques later in high school, Kevin acted like he didn't mind. But he would cry as softly as he could into his pillow at night, hiding the tears from his grandparents and brothers.

After he graduated, Tom had moved away without looking back. Returning when it suited him, wanting to hang out as if no time had passed. Kevin pretended that it didn't bother him, but of course it did, especially when the cycle repeated itself over and over again.

"Tom?" he whispered.

His friend didn't move, just kept staring, dead eyed, at the screen in front of him. Kevin and Kroll reached the desk, and Kevin glanced at the monitor. To his surprise, there were no accounts pulled up, no spreadsheets, only a blank screen, its brightness fluctuating slightly. He'd never seen anything like that before—dead computer screens were usually black, not this blaze of sickly, pale, bluish light.

Kroll shouldered past him, drink sloshing over his fingers, and slapped Tom hard on the back. Tom didn't flinch, didn't even blink.

"There's my fucking sales monster!" Kroll shouted. He turned, and Kevin could see his attention focus on the strange computer screen. "Uhh . . . working hard there, Decker?" He laughed and clapped Tom on the back again.

"Your boy is either drunk or fucked in the head," he said to Kevin. "And you know what? That's fine with me as long as he keeps the deals rolling in!" Laughing, Kroll walked away, yelling over his shoulder, "Keep it up, Tommy boy. Keep it up!"

Taking a close look at Tom for the first time in weeks, Kevin was shocked. His best friend's face was as pale as a corpse's, especially in the computer's odd light, and covered in yellowed bruises and small scabs. He was wearing a nicely fitted suit, but his hair was a wild mess, and his beard had grown in. Was he going gray, or was that a trick of the light? Gray hair or not, the man looked older and worn. Withered. A husk of the person Kevin had known most of his life.

"Tom," he said quietly, just loud enough to be heard over the music. "I don't know what the fuck is going on, but enough is enough. You're scaring me, man."

There was a long moment of silence. Tom still didn't blink, didn't even seem to be breathing. Kevin glanced back at the party, which was like looking into an alternate reality. People having fun, dancing, singing, making out in the shadows. The dark corner that Kevin and Tom inhabited felt like an inverted hellscape.

"Please," Kevin said, turning back and placing one hand gently on Tom's shoulder.

His friend jumped as if he'd been prodded by a live wire, hanging up the phone with a robotic smoothness. "Get your hand off me."

Kevin's mouth gaped open. The voice that had emerged from the person in front of him sounded as if it had been dragged unwillingly from a grave.

"What . . . ?" was all he managed to get out.

"You fucking my wife, Jenkins?"

Kevin wasn't sure he'd heard right. Tom's lips barely moved as the words escaped, the voice still foreign.

"I can smell her on you. You fucking Jenny, Kev? I know you've always wanted to."

Kevin felt something harden inside himself as his mind flashed back to the moment he'd pulled Tom down that flight of beaten-up wooden stairs. It was shocking sometimes how fast a friend could become an enemy.

He took a breath, tried to contain his building anger. "I know you've been going through a lot . . . but watch your fucking mouth. Jenny is worried about you."

Tom's head swiveled unnaturally, as though he were a machine attempting to approximate human movement, and his gaze focused on his coworker. He rose with that same bizarre smoothness, only inches from Kevin, who fought the urge to step back. Almost exactly the same height, the two men stood face-to-face, inches from each other.

"Is that right," Tom said flatly, his voice gravel.

"Tom . . . I'm worried about you, too."

Recognition flickered behind Tom's eyes, and Kevin longed to reach out, to shake him or hug him, but something held him back.

Tom's eyes deadened. He leaned forward and spoke, his fetid breath curling against Kevin's face. "You should worry about yourself, you fucking piece of low-class orphan shit."

Without even thinking, Kevin punched Tom in the mouth. He'd always struggled with his humble beginnings, with his constantly absent parents who had then died in a car accident when he was very young. He'd always felt responsible for his three younger siblings, felt hemmed in by his overly strict grandparents and the family's almost complete lack of money. Tom knew that. Knew it better than anyone.

Kevin had tearfully poured out his insecurities and frustrations over the course of more than one sleepover when they were kids, lying on a sleeping bag on the floor of Tom's bedroom. Tom had vowed never to tell anyone about it, never to make fun of him or make light of his feelings. And he never had. Until now.

The blow threw Tom back and sent him toppling over the small desk. The computer monitor smashed to the floor, but its light continued to shine, now at a bizarre angle, like a demented spotlight.

Kevin looked down at the dark crumpled mass that was his best friend.

Behind him, the music and shrieking continued. No one had even noticed their altercation.

Tom rose, wraithlike, into the sickening light. He smiled, blood running through his teeth and into his beard. Lunging forward, he tackled Kevin, knocking the breath out of him. Stars danced in front of Kevin's eyes. His mind flashed back to the last time he'd been lifted off his feet, during a wrestling match in college.

He'd been an All State wrestler in high school and snagged a partial scholarship to a small Division III school, making him the first person in his family ever to get a college education. His grandmother had shed giant tears when the acceptance letter arrived.

Undefeated in high school, Kevin had entered his first college match like a returning champion rather than the freshman newbie he really was. His opponent didn't look like much, and his teammates patted him on the back, excited for the high school phenom to take that skinny little fucker apart.

But within seconds of the ref's blowing his whistle, Kevin found himself in the air, the victim of a painful move he'd never even heard of before. Then he was on his back, blinking in confusion as the ref counted to three in slow motion; his teammates refused to make eye contact with him when he looked at them, pleading silently for affirmation that never materialized.

The memory shut off like a switch had been thrown as Kevin and Tom crashed into the makeshift DJ area. At the impact, the digital music glitched and skipped; the DJ shouted and jumped aside. The fighters smashed into a string of Christmas lights, getting tangled up as partygoers backed away from the melee.

Kevin tried to roll away from Tom but was unable to get far due to the lights tethering them together in some kind of sick display of holiday cheer. In great shape from hours spent at the gym, Kevin was on his feet almost instantly. To his surprise, Tom was, too.

"Look . . . Tom . . . I didn't mean to—"

A fist came out of nowhere and connected with his cheek. Kevin thought he heard something crack in his face and fought to keep his balance; another fist landed in his gut, driving the breath from his lungs. As Kevin doubled over, gasping for oxygen, Tom brought his knee up and smashed it into his friend's face. Kevin nearly blacked out; the intensity of the pain told him that his nose had been broken. Blood filled his mouth and he sputtered, somehow managing to avoid another blow to the head.

People had formed an unintentional circle around the fight; most were too shocked to help or even call for help, though Kevin thought he saw one or two using their phones to record the fight.

"Stop it!" Kevin shouted, throwing a vicious uppercut into Tom's chin. Tom's head snapped back, trailed by a thin stream of blood. To Kevin's amazement, Tom laughed as he staggered back, then wiped his bleeding mouth on the sleeve of his expensive white dress shirt. Tom looked at the bubbling stain for a moment before smearing the blood all over his face. Grinning, he started walking slowly toward Kevin, hands at his sides.

"No, Tom, no . . ."

His entire body raging with pain, Kevin managed to throw another punch, catching Tom in the left eye, which immediately began to swell and turn purple. Tom was still laughing. Tears ran down Kevin's face as he smashed a fist into Tom's other eye; his friend retaliated by grabbing the string of lights that connected them and wrapping it around Kevin's throat.

The attempted strangulation seemed to shock the party guests into life. Led by Kroll, they surged forward. Kevin's eyes bulged as he gasped for air, arms flailing. Were they kids again? Had everything that seemed to have happened over the last twenty years been a bizarre flash-forward or some kind of wish fulfillment made up by his subconscious? Was he actually falling asleep at Tom's house after hours of video games and comic books and gossip about the girls in school who they thought were cute, fading out of consciousness in a sleeping bag on his best friend's floor?

With a sudden surge of strength, unwilling to surrender, Kevin whipped his head forward, smashing Tom's nose with a sickening snap. Somehow, with blood streaming down his face, Tom kept laughing, though his grip on the Christmas lights faltered and Kevin shoved himself away.

"I loved you, man. I *loved* you," Kevin said, his voice as rusty as an old tin can, while the non-music kept playing and the twinkling lights blinked on and off, bathing their distorted, battered faces in waves of color. "But we're done. Do you hear me? We are fucking *done*."

He shrugged out of the string of lights, spitting a glob of phlegm and blood onto the floor, keeping a wary eye on his opponent the whole time.

But Tom just stood there, grinning and giggling, staring intently at Kevin as if attempting to drill a hole into his head with his eyes.

"I'm sorry," Kevin said to Kroll, swaying slightly. "This is my fault. I threw the first punch and I'll pay for the damage. But if this motherfucker is still working here after the holiday break, you can bet your ass that I won't be."

As he limped out of the office, the room lapsed into near silence, except for the strange, skipping music. Even Tom had stopped laughing, his head cocked to the side like a confused animal, staring after the man who had once been his best friend until the door closed behind Kevin.

After a long moment, someone coughed and Tom snapped out of his stupor, looking at the other party guests as if seeing them for the first time. He glanced around the room and then removed the rest of the string of lights from his body. He smoothed his suit and straightened his tie. Several people stepped away from him, unsure what this blood-streaked crazy person was going to do next.

Tom reached into an inside pocket of his suit jacket and withdrew his Zippo and a pack of cigarettes, then tapped one out and lit it with a shaking hand. He inhaled a long puff, then exhaled, a giant smile crossing his face as smoke billowed into the air.

"What are you fucking pussies waiting for?" he shouted. "Let's *party*!"

MONTH
EIGHT

The last few weeks had been a blur for Jenny.

At the end of her lunch with Kevin, feeling so hopeful, she'd stayed in the restaurant when Kevin left, telling him she needed to use the bathroom—which she did. When she returned to the table, which the busboy was already clearing, she'd ordered a second beer. She'd sat quietly, savoring every sip, picturing her future. She and Tom would reconcile after nights of tears and apologies, and she'd move back home. Once their beautiful baby was born, they'd focus completely on their brand-new family, wrapping themselves in a cocoon of blood and darkness.

Jenny had nearly choked on her beer at the image that suddenly soaked her mind in crimson. Her stomach went sour; she stood quickly, almost knocking over the half-empty bottle, threw a ten-dollar bill on the table, and rushed out of the restaurant.

For the rest of that day, she'd tried to shake the images that had assaulted her at the restaurant: being consumed and choked with blood as she held her baby and was held in turn by Tom. This waking nightmare echoed the kinds of dreams she'd been having lately—horrible, gore-soaked visions often set in the basement of their house. She tried to laugh them off, to chalk them up to her accident on the basement steps, months earlier. A single small scar on her leg served as a permanent reminder of that day. But each time she had the dream, it got worse . . . and harder to dismiss the following morning.

She spent the day after her lunch with Kevin in bed, waiting for him to call. She hadn't had the patience to read a book or magazine or even to watch TV. Victoria had knocked a couple of times, but Jenny remained silent, unwilling to engage in small talk, or any talk at all. She refused to cry, though. She was sick of crying.

A little after ten o'clock at night, with the world outside drenched in blackness, her phone had vibrated against her arm. She blinked awake.

God damn it, she thought. How could she have fallen asleep? How many times had Kevin called before she woke up? And why had she turned her ringer off? She had no recollection of doing that. In fact, she'd been having weird memory lapses lately, often directly correlating to the hallucinations. It was maddening.

"Kevin?" she said, picking up.

After a moment, a weak voice echoed in her ear. "Yeah."

"Kev, what's wrong? Are you okay?" Fear thrummed through her and she heaved herself to her feet, struggling with the bulk of her pregnancy.

"No. I'm not. I'm not even close to okay. Tom has lost his god-damn mind."

Jenny stared out the window at New York City. Victoria's apartment was on the twenty-third floor, and the view of Down-town Manhattan was usually spectacular. But tonight, as the rain washed down, the lights of the city were muddied and hard to make out.

"What . . . what happened?" she stammered.

"It doesn't matter. But I'm done with him. You hear me? *Done*. Forever. And . . . I know it's not your fault, but I don't want to see you ever again either. Whatever's going on with you two, leave me out of it."

Her vision swirled and she backed up, dizzy, until her legs hit the bed and she sat so abruptly that she nearly toppled to the floor.

"I don't understand. Tell me what happened."

"The only thing you need to know is that your husband is gone. The guy you fell in love with—the guy I grew up with—I don't know where he went. But he's not the psycho who beat the shit out of me yesterday afternoon at our office party."

"Beat the shit out of you?" Jenny repeated in a whisper, unable to process what she was hearing.

Kevin sighed. "Look, I'm sorry. I'm in the fucking hospital, Jenny."

"You're in the . . . ? Where? I'll be right there."

"No. *No*. Aren't you hearing me? I don't want to see you! I don't want you or Tom anywhere near my life. He is *toxic*. If you're smart, you'll stay the fuck away from him. If I never see him again, it'll be too soon."

"But . . . what about at work?" She knew it was an odd question, but she couldn't think straight.

"Jenny, Kroll called me this morning, told me he'd fired Tom. Your husband was lying about all those deals, making shit up. Filing reports that were full of gibberish once you looked deep enough into the contracts and purchase orders. Kroll was not amused. Since I brought Tom in, I'm lucky *I* still have a job."

Jenny sat on the bed, watching the rain wash against the windows. Her pleasant visions of the future had disappeared as Kevin spoke. What the hell had happened?

After a long silence, Kevin said, "Sorry, Jenny, but I have to go. Maybe I'll call you when I get out of here, when I get back to work. I just need time. I might get out of the city for a little while. Go see my grandparents. And Jenny . . ."

"What?" she asked, terrified.

"Stay the hell away from Tom. He's a monster."

With that, the line went dead.

Jenny had immediately tried calling Tom, hoping whatever Kevin was talking about was a mistake, but the call went straight to voice mail.

Over the next few weeks, she ignored the advice of her sister and kept trying to reach Tom, without success. Eventually, his voice mail wouldn't accept new messages and she stopped calling. On the days that she worked at her studio, if it wasn't too teeth-clenchingly cold, she would walk past their house on her way to or from the train station, but she never saw anyone inside, never even saw a light on. Even the used car they had bought all those months ago was gone. Had Tom sold it? She had no idea.

Jenny almost knocked a couple of times but could never quite work up the courage. She was afraid of her own house and her own husband. When the hallucinations hit, she was even afraid of herself.

One late afternoon, as she neared her old Victorian, she'd seen Andrea and Paige coming out of their house nearby. A light snow was falling; the setting sun was shining through the clouds and it was a beautiful day despite the cold. Paige, dressed in a thick snowsuit, was jumping into giant piles of snow on the sidewalk. When Andrea and Jenny made eye contact, Andrea's mouth fell open in surprise.

Jenny smiled and raised her hand slightly in a nervous hello, but Andrea didn't reciprocate. Instead, she turned away, leading her daughter into the garage. Moments later, their car pulled out and they drove past Jenny, who was still standing in the same spot on the sidewalk. This time, Andrea completely avoided looking at her.

Sitting in the back, Paige grinned, eyes widening in excitement, when she saw Jenny. The girl waved enthusiastically at first but stopped when Jenny didn't move, just stared at her, sad and forlorn against the gunmetal sky.

To her horror, Jenny saw blood start gushing from the child's eyes as the car pulled away. She knew it couldn't really be happening, but it seemed so real. She quickly made her way to the train station and back to Manhattan.

Victoria had told Jenny on more than one occasion that she should relocate her studio, move it into the city, but Jenny disagreed. She couldn't afford a New York City rental, she was going to have a baby soon, and finding a new space and setting it up would take time she didn't really have. But the real reason was that she hadn't given up on Tom, *refused* to give up on him—a conversation she didn't want to have with Victoria. Not yet. Everything was too raw.

She hadn't reached Tom, but she remained certain that eventually he would talk to her, that he wasn't too far gone. She knew in her heart that he would come around, despite Victoria's insisting that Jenny file for divorce and sell the house.

Finally, Jenny had been forced to tell Victoria to "shut the fuck up" on the topic—right in the middle of dinner one night, while they were enjoying Lakshmi's phenomenal homemade stir fry. Her sister hadn't mentioned Tom since then.

Through it all—her anguish and despair over the state of her marriage, her worry about her husband, her continual arguments with her sister—Jenny clung to her studio. Despite Victoria's earlier warnings, her client list had grown steadily. The advent of winter and extreme cold had been especially kind to business, with people eager for physical release after days trapped inside. She was offering some group classes and fewer one-on-one training sessions; she'd even started a kids' class on Saturday mornings, which had filled up within a day of her announcing it online. An additional Sunday morning class filled just as quickly.

Her clients were a mix of people, in refreshing contrast to the never-ending stream of bankers she'd worked with before. Various ages and fitness levels; different ethnicities and backgrounds, and, she assumed, different sexual orientations; some snooty housewives, some part-time athletes who said they were sick of the mega-gym a few towns away, even one former professional baseball player who was sixty-three years old and in pretty remarkable shape.

And then there was Chad.

He'd shown up again a couple of weeks earlier, on the coldest day Jenny could remember in years, while she was still reeling from the call with Kevin. The studio had been empty all day, her only two appointments having canceled due to the snow that had fallen the night before, not to mention the life-threatening temperatures. She'd received their texts, back to back, while already on the train to New Jersey, immediately annoyed that she'd woken up early on a Monday morning for nothing.

Stepping onto the nearly empty platform in Springdale, Jenny had weighed her options. Since she didn't have any other appointments until late Tuesday afternoon, she could catch the next train back to New York City, then get into bed and stay there for almost twenty-four hours, watching bad TV, eating junk food, and wallowing in depression.

Or she could suck it up and go to the workout studio anyway.

Do some cardio. Lift some weights. Nothing too crazy so late in her pregnancy, but still. Afterwards, she could grab a coffee, maybe even some lunch at the cute little sandwich shop that had recently opened a few doors down from her place. The owner was a retired businessman who smiled and made corny jokes whenever they saw each other.

Maybe she would stop by the house. Try once again to see if Tom was home and make sure he was okay. Try to get a sense of what exactly was going on with him, even if the ultimate answer was a painful one.

Her workout had been going great, loud rock music blasting from the sound system, when Chad walked in. He seemed sort of sheepish, almost shy, saying that he wanted to sign up for a class. Sweaty, out of breath, and a little embarrassed, Jenny had grabbed a hand towel and mopped her face and the back of her neck, aware that she was pretty ripe. If Chad noticed her sweat or her big stomach when she brought him the paperwork, he didn't mention it.

He jotted down his address and credit card number and insisted she run the latter before he took the class, which made her laugh. Somehow, slightly abashed Chad was even more attractive than confident Chad. As he checked the box next to the liability waiver and signed his name on the bottom, he admitted that he'd never had a one-on-one fitness class before. When he handed her the clipboard, she nearly dropped it—probably not the best impression a fitness instructor could make. The entire exchange was awkward and fumbling, and took less than ten minutes. Chagrined but buzzing, Jenny had watched him go and sighed.

Today was Chad's first individual session.

Jenny gently placed her hands on his bare shoulders. She couldn't believe she was alone with him. Despite being eight months pregnant, she felt amazing. Over the last several weeks, her senses felt as if they had exploded. Tastes were more complex than ever, her hearing seemed better than it had been even when she was a kid, her ability to identify things based on their scent alone felt uncanny. She had heard that this was a common "symptom" of pregnancy, but she never expected it to be quite like this.

Not to mention her sense of touch.

Chad's warm skin felt incredible against her fingers. It had been months since she had touched a man, let alone been touched by one. The nightly hugs from her sister were nice, definitely appreciated, even if she didn't always want to reciprocate, but it wasn't the same. She missed Tom's hands on her, missed his small gestures, like when he would touch her cheek gently as he pushed a strand of hair behind her ear. She missed feeling his scruff against her face when they kissed. She missed his smell, his smile, the way his mouth tasted, even the look in his eyes when he got frustrated or mad.

Jenny pushed the bittersweet thoughts of her husband out of her mind.

Chad seemed less shy than on the day he'd signed up, more talkative and flirty, as he'd been when they met at the Deckers' big housewarming party, a million years ago.

When he arrived at the studio and took off his coat, Jenny had seen that he was dressed in a tight tank top and a pair of running shorts, an outfit that showed off his impressive but not over-the-top physique. They'd chatted lightly, Jenny feeling butterflies in her stomach. As he began stretching, she shifted from nervous to professional, realizing that Chad had learned all the wrong things about how to warm up before a workout. She sternly told him to stop, then walked over and placed her hands on his shoulders— and both she and Chad went still and silent. There wasn't even any music—for some reason, Jenny had forgotten to turn on the sound system even though that was always the first thing she did before a workout.

The moment stretched on as Chad stared into her eyes, and Jenny found herself unable to speak. She hadn't realized how blue his eyes really were, or that they were speckled with tiny flecks of green-gray unlike anything she'd ever seen before. His breath smelled amazing, minty and sweet. A self-assured smile spread across his face.

"What next, Coach?" he said quietly, practically whispering.

The hair on her arms stood up in excitement. She blinked and got hold of herself. Years of on-the-job training kicked in, and she flashed a confident smile to match his.

"Whoever taught you to stretch did a terrible job," she said, forcing herself to reposition his arms. "If you don't stretch correctly before a workout, you could do long-term damage to your muscles. You might not realize it right away, but eventually it's gonna come back to bite you in the ass."

"Well," he said, "my dad taught me how to stretch. He was my Little League coach. So, are you saying he was a terrible coach?"

Jenny laughed and kicked his legs open, a little harder than she'd intended. He looked surprised at the impact but quickly recovered and smiled again. "Legs farther apart," he murmured. "Got it."

She almost apologized for kicking him so hard but thought better of it. If he wanted a real workout that was going to make a difference, he was going to get it. She walked over to the stereo and turned on the music, nice and loud.

For the next hour, Jenny pushed Chad hard. He seemed to relish the challenge, and she came to realize that the guy was in fantastic shape, even better than his appearance suggested. By the end of the session, they were both sweating heavily and even pulled off a non-ironic high five after he did his last jump rope set. She threw him a towel and handed him a bottle of water.

"Thanks," he managed to get out between greedy sips.

"Not a bad start. For a newbie." She was barely out of breath, despite being so far along in her pregnancy and pushing herself a little too hard to impress him.

Leaning against a wall, he chugged the rest of the water; some spilled down his chin and ran along his throat. She watched his glistening Adam's apple bobbing up and down and felt a rush of attraction flow through her body. When was the last time she'd had sex with Tom? Probably that time in the restaurant bathroom. That had been amazing, but it had also been months ago. She tried to calm her breathing as Chad wiped his mouth with the back of his hand.

"What?" he said with a smile, watching her closely.

She forced herself out of the almost-fugue state she'd descended into and walked over to him, snatching the towel out of his hand. He laughed in surprise. "You aren't done yet, Forsythe. Time to fix your post-workout stretching now."

Chad mock-saluted. "Yes, ma'am."

He stepped away from the wall as she took another step toward him. Her earlier playlist was done, and it had grown quiet in the studio. There were no cars driving past; there was no one on the street outside. It was as if they were the only two people in the world.

They stared into each other's eyes. Jenny told herself to say something, to get back to business, but was unable to. Chad gave her a half smile, a delicate curve of the lips that crinkled the corners of his eyes. Somehow, despite his intense workout, his hair was still perfect. He looked as though he'd just stepped out of a fashion magazine.

Chad inched closer. Jenny held her breath, unable to speak, barely able to even think.

"Jen . . . ," he said plaintively, almost desperately, and then he was kissing her.

His mouth tasted so good—Jenny felt as if she'd left her body and was observing the situation from a distance.

Tightening his arms around her, Chad kissed her more deeply. Jenny wasn't exactly kissing him back, but she hadn't stopped him either. Her brain didn't seem to be able to communicate with the rest of her body. Her arms hung languidly at her sides while goose bumps shot up and down her spine. His stubble against her face, his soft lips, his strong hands on her back. It felt incredible to be touched like this.

"Wait . . . ," she managed to say as he pulled away for a second. Even the feeling of his breath so close, gently caressing her mouth, made it hard to think. He was so fucking hot.

"You're beautiful . . . ," he whispered, and her body flushed yet again. "All of you," Chad said, placing his hands on her stomach and leaning in for another kiss.

The feeling of another man's fingers on her pregnant belly snapped Jenny back into reality. That was her baby in there. Hers and Tom's.

She fought against the pleasure coursing through her and managed to get out a loud "Stop."

Chad either didn't hear her or didn't care, because his attempted kisses became more intense and he forcefully slid his tongue into her mouth, moving his hands around to the small of her back and pushing his pelvis against her. Jenny felt as though she were trapped in the nightmare she'd had months earlier, when she dreamed of being covered in body parts. Chad's wet, probing tongue reminded her of the bloody finger that had been lodged into her mouth, its ragged nail tearing at the inside of her cheek. Her vision turned red, and she wanted to vomit.

Despite the blood pounding in her ears, Jenny calmly wrapped the fingers of her right hand around Chad's neck. He moaned in pleasure and murmured, "Yeah, baby . . ." When she started squeezing, it took him a moment to realize what was happening. Then his eyes opened wide and he stared at her in confusion.

"I said *stop*," she hissed, lifting him into the air by his neck, one-handed, his feet dangling off the ground. He gasped for air but there was none to be had, even when he started clawing pointlessly at her fingers.

Jenny could hear screeching in her ears even though she knew it was silent in the studio, except for Chad's pathetic gurgling. The high-pitched noise got louder and louder until she couldn't take it anymore. She threw him against the nearby wall, slamming his body hard against it. Chad collapsed in a breathless heap, grabbing at his throat, taking long, deep breaths, tears rolling down his face. His perfect hair was a mess.

"Fuh . . . ," he sputtered, staring up at her. Jenny blinked rapidly. The shrill screaming in her ears was gone, replaced by Chad's rapid breathing. *"Freak,"* he finally managed to get out. "You're a fucking *freak*! Just like your psycho husband!"

Jenny looked around the studio, then out the window. Nothing had changed. Everything was quiet; no one outside had noticed. She swiveled her head back around, almost insectlike, and stared at Chad with curiosity, then glanced at her hands. Had that all really happened?

Wobbling, Chad got to his feet, using the wall for support.

Jenny snapped out of her trance, the echoes of the screeches still reverberating in her ears; her eyes widened. "Oh my God, Chad . . . ," she said, taking a step forward.

He stumbled along the wall, toward the door, throwing his arms up in a defensive gesture, fear blazing in his eyes. "Stay away from me!" he yelled, sounding like a little boy. Jenny stopped in her tracks. "Stay *away*," he repeated, a thin hiss. He continued to slide along the wall, as if afraid to make a direct bolt for the door, clearly not wanting to get any closer to Jenny than he had to. She stood still, watching him go, her gut twisting with fear, excitement, and nausea.

After what seemed like a very long time, Chad reached the door. He threw it open and flung himself outside, shooting one last glance back at the woman he had just been kissing, abandoning his coat despite the frigid temperatures. His gorgeous eyes were full of terror.

The darkness outside swallowed Chad almost immediately. The door was still open in his wake, admitting cold air that swirled about Jenny. She closed her eyes and let the wind roll past her face, through her hair. It felt incredible.

A voice whispered in her ear.

"Good girl. . . ."

Jenny's eyes whipped open and her feeling of ecstasy vanished, replaced by an almost inhuman fear, her heart slamming against her rib cage. Her stomach ached and she placed her hand on it as she looked for the source of that horrible voice, a voice pulled from every nightmare she'd ever had. The studio was empty. The wind grew stronger, colder, and more bitter.

Jenny surged forward, still clutching herself, and pulled the door shut with more violence than she'd intended, a thin crack erupting in its wood.

Tears began to roll down Jenny's face, unbidden, but she felt strangely empty inside. She stepped away from the door, backing up to the center of the room, where she had been kissed by Chad Forsythe. She sank down into a fetal position, clutching her stomach and the baby inside, and wept, loud and messy, for a long, long time. Despite her tears, she felt nothing, absolutely nothing inside, which made her cry even harder.

Another storm was threatening when Ray Dallesander pulled up to the Decker residence a little after five o'clock in the evening. Ray grumbled under his breath as he clambered out of his messy truck, toolbox in hand, cursing himself for wearing only a T-shirt under his barely adequate winter coat. He'd gone through an ugly divorce a year earlier and had trouble concentrating on much these days, let alone what clothes to wear. Theresa, that fucking bitch, had destroyed him with her expensive lawyers and bitter, scrunched-up face. He had no idea how he was going to pay his bills, not to mention the tabs he kept racking up at the various bars he ended up at every night of his life.

Thank God he didn't have any kids. A monthly child support check would have been the death of him. Maybe literally. And it wasn't like the inheritance he'd received from his recently deceased mother was doing much to help. It had barely covered her own funeral expenses.

That's why he had accepted the furnace job when that Decker loser called. Sure, it had been odd, months ago, when the long-haired freak refused to let him into the basement . . . but really, what did he care? It was annoying to the small part of Ray that was a completist, but as long as the weirdo signed the paperwork that relieved Ray of any legal exposure, Decker's money was as green as anyone else's.

This new call had come just in time. The inspection jobs had dried up in November and especially December. He hoped that people would start buying houses again in the new year, flush with holiday cash or bonuses from work, but either the economy or the weather, or both, was proving otherwise so far. Ray had been thinking of advertising his services as a general handyman, but hadn't done it yet and at the moment was almost entirely out of money.

Still, it meant working for Decker. He'd despised the guy on first sight . . . the greasy hair, the tattoos, the general air of being too good for everyone else . . . that bullshit hippie sensibility had always bugged the crap out of Ray. He was a simple guy, liked simple things, pined for a time that had long since passed, when hardworking men could make a living, keep a happy home where people knew their roles, and maybe even have a kid someday, preferably a son.

But if this Decker job worked out, it might be the start of Ray's new handyman business. Decker was odd, there was no doubt about it, but he'd probably give a good recommendation based on a job well done. The wife had seemed nice on the phone, all those months ago, and she looked pretty hot in the pictures that Ray had found on the internet. The Decker job could change everything. Ray just had to be on his best behavior. Even if it killed him.

Shivering, Ray stomped up the wooden stairs, knocking the snow off his threadbare boots as he went. He noticed that the paint was peeling in the spots that weren't covered in ice or snow and the wood underneath was cracked or buckled in several places. Ray's mind calculated what he could charge a rube like Decker for this kind of work, let alone all the other problems the ancient house must be hiding. This place and its ignorant residents were a virtual gold mine. This could solve everything.

Ray pushed the dimly glowing button of the doorbell. If it rang inside, he didn't hear it. He tried to recall if he'd even checked it during the inspection all those months ago. He'd taken a few nips from his always-present flask that morning, and the inspection, if he were being honest, was a bit hazy. As he waited, freezing, he rubbed his hands together.

It had begun to snow again and the world grew much darker as a result, as if it had been draped with a funeral shroud. He turned to look at the snow and noticed that his tracks to the porch were already filling up. The dead-end neighborhood looked beautiful in the falling snow, the light fading behind a row of annoyingly large houses, some with smoke lazily curling from brick chimneys. It was like a postcard from a lost era, and something about it made Ray's heart ache. He missed his wife . . . his *ex*-wife . . . and that realization made the breath hitch in his throat.

The front door suddenly swung open behind him with a sharp creak, causing Ray to jump. *God* damn *it*, he thought. The last thing he wanted was to appear weak in front of this guy. He turned to face his customer, his best hope for a second chance at life.

Decker stood in the shadowy doorway, wearing a ratty, stained, not-white-anymore T-shirt and a pair of ripped jeans. No shoes or socks despite the cold. His hair was shorter than the last time Ray had seen him but was even more greasy and wild, and he sported a full beard of patchy salt-and-pepper. Dark bruises stood out in contrast to the shocking paleness of his face, and his nose looked weird, bent at an unnatural angle.

A strange odor wafted out of the house, like nothing Ray had ever smelled before. It was an earthy scent, similar to newly cut grass or dirt on a hot day after a brief rain, but there was something underneath that, something he couldn't quite put his finger on, that made the hair on the back of his neck stand up. *A gold mine*, he reminded himself. *You need this.*

"Tom . . . uh, hey, how are you? Sorry I'm a little late. The roads . . ."

"No problem," Decker responded, a forced smile enveloping his face. "Please. Come in."

Ray attempted to do so, but Tom barely moved, forcing the more rotund man to shimmy past, sucking in his breath and large belly, stepping over a pile of envelopes as he did so, many of them emblazoned with the words FINAL NOTICE. Decker closed the door behind them, sinking the dining room into darkness.

"So . . . ," Ray said, heading for the kitchen. "Having some trouble with your furnace, huh?" Decker followed him, silent. It was unnervingly dark in the dining room.

"Well, it's definitely cold in here . . . no question *something's* wrong with your furnace." There was even a nasty draft in the house. He looked at Tom's outfit again. "Aren't . . . *you* cold?"

"Honestly, I hadn't noticed," Tom said, that stupid smile still on his face. "I've been painting, getting the blood going. I lose my mind a bit when I'm working."

"Yeah, sure."

The two men stared at each other in the pale light from the kitchen fixture overhead. Snow tapped gently against the windows. Ray glanced down again at Tom's shirt. Those weird, blue-black stains didn't really look like paint, but what the hell did he know? When it came to art, he was clueless, never really understood why people went to museums or galleries when there was an entire world of *real* shit out there, not to mention the beauty of women and the excitement of sports.

"How's Mrs. Decker handling the cold?" Ray asked, thinking of beautiful women.

Tom's odd smile faded and he looked down at the floor, eyebrows beetling. Ray noticed that Decker was standing directly on top of that strange brown splotch that he'd dismissed during the inspection. He could probably charge a thousand bucks, at least, to redo this shitty old linoleum floor.

"She's . . . not here," Tom said, his voice sounding dead. The lack of emotion sent an inadvertent chill of sympathy along Ray's skin. *Oh shit. This poor bastard got dumped, too. Look at that, we have something in common after all.*

"Roger that," Ray replied, moving forward and clapping Tom on the back, a manly gesture he had performed hundreds, if not thousands, of times before, a way of telling another guy that you were on his side without being gay about it.

Tom's head snapped up and he knocked Ray's arm away, his eyes burning with violence.

Ray's fingers curled into fists, and a switch flicked on deep in his gut, the instantaneous change from lovable teddy bear Ray to terrifyingly violent Ray. Even as a kid, he would routinely punish other kids for any perceived slight. A reverberation of the violence his father visited upon him, perhaps. He hated that part of himself, even if he sort of reveled in the fights. He was aware that his temper had driven away everyone he had ever cared about, and he knew he should be sorry about that, but secretly he loved that rage. *Needed* it.

He was ready to pop this wild-haired fag in the face, another manly gesture he had performed on many a drunken night.

The odd smile returned to Decker's face.

Ray worked to slow his breathing. *Calm down,* he told himself. *You're here to do a job. So, do your fucking job.*

"Sorry," he forced out. He *never* apologized, a point of immense pride for him. "Look, let's . . . can you just show me the furnace? I'm sure you don't want it broken tonight . . . supposed to get down to zero, probably way below with the windchill."

Tom nodded and turned toward the closed basement door. "Downstairs," he said solemnly.

Yeah, Ray thought, *No shit.*

The door glided open with a creak that echoed in the kitchen and made Ray notice for the first time how quiet the rest of the house was. The snow had stopped and there was no wind, or none that he could hear.

"Come on," Tom said before disappearing down the stairs. Ray shook his head, laughing quietly to himself. This guy was clearly off his rocker . . . had probably been dumped by his wife right around the holidays and lost his shit as a result. Had let his appearance and house go. A part of Ray wished that he could just walk out of there. The thought of Decker, standing alone in the basement for who knows how long, waiting for Ray to appear, was hilarious to contemplate, almost too good to pass up. He could drive home, open that new bottle of good tequila he'd treated himself to earlier that day, drink himself into a multiday stupor. But the thought of the tequila, of how many twenties he'd had to peel out of his wallet to afford it, also made him think about the pile of bills he had thrown across his piece-of-shit apartment the night before.

Everything was riding on this job.

Sighing, Ray headed down the basement stairs, nearly tripping over a large, jagged hole in the middle of one step.

"Whoa!" he shouted. "Holy shit, you could warn a guy!" He closed his eyes as he caught his balance and tried to swallow his simmering rage. "I could fix this for you, too, wouldn't take long at all," he said, trying to sound friendly and helpful. Employable.

He stepped over the broken step and walked the rest of the way down, surprised by how dark it was in the basement. How warm. And packed with garbage.

"Decker?" he said, unable to see the man in the oppressive gloom.

"Here," Tom said.

Ray peered toward the voice, squinting, barely making the guy out in the nearby shadows. "Aren't there any other lights down here?" Ray asked.

"Broken," came the muddy reply.

Of course they are.

"That's okay, I have my flashlight." Ray reached down to his belt, but the flashlight wasn't there. *Fuck.* He'd gotten into the bad habit of taking it off when he got into the truck. Didn't like the way it pressed into his side when he was driving. "Shit, I . . . left it in the truck. I can be back in a minute."

He worried that a break in momentum, even such a small one, might kill the deal, but Decker smiled at him.

"Just come see it first," the guy said, his voice clear now and maybe a little urgent. Ray liked that sound—it meant Decker was more desperate than he'd been letting on. The aloof attitude, the one-word answers, that stupid smile . . . the guy was probably hiding how inept he was, putting on a brave face so Ray couldn't take advantage of him. But Ray saw what was going on.

He was going to *gouge* this pretentious motherfucker. Served him right.

"Yeah, okay, sure," he said, and began to follow the home-owner through a maze of junk, noticing that unlit Christmas lights had been strung along the makeshift path. He marveled that Decker had been living here for however many months and hadn't cleaned this hellhole up. Or maybe this shit was all his? Some kind of obsessive hoarder or something? Whatever. Ray didn't care. Not his problem.

It was impossible to see much of anything in the darkness of the basement, so he focused on Decker, whose white T-shirt was less dirty in the back, helping Ray navigate the twists and turns. He tried to keep his breath even. He had never loved dark, en-closed spaces. His mother used to lock him in a tiny closet when he was a kid and had done something wrong. She'd leave him in there for hours. He remembered with shame how many times he had pissed his pants in there.

"The furnace . . . is *this* way?" he asked. He had an uncanny sense of direction, an innate instinct and understanding of where things were and where they were supposed to be, and something about this didn't seem right. If he had built this house, he would have put the furnace and the hot-water heater on the other side of the basement, closer to the street. Every nerve in his body told him to turn around and walk, if not run, away—but he overrode the feeling. That was the terrified kid in the closet talking. If this was a harebrained scheme to get Ray down here so Decker could play some trick on him, the weak little hippie had another think coming. Besides, the internal structure of some of these old houses didn't always make sense. People were idiots back then.

Ray tripped over something and instinctively put his hands

out, inadvertently using Tom's back as support. He waited for another disproportionate, even violent response, but Decker simply said, "It's okay. I've got you. We're almost there."

Sure enough, they were approaching the far wall and there *was* something there . . . but it didn't look like a furnace, at least not one Ray had ever seen before. No pipes extending up into the house, no pilot light gleaming out from underneath. If this was the furnace, no wonder the house was freezing.

"That's not . . . ," he said, then realized that the thing in front of Decker was an ancient refrigerator. The path ended in front of it.

Decker smiled at him and said, "I just want to show you something first. I found something behind this refrigerator and I'm not sure what it is. But it's *amazing.*"

Ray's imagination instantly ran wild. Had Decker found something rare and valuable—something whose worth the hippie didn't understand? He'd tell the guy that he would take care of the situation, make it sound like a problem even if it wasn't, and then abscond with the treasure, move away from this horrible part of the world. He was sick of snow and ice. Sick to death of it.

"Let's see," he said, trying to contain his enthusiasm.

Nodding, Decker took hold of the old fridge and strained to move it. His face turned red with the effort.

For fuck's sake, Ray thought. *This guy really is a pussy.*

"It . . . sticks sometimes," Tom huffed.

"Here, let me," Ray commanded, placing his toolbox on the floor and shouldering forward, none-too-gently shoving Tom out of the way.

Decker shrank behind him, probably embarrassed. "Of course," Tom said. "I'm curious to see what you think of it."

Ray's fingers were slick with sweat. He wiped his hands on his jeans before grabbing the refrigerator, bracing himself for its massive weight.

Surprisingly, the giant appliance swung forward with almost no resistance whatsoever. Ray had pulled with so much effort that he almost lost his balance. He leaned into the fridge to stay upright, stopping its movement. He could hear Decker breathing behind him.

It was dark back there, behind the refrigerator, but he could tell that the wild-haired, batshit-crazy-eyed wackadoo hadn't been lying. There *was* something there. The way it caught what little light reached it made Ray think it might be something valuable after all. It glistened, practically sparkling, and his mind conjured up images of rubies or emeralds hidden in this ancient wall decades earlier, of Decker accidentally unearthing them somehow in his utter stupidity.

But no. As Ray's eyes continued to adjust, it became clear to him that this was no odd collection of jewels. A huge, dark mass clung to the wall. It looked *moist*, which explained why it glistened. Ray abruptly realized that the thing was moving slightly, kind of throbbing, and that it gave off a strange but not unpleasant odor. It also seemed to be . . . wheezing? Ray's brain tried to process what he was looking at, and failed.

"What the hell—?"

Hands on his back shoved him forward. Ray pushed back against the force, but his feet slipped on what felt like dirt on the floor, and he moved inexorably closer to the thing on the wall, realizing that it was some sort of pod. Was it alive? It seemed to be expanding toward him.

I'm going to fucking kill this guy, he thought, furious. But his anger turned to terror as he stared at the pulsating veins that covered the thing on the wall and realized that it was very possible that he, himself, was about to die.

"Get the fuck *off* me!" he shouted as his fear spiked and warm piss ran down his legs, staining his pants. He tried to get away, but Decker's hands were clamped on to his shoulders, unbelievably strong and unyielding. *"Please!"* he cried, only inches from the mucus-covered mass. "I'm sorry! I'm *sorry!*"

His forward momentum seemed to slow, and for a moment, a glimmer of hope crossed his mind. Maybe this *was* a prank after all. An elaborate one, but a prank nonetheless. They could laugh about it upstairs in the kitchen, later, before Ray beat Decker within an inch of his life.

He felt Tom's breath on his ear. "I'm sorry, too."

With that, Decker pushed him one last time and Ray's face made contact with the thin, clear membrane that encased the dark *thing*. The pain of that touch was the worst he had ever experienced, bright and flaming agony.

Ray Dallesander screamed, a pitiful sound, the scream of an animal or a child. A final scream.

Tom held the man's yammering, shuddering body in place, watching dispassionately as the chrysalis began to consume it. Ray's one still-visible eye was going wild in its socket, and Tom leaned forward, feeling that the man deserved human contact in the last moments of his life, even if it was difficult, almost impossible to experience. Part of him wanted to walk away. But he couldn't. It wouldn't be right.

They made eye contact and Ray emitted a garbled shout, desperate, as if he could still somehow get out of this. It reminded Tom of that first squirrel from months earlier, and of all the animals since then.

He hated this.

But if the chrysalis didn't feed, it didn't give Tom what he wanted. What he *needed*. He could only imagine the reward for a meal this large.

The chrysalis continued to feed as Ray flailed wildly. More of his face vanished. One of his arms. His nose. Tom grimaced while he watched. This was so much worse than he had expected. But it was important, he told himself. *Necessary*.

The man's unbearable screeching abruptly ended as his mouth was enveloped. The only part of his face that was still visible was that one damn eye.

Tom made himself keep watching. Forced himself not to help.

"I'm sorry," he said again.

At last Ray's face was gone completely, followed quickly by his entire head.

The home inspector's large body began to spasm, and Tom stepped back, afraid he'd be hit or kicked. The body . . . the corpse . . . went slack within seconds. That always happened. First the struggle, then a horrible limpness.

Tom started to look away and then stopped himself. He clenched his jaw and tried to focus on what was left of Ray's body, forcing himself to watch the entire process.

As the chrysalis continued to feed, Tom noticed something bulging in Ray's back pocket. When his brain processed the shape, he panicked and lunged forward, reaching into the pocket and scrabbling for its contents. His hand wrapped around the object just as the chrysalis's membrane swept over that part of the man's body—and Tom's hand.

Tom had touched the chrysalis dozens, if not hundreds, of times, and it had never hurt him. But as the dark mass wrapped itself around Ray's waist and Tom's hand, wrist, and part of his forearm, a shooting pain raced up his flesh, as if he'd shoved his fingers into a raging fire.

Yelling in agony, Tom fought to pull his hand free, keeping his fist clenched around the object he'd found in Ray's pocket. The small, fast-disappearing, logical part of his brain insisted this was important, that it was essential, though at the moment he couldn't remember why.

The pain was almost unbearable.

Jerking away from the chrysalis, Tom yelled again as his hand came free.

He tried to catch his breath as he stared at the blackened husk of his forearm, reeling from the pain. Closing his eyes, he breathed through his nose, trying to clear his mind . . . Ray's eye kept appearing in his inner vision, staring directly at him.

After a few moments, Tom opened his eyes and frantically swiped at his wounded arm with his free hand. Most of the blackness seemed to be detritus from inside the chrysalis, but the skin beneath the muddy soot was charred red and oozing pus. The pain was breathtaking.

He looked up at the chrysalis, surprised that it had hurt him, even a little offended. Thinking it through, he decided it must have confused him with Ray. The chrysalis would never hurt him intentionally.

Tom Decker smiled and opened his scalded hand.

Ray's keys were unharmed.

Thank God, Tom thought, knowing full well that God was nowhere to be found down in this particular darkness.

MONTH NINE

After her week of nightmares about it, Jenny was shocked to discover that the psychiatric hospital was nondescript, looking pretty much like any other medical building she'd ever visited. But staring at it, shivers running up and down her spine, she knew better. This place was different.

Wet snow fell against the windshield of the rental car, blurring the building before obscuring it completely. She hit the wipers, making the building reappear, then watched it vanish again. She'd lost count of how many times she'd done this. Twelve? Twelve hundred?

She found herself descending into this sort of fugue state more and more. She was barely eating or sleeping, barely talking to her sister. Victoria pleaded with her to get help, said she knew a great therapist only a few blocks away, but Jenny just shook her head. Sometimes Victoria would angrily say that Jenny should be the one living in the house, that Tom should be crashing on someone's couch. Then she would quickly apologize and say that Jenny was welcome to stay as long as she wanted. Whatever she said, Jenny would simply nod and try to smile, then retreat into her room, spending hour after hour in bed, staring out the window at the sky, at the ice and snow. Feeling nothing. Or next to nothing. Ever since the incident with Chad at her studio . . .

She hadn't been back since. She'd managed to keep the place going by finding some part-time help, a nice college girl who was studying physical therapy. Try as she might, Jenny couldn't remember how that had happened. Had she run into the young woman somewhere? Advertised the job somehow? Still, the college student called every couple of days to report on what was going on, and Jenny would repeat "uh-huh" into the phone until the call was over. The details of what was said vanished immediately from her consciousness.

Jenny tried to purge the incident with Chad from her memory but failed. If anything, the images from that day had grown even clearer in her mind. The feel of his fragile throat against her fingers. The sound of his choked breathing. The reverberation of his body hitting the wall, which she had felt running along the floor and up her legs, turned her on even more than being kissed by him.

The look on his face as he practically crawled to the door, toward the freedom that she could have denied him at any moment.

She loved that feeling of absolute power over another human being. And hated it. She had no idea *what* to think of it.

Often, she closed her eyes against the memories and waited for sleep to come, though it rarely did. She'd try to cry but had no more tears, so instead she would lean against the headboard, gently hitting her head against it, just enough to feel something. To know that she was still there.

She found herself walking the streets of Manhattan, underdressed for February's chill, staring at the people she passed. Wherever she turned, she saw blood leaking from their ears, or lips curling back to reveal jagged fangs. A blink and the images would be gone, if only for a few minutes. Often, she would stand in the doorway of a bar, wanting so badly to go in and drink until she was completely wasted. If anyone looked at her and at her bulging belly, she would hurry home and shower, trying to wash everything off her, out of her mind. And failing.

Her nightmares increased in the weeks after the incident with Chad, becoming horrifying, blood-drenched dreams, usually of disfigured children, that left her gasping for breath as she awoke. Almost all the dreams took place in her house's basement or kitchen; sometimes instead of children, the dreams were about an older couple. Jenny assumed that she was envisioning the people who lived there before she and Tom had moved in. Because she didn't know what they looked like, her mind created different faces for them each time, often distorted and covered in gore.

Jenny grew increasingly obsessed with the woman who had murdered her husband in their kitchen. She wanted to know everything about the old couple, how they had lived, how he had died, where the woman was now. When she'd looked into the house's history, months earlier, she was preoccupied with crucifying Chelsea, so she hadn't gone much beyond the basic facts.

Late one night, a little after three o'clock, Jenny had crept into her sister's room to borrow her laptop. She watched Victoria and Lakshmi sleeping peacefully, their limbs intertwined, until she felt an urge to smash their faces in with the computer. Shaking her head, trying not to scream in terror and frustration, she backed away, clutching the laptop to her chest as if it were the only thing keeping her sane.

Back in her bedroom—the guest room, she corrected herself;

her bedroom was in New Jersey—Jenny booted up the computer, got online, and began to dig for information. She quickly found the short article she'd read before; then, using key words from that article, she widened her search. For almost three hours, Jenny scoured the internet, scribbling notes onto a pad she'd taken from Lakshmi's desk.

At nearly six in the morning, she decided that she'd tracked down as much information as she could. She cleared the browser's history, closed and returned the laptop, and reviewed her notes.

The house's previous inhabitants were Abigail and Spencer Gilchrist; she was a retired archaeologist; he, a retired schoolteacher. They'd had three children but, heartbreakingly, all had died, two in separate car accidents and one due to a health condition. *That explains the big house,* Jenny thought. Although Abigail was retired, she had still gone on occasional digs with students or elder groups, judging by an old newspaper photo Jenny had found on someone's social media page, showing Abigail returning from a trip with a group of college students.

It was much harder to find information about Spencer. He'd been a high school science teacher for decades and coached the boys' varsity baseball team for most of that time. One year, the team had pulled off a string of major upsets and won a state championship, but otherwise Spencer's career had apparently been uneventful.

The most interesting information appeared in a news story on an obscure true crime website. A follow-up on the case, it contained a lot of the same information Jenny had found elsewhere, but one tidbit was a game changer: Abigail was practically comatose after the murder and largely unresponsive throughout the beginning stages of the trial. In the end, she had been found "not responsible by reason of insanity" and was remanded to Valley View, a state psychiatric facility about forty miles from Springdale.

Now Jenny was sitting in the Valley View parking lot. She wasn't sure why she had come; she only knew that she had to talk to Abigail Gilchrist. She'd parked as far from the entrance as possible—just looking at the front door of the hospital made her nauseated, as if it were the entrance into every nightmare she had ever experienced.

She'd called the facility a day earlier and asked to speak to Abigail. The receptionist asked for her name, and when Jenny hesitated before trying to stutter out a lie, the woman said neither the hospital nor its patients spoke to the media and hung up. Undeterred, Jenny called the closest rental car place and made a reservation.

Sitting in the car wasn't getting her any nearer to her goal, so Jenny got out and trudged through the snow to the front door, fighting unease every step of the way. She felt her cell phone buzzing yet again. Victoria had been calling regularly all day, but Jenny ignored it. She had to do this by herself.

By the time she reached the portico, she was cold and wet—her coat wasn't warm enough for the weather, and she wasn't wearing a hat, gloves, or boots. She stopped under the parapet to catch her breath. Though she hadn't been hurrying, her heart was pounding.

Even on the doorstep of the building, Jenny wasn't exactly sure what she was doing, had no idea what she was going to say if she was allowed to speak to the previous inhabitant of her house. But her life had fallen apart completely, and every fiber of her being told her that Abigail was essential to understanding what was happening.

———

"Can I help you?"

The young woman sitting at a desk behind a thick plastic partition had kind eyes. In her early twenties, she looked at Jenny with genuine warmth and curiosity, a pen in one hand and papers strewn across the desk. If not for the intermittent shrieking from behind the nearby walls, this could have been a reception area in any office building, anywhere. Tinny music played from unseen speakers.

"I . . . ," Jenny began, then found that she had no idea what to say. If she told this woman the truth, they'd probably lock her away. She fantasized about breaking the receptionist's nose with her fist.

She blinked several times, then tried again. "I'm here to visit a guest," she said. "A patient."

"I see," the other woman said. "And who would that be?"

"Abigail Gilchrist."

The young woman turned to her computer and started typing. "Do you . . . have an appointment?"

Jenny hesitated again. This was the part she'd been dreading. "No."

The smile vanished for a second, then reappeared when the receptionist looked back at Jenny. "I'm so sorry, but we require patient- or doctor-approved appointments for any visits. I'm sure you understand the . . . the delicate nature of our residents. Would you like to schedule something now?"

"I . . . It's really quite urgent that I see Abigail. Today. Now."

The receptionist made a clicking sound with her tongue and shook her head. "I'm sorry, it's just not possible."

Jenny looked at the floor and tried to push down the unnatural rage that was building inside her. Losing her temper wouldn't help at all, would probably just get her kicked out.

"Can you deliver a message to her? I think it would convince her to see me."

The woman nodded. "All messages have to go through her doctor, but I can do that, and you're welcome to wait for a response, if there is one. I can't guarantee that you'll be able to see her today, even if the doctor is here."

"Thank you," Jenny said. "Please ask the doctor to tell Abigail that my name is Jennifer Decker and that I'm here about the house. Her house. Where I live now. I think she'll know what I mean."

The receptionist nodded again. Jenny walked over to the row of guest chairs and sat down. The woman picked up a phone and dialed with beautifully manicured fingernails. After a short conversation, she hung up and turned to Jenny.

"I'm not sure how long it'll take to get an answer. Like I said, we may not even hear anything before the end of visiting hours."

"Okay," Jenny said. "Either way . . . thank you."

The young woman nodded and went back to work. Jenny closed her eyes and tried to clear her mind. She didn't know what she would do if Abigail wouldn't see her. She imagined bursting past this button-nosed receptionist and smashing down doors until she found Abigail Gilchrist.

She wished Tom were with her. She had never felt so lonely in her life. Even growing up, after Victoria left for college and Jenny was alone in the house for a couple of years with her parents, who were focused on their own lives and careers, Jenny had a close circle of friends. They took advantage of their final high school years, partying hard, committing minor crimes around town, usually when drunk or high or both, and skipping school whenever and however possible.

Those years were some of the best of Jenny's life, and she

found herself in that moment, sitting in the waiting room at a psychiatric hospital, wondering what had happened to those friendships. Sure, she was still connected with most of them on social media, but she rarely spoke to any of them and never saw them at all, even though at least one lived in New York City. After all this insanity was over, after she had the baby and figured out her life, whether Tom was in it or not, she promised herself she would fix that. She would rekindle those relationships. They would be part of her own rebirth.

A clock on the far wall clicked away, the passing of seconds a constant punishment. Jenny had to stop herself from freaking out. How much of this could she take before losing her mind for good?

The receptionist made no sound whatsoever, even as she moved papers around. Jenny stared at her. How the fuck was that possible? The woman started laughing, but there was still no sound. Jenny shook her head. Had she gone deaf? Was that also a part of late pregnancy that she had missed in the books she'd read? No, that was ridiculous. She could still hear the clock.

The laughing receptionist picked up a metal letter opener and shoved it into her own neck, blood spraying out all over the desk. Jenny tried to stand up, wanting to help, but was rooted to the flimsy plastic seat, unable to move. The young woman bled out, the smile slowly fading from her pale face before she slumped onto the desk. Jenny closed her eyes against the image, but it was burned into the darkness behind her eyes.

"Miss?"

The voice seemed to come from across a huge expanse. Jenny felt herself clawing toward it, as if it were leading her out of a deep pit.

"Miss . . . ?" the voice said again.

Jenny's eyes shot open. The receptionist was sitting behind the glass partition, unharmed, with the same pleasant look on her face. Had Jenny fallen asleep? She glanced at the clock. At least an hour had gone by.

"Sorry. I guess I dozed off. Pregnant-lady thing." The young woman didn't laugh, so Jenny soldiered on. "What did the doctor say?"

"Well, the good news is that Abigail's doctor *is* here this evening, but unfortunately, he was unable to get a response out of Mrs. Gilchrist. He did say that if you make a more formal request, a short visit could possibly be arranged. But the process can take several weeks, if not longer. I can print out the paperwork for you now if you'd like?"

A deafening white noise filled Jenny's head. *No.* She was not leaving here without talking to Abigail.

"I'm sorry, but I *have* to see her. It's urgent."

"Miss, I'm not authorized to—" the woman started to say, but Jenny stood up and walked forward, then leaned down and spoke directly through the small circle in the thick plastic.

"I understand that you have a job to do, and I respect that. I really do. But when I say that it's a matter of life and death that I talk to Abigail Gilchrist, I'm not exaggerating. Not even a little bit. If I told you what's been going on in my life, you wouldn't believe it."

Jenny could feel an energy pulsing off her skin, more than just desperation, something alien and powerful. She could see the young woman's eyes glazing over slightly.

"I'm throwing myself on your mercy," she continued. "Please. *Please.* If you could get one more message to the doctor, to *her,* I'll sit down in that chair and I won't say another word. And if she still doesn't want to talk to me, I swear that I'll leave and never bother you again. But for my sake and the sake of my baby, I am begging you to do this."

The receptionist stared at Jenny for a long, uncomfortable moment. Her smile had vanished completely, and she seemed confused but then slowly opened her mouth and spoke.

"What's the new message?"

Everything depended on this. If she failed, she might as well give up on Tom forever.

"Tell Abigail that I'm here to talk about the basement."

Within ten minutes of this second message's being delivered, Jenny was signing paperwork to enter the facility, her hands trembling.

During her research back at Victoria's, she had found some pictures of Abigail online. She'd thought the woman was attractive in a handsome, matronly kind of way. Jenny wondered how much murdering her husband and being thrown into a psychiatric institution would have changed Abigail's appearance.

A guard arrived and buzzed Jenny through a plain first door and a second, heavier-looking one that had the words AUTHORIZED PERSONNEL ONLY stenciled onto it. Then she had to go through a metal detector; all she had on her were her wallet and the rental car keys.

The guard was huge, probably in his fifties, dressed in a dark uniform, hair buzzed short and face chiseled, a large walkietalkie strapped to his belt. Jenny guessed he was an ex-cop or a former prison guard. There was no humor in his eyes. He silently led her down a long, brightly lit hallway lined with doors, most of them closed. Jenny saw patients in a few rooms, some in bed, others standing or seated. In general, they seemed harmless, even happy. Maybe this wouldn't be so bad after all.

They reached the end of the hallway, and the guard swiped his ID over a security pad, then pushed an elevator call button, which didn't light up. Jenny wondered if the elevator was working as an image of a spider hatching from the man's finger flashed through Jenny's mind. She shook it away. She needed to keep her shit together, now more than ever.

After several minutes, when the elevator still hadn't arrived, Jenny turned to the man. "Maybe it's—" she began. The doors creaked open at that moment, as if her voice had unlocked them.

The guard swiveled his head and raised an eyebrow at her, then stepped inside. The doors started to close and Jenny rushed forward; one panel banged against her shoulder before reopening. The impact didn't hurt, but the guard snickered ever so slightly. Jenny felt the white-hot rage reemerging and didn't fight it this time.

"You don't have to be such a fucking asshole," she growled at him.

The man's gaze remained impassive, but he smiled at her comment, then pressed the button for the top floor, the fourteenth. He crossed his arms over his chest and stood stolidly as the cab moved slowly upward.

The elevator was probably the slowest one she had ever been in. It felt as though the cables would snap at any moment and they'd tumble down into the darkness until they smashed to pieces at the bottom. In her imagination, the guard's face never changed from its glaze-eyed, bemused expression, even on impact, even in death. The guy had probably never once had trouble falling asleep in his entire life. Jenny wanted to claw his eyes out with her bare hands.

After what seemed like an eternity, the elevator stopped with a disturbingly loud clank. There was a long pause and then the doors squealed open. Jenny waited for the man to walk out, since he clearly wanted to be in charge, but he just stood there, extending one arm to indicate that she should exit first.

Jenny gave him her best *fuck you* stare and stepped out, glancing back over her shoulder to see how closely the guard would follow. As he stepped forward, his walkie-talkie suddenly blared to life, a frantic voice shouting something unintelligible to Jenny's ears.

"God damn it," the man said, and then hit the device's button and said angrily, "I told you to keep an eye on him. I'll be right there."

"We need to go back downstairs," he said to Jenny. "There's an issue on the third floor, and I can't leave you here alone."

"I'm not going anywhere," she responded forcefully, taking a step back from the elevator. He looked at her, seeming surprised by what was happening, and the doors shut, leaving Jenny alone in the fourteenth-floor hallway.

She turned around. Where the first floor had been brightly lit, this one was much darker, the fluorescent light barely reaching the floor. There were rows of closed doors on either side of the hall until the end, where the hallway turned to the right.

Jenny's pulse quickened. She clenched her jaw, feeling her teeth grind against each other painfully, then started down the hall, determined to find Abigail.

The first door had a small, square window. She stood on her toes to peer in. Against the far wall, a man with a shaved head stood with his arms at his sides, face pressed against the padding. She stared for a long moment, waiting for him to move, even the

tremble of a finger, but the man seemed to be completely immo-
bile. Jenny knew she shouldn't, but she tapped on the small window with a fingernail. Almost instantly, the man's head swiveled
180 degrees, an impossible angle, and a bloody smile crossed his
face; his eyes were black dots.

Jenny stepped back, terror seizing her, and fought not to scream,
fought against the almost overwhelming urge to run to the elevator and pound the call button. Instead, she slowly moved back to
the window. The man was exactly where he had been, face pressed
up against the wall, arms loose at his sides. Another hallucination.

Jenny moved on.

She looked into each of the rooms as she passed, her stomach
starting to hurt. She couldn't even remember the last time she'd
had anything to eat or drink.

Most of the padded rooms were empty. In the occupied ones,
the patients were either sleeping or passed out. None were Abigail
Gilchrist.

Jenny reached the end of the hallway and was confronted with
the turn, which led into darkness. She squinted into the shadows
and determined she was looking into a small area with an emergency exit at the end, a bright-red fire alarm bar across its front.
Jenny's forehead wrinkled in frustration. Where the hell was
Abigail?

She felt a sudden stab of pain in her groin and was unable to
catch her breath as she bent over slightly. *Was that a contraction?*
she wondered.

"Hello?"

The high-pitched voice made Jenny jump, and she quickly
turned around, her fingers balling into fists. Back by the elevator
stood a bald man in a lab coat, his eyes hidden behind a pair of

round-rimmed glasses. He had a clipboard tucked under one arm.

Where the hell had he come from?

"I'm sorry I was delayed," he called down the hallway, "but I'm surprised that Security left you up here all by yourself!"

"Am I on the wrong floor?" Jenny asked, walking toward him.

She was gripped by unreasonable terror as she neared the man, presumably Abigail's doctor. She still couldn't see his eyes through the glare on his glasses, though there didn't seem to be enough light in the hallway to cause such an effect. She felt as if her feet were sinking into the floor as she walked, as if the concrete were melting, the hallway stretching, keeping the man continually out of reach. The smell of blood and shit filled her nose, and she fought back a jolt of nausea.

With a sense of time snapping back into place, she found herself standing right in front of him. He was short, and there was a big, warm smile on his face. She could see his eyes now. They were brown, and kind. Jenny relaxed. She was exhausted and letting her imagination run away with her. After she finished visiting Abigail, she promised herself, before she made any more rash decisions, she would go back to Victoria's, eat a big healthy meal, run a hot bath, and get a good night's sleep. Then she could figure out what to do next.

"No, you're in the right place. I'm Dr. Phillips. You must be—" He glanced down at his clipboard. "—Ms. Decker."

Jenny looked down at her hand and realized she wasn't wearing her wedding ring. It was sitting on the dresser in her room at Victoria's. She couldn't believe she'd forgotten it. She shook her head and looked at Dr. Phillips.

"Mrs. Decker. Jenny. Yes, that's me."

"Great. I'm so sorry again about the delay. Honestly, I didn't think Mrs. Gilchrist would respond at all. When she first arrived here, there were a number of visitor requests, but they were all from members of the media. She never responded to any of those at all, not even with the blink of an eye, and we prefer not to dignify those requests anyway. And in the months since then, we've heard nothing. No one's interested in her anymore.

"Tonight, when I told her about your first message, I was surprised because she actually made eye contact with me. But she didn't say anything. I've been working with her since she arrived after . . . well, after what happened. Such a tragedy. I've worked with similar patients during the last couple of decades, but Mrs. Gilchrist is one of the most shut-down people I've ever treated.

"So, I was thoroughly surprised when I delivered the second message, the one about the basement, and she spoke! She immediately asked to see you. Don't you think that's amazing?"

"Yes . . . ," Jenny agreed, trying to take the man in. He was talking almost faster than she could process.

"I've never even heard her voice before today!" he nearly shouted. "She didn't talk during the trial evaluations, or when the lawyers had her sign all kinds of paperwork after the trial, and hasn't spoken a word since the day she was brought here. I had practically given up on her, the psychosis seemed so deep. Anyway, we had to make some preparations to ensure that your visit was safe, even though I don't suspect she would ever harm you. She actually seems like a very gentle woman.

"I think she and her husband must have had a very serious argument that escalated to a most terrible degree. However, even though I don't believe she would ever harm you, or me, we did take the precaution of fitting her with a straitjacket. She didn't seem to mind, and I felt bad about having it placed on her, but . . . you know . . . rules are rules. Mr. Gerritsen . . . the guard who escorted you up . . . had to run downstairs to attend to another matter, but he'll be right back up and then we can go to the visitation room and see Mrs. Gilchrist."

Jenny felt her jaw clenching again, her momentary sense of peace instantly vanishing. She couldn't wait another fucking second to see Abigail and get some answers. Who knew how long it would take that walking steroid shot to get back up here, especially on this place's nineteenth-century elevator?

She pasted her most charming smile across her face and leaned in a little closer, locking eyes with the short doctor. "Is there *any* way we can go into her room first? I promise this won't take long. I just have a simple question for Mrs. Gilchrist." She leaned in even closer and placed her hand gently on his shoulder. "Please?"

She could feel the sexuality oozing from her pores, and the sense of power it engendered caught her by surprise. She had never felt this way before. It must have been the pheromones from the pregnancy or something. She'd couldn't remember ever getting this kind of reaction from a man before, not from Tom, not even from Chad.

Behind the glasses, Dr. Phillips's eyes seemed to glaze over, much like the receptionist's downstairs, and beads of sweat broke out across his forehead. His breathing became ragged as he stared at her mouth. He wiped at the sweat on his bald head, causing it to gleam slightly in the dull light.

"Of . . . of course," he said. "I don't see why not. The guard will join us shortly. What harm could come of it?"

Jenny leaned back, feeling sick about what she had just done, but she told herself that she *had* to see Abigail as soon as possible. "Thank you," she whispered.

Dr. Phillips pulled a large key chain from an inside pocket of his lab coat and stared at the dozens of keys on it before selecting one with the precision of a surgeon. He smiled nervously at her, looking like a smitten schoolboy, then turned and jammed the key into the lock of the nearest door.

Jenny's forehead wrinkled. Abigail was on this floor? In that room? It didn't make any sense. She had looked into every single window and hadn't seen her—or anyone in a straitjacket. Unless the woman had been clinging to the ceiling like some kind of giant insect . . .

The door creaked open and Dr. Phillips stepped aside. "Ladies first," he murmured.

Jenny felt rooted to the spot. This was what she wanted, so why was she so terrified? Under the gaze of Dr. Phillips, whose eyes had vanished again behind the glare of his glasses, Jenny forced herself into Abigail Gilchrist's room.

When she stepped across the threshold, the temperature seemed to drop several degrees and the air felt unnatural, as if there weren't enough oxygen, or too much. A woman with a rat's nest of gray hair stood against the far wall, arms hidden in a dirty straitjacket. The smile of a twentieth-century homemaker or talk show host was splayed across her face, and her brown eyes twinkled as if she'd been waiting for this encounter for her entire life.

Jenny stopped a few steps inside and felt Dr. Phillips push up against her as he closed the door behind them. She wondered if he really needed to get so close in order to be clear of the door or if he was hungry for contact because of her pheromone attack. She guessed the latter when he walked around her, his shoulder gently brushing against hers.

"Mrs. Gilchrist," he said, his voice as gentle as if he were talking to a toddler, "I'm back. And I'm sorry about the straitjacket."

Abigail said nothing, her gaze locked on Jenny. Her eerie smile didn't waver. Jenny swallowed, steeling herself. *This is what you wanted,* she told herself. *This is what has to happen.*

"I'd like to introduce you to Mrs. Decker," Dr. Phillips said. "She lives in the house you used to occupy. She's eager to talk to you, but there is no pressure, from either of us, for you to say anything. If you feel like talking, that's *great*. But if you don't, that's fine, too." He matched Abigail's smile and nodded, then glanced at Jenny, as if to say, *Your turn.*

She stepped forward and the doctor moved slightly to the left, clearing the space between the two women. The patient in the straitjacket didn't move, didn't even seem to be breathing.

"Abigail," Jenny said after a long pause, "thank you for agreeing to see me. I'm sorry to bother you. I'm not a reporter . . . I'm not trying to exploit you or make you say anything you don't want to."

The older woman didn't even blink. Jenny looked at Dr. Phillips, who shrugged. *Yep, this is what I go through every time.*

Jenny smiled and stepped a little closer to Abigail. "I live in your old house on Waldrop Street. It's a beautiful house, even with that big bloodstain on the kitchen floor."

The woman's eyes flickered, and Jenny heard Dr. Phillips draw a breath. "Please . . . be careful what you say to her," he whispered.

Jenny nodded, though she had no intention of being at all careful. She had to keep pushing.

"We tried over and over again to get that stain out, but even though it fades and fades . . . it's still there. There was just so much blood. But you already know that, don't you, Abigail?"

Slowly, the woman nodded her head. Jenny could feel Dr. Phillips tensing next to her.

"Maybe we should step outside and wait for the guard . . . ?" he suggested, but Jenny barely even heard him.

"But that's not what I'm here to talk about."

The older woman's eyes went wide, anticipating.

"I'm here to talk about the basement."

A wheezy, croaking sound emerged from the back of the woman's throat.

Jenny knew she shouldn't, but she moved even closer. "I can't hear you, Abigail," she whispered.

The woman blinked bloodshot eyes and said, "Miiiiiiiiine."

Dr. Phillips took a step forward, but Jenny blocked his path. She was too far along to let this little man fuck things up.

"*What's* yours, Abigail? The basement? Or is there something down there?"

"Mrs. Decker," Dr. Phillips interrupted, "please. I really think it's best if we—"

"It's *mine*," Abigail growled. "*I* found it. All by myself. In the desert on the other side of the world. It was so small, so beautiful. I was going to show everyone, show the students . . . I knew they would get a kick out of it . . . a strange artifact that their doddering old chaperone had dug up . . .

"If they even noticed before they went back to their drinking and their fucking. They were all fucking, even the other adults. Did they think I didn't know what they were doing? *Did they?*"

Dr. Phillips touched Jenny on the shoulder, but she shrugged him off.

"What did you find? Why didn't you show it to anyone else?" Jenny asked, staring directly into the woman's eyes.

"The more I touched it . . . ," the woman said, her eyes rolling back into her head, her expression practically orgasmic, "the more it opened up things in me I had never known were there, showed me things I didn't know were possible. No one else deserved it. Not then. Not now. It's *mine*."

The woman's head cocked as if she had smelled or heard something strange. She leaned forward slightly. Jenny's gut told her to run, but she forced herself to remain motionless. She could see Dr. Phillips fidgeting out of the corner of her eye.

Abigail sniffed near Jenny's face, and then her eyes went wide. A look of absolute clarity filled her eyes as she looked down at Jenny's stomach.

"It's . . . *inside* you?"

Goose bumps exploded across Jenny's flesh. "I—"

"Mine!" Abigail shouted, lunging forward and trying to bite Jenny in the face. Jumping away, the pregnant woman fell hard into Phillips and they both collapsed in a heap, the clipboard falling out of the doctor's hands and clattering to the floor. The old woman leaped onto them, attempting to get to Jenny. Phillips, flailing, was in the way; Abigail fastened her teeth on the doctor's nose and bit down, chanting "Mine" over and over again.

Blood spurted out as the woman ground her jaws together. A horrible cracking sound filled the space, accompanied by a piercing shriek. Jenny and the doctor were still tangled together, leaving Phillips unable to stop his attacker. Abigail tore his nose clear off his face and spat it into a dark corner, still saying "mineminemineminemine" and beginning to laugh in a horrible way Jenny had never heard before. Blood ran down the crazy woman's chin and shot out of the ragged hole in the man's face; screaming, he clapped his hands over the wound, but the liquid continued to seep between his fingers.

Dr. Phillips rolled away and Abigail stared at Jenny, a sick smile spreading across her spattered face, her eyes sparkling. Jenny felt paralyzed. As Abigail tensed, preparing to leap to her next victim, the security guard burst into the room and tackled the old woman. He pushed her face against the floor until something cracked and blood gushed out of her nose.

The guard called for backup on his walkie-talkie, then shouted something at Jenny, but she couldn't make sense of it and stared at him dumbly. The guard shouted again, and this time she understood.

"Lady, are you okay?"

She didn't answer, just watched the two rivers of blood meet and mingle, becoming indistinguishable from one another. Images filled Jenny's head: an ancient stretch of sand, fusing into fire, into stars, her body rising up and shooting through the sky, then falling and landing near her house, being pulled against her will through the front door, through the kitchen, down the stairs, and into the darkness of the basement.

She returned to herself when two more guards raced into the room, along with a medical doctor, who started to bandage Dr. Phillips's face, shouting that they needed to get him out of there and into surgery, asking where the man's nose was. Abigail Gilchrist was pinned to the floor by the original guard's giant knee. Though that had to be painful, she was laughing hysterically. And crying at the same time, with blood, tears, and snot smeared across her face.

"Mine. Mine. Mine. Mine," the older woman repeated steadily despite the chaos.

Jenny stared at her, then slowly and carefully got to her feet and straightened her clothing, absentmindedly stroking her nine-months-pregnant belly. Her scarred leg hurt slightly from the fall, but other than that, she was unharmed. For the first time in weeks, if not longer, her mind felt clear. Abigail's words rang in her ears. She knew exactly what she had to do. As soon as they let her out of this place.

She had to go home, find Tom.

And visit the basement.

It was the middle of the night by the time Jenny was done answering questions.

The local police had been called in, but Jenny's story checked out, backed up by what little they could get out of a drugged-up Dr. Phillips. It was clear that the doctor had broken protocol by allowing Jenny into a patient's room, especially without security present. After he recovered, if he continued working at the institution, he would face significant repercussions for his actions.

The young woman at the front desk glared at Jenny as she left. Jenny ignored her, hoping she would never have to enter this building again for the rest of her life.

The rental car didn't start at first, nearly giving Jenny a heart attack—she'd left one of the interior lights on—but after several tries and a few violent bangs on the steering wheel, it roared to life. She tore out of the parking lot as if the building behind her were on fire.

The highway was empty, making Jenny feel as though she were completely alone on the planet. She tried to ignore the sinking feeling that she was hurtling toward the end of everything that mattered to her.

For some reason, during the drive, her mind went back to her honeymoon with Tom. They hadn't had a lot of money, so they'd rented a house on a lake in Pennsylvania, not far from where Tom grew up. He had been irrationally fearful that he would run into someone he knew, but she talked him into it. Not only was it a beautiful lake, but a part of her thought it would also be good for Tom to confront his past a little bit, to say goodbye to the things that seemed to be holding him hostage. They were starting their new life together, and what better way for him to unburden himself from his own past?

They'd had an incredible week. They completely unplugged, divorcing themselves entirely from the outside world and focusing solely on each other. Taking long, lazy trips out to the middle of the lake in the tiny boat that came with the house; sitting in the sun and reading the beat-up paperback novels that someone else had left behind; cooking multi-course meals, something they never did in their normal life; spending half the day in bed, talking and making love. It had been a wonderful time, a magical start to their marriage. She longed for those days and was determined to get them back.

I'm going to find Tom, she told herself. *And we're going to make everything okay. Together.*

The house waited, looming, in the darkness.

The driveway was covered in snow, so Jenny parked on the street. She got out of the car and leaned against it, staring at the place that was supposed to signify a new beginning for her and Tom. It had stopped snowing during her drive, and the temperature had dropped again. It must have been three or four o'clock in the morning.

Jenny placed her hands on her distended stomach, slightly out of breath. *You're terrified of talking to your own husband*, she thought.

The walkway to the porch was covered in snow and ice; Jenny wondered when Tom had last shoveled. If he'd ever shoveled. The empty tree branches overhead reminded her that she'd raked up their leaves only a few months earlier; the memory almost broke her completely.

Jenny glanced down at the sidewalk, blinking away tears, then looked back at the house as her resolve returned. She was here to find her husband. Reclaim him. For her sake and the sake of the baby that was almost ready to be born. She walked slowly along the uneven, frozen walkway, careful to set each foot before moving the next. She'd heard of people taking nasty spills at night in the dead of winter, being knocked unconscious, and freezing to death. Not her. Not today.

Jenny reached the porch and pulled herself up the steps, using the railing for support. The feel of its cold, chipped wood against her fingers was both sobering and exhilarating. The swing swayed slightly at the other end of the porch, its metal chains creaking quietly.

She almost rang the doorbell before deciding that it was her house, too, God damn it. Reaching into her back pocket, she fished out the key that she always kept on her, through all the weeks since the night Tom had knocked the glass of wine out of her hand. She'd known she would need it eventually.

As Jenny neared the door, key in hand, the door creaked open. There was no one in the entryway—perhaps the door hadn't been completely shut by whoever had last passed through it. Her stomach tightened. *Here we go.*

She entered the house.

The dining room was dark, but the kitchen threw off enough

light for Jenny to see where she was going. Everything looked foreign, as if she'd never been in the house before. Nothing had changed but everything felt different, as if the place were radiating evil or danger, or both. Jenny felt a twinge in her abdomen but ignored it. She was having trouble catching her breath. Her heart was pounding.

"Tom?" she called weakly.

There was no response.

The overhead light in the kitchen seemed brighter than ever when she entered the room. Had Tom replaced the bulb? The bloodstain also looked brighter, almost as if new blood had been spilled, filling the exact same pattern. It had to be a trick of the light. As she stared at the stain, it seemed to lift off the floor and rise toward her. She closed her eyes and shook her head, stepping blindly toward the open basement door.

When she opened her eyes, at the top of the stairs, she called her husband's name and peered down into the darkness of the basement. The bulb in the stairwell seemed dimmer than she remembered, especially after the brightness of the kitchen, but she could still easily see that damn hole in the fifth step.

At the sight, Jenny's blood boiled. Her vision clouded with rage and she tried to calm down as her head began to spin, afraid she might fall down the stairs and break her neck. Steadying herself, she was surprised to hear a rhythmic sound rising from the basement. Was that . . . *breathing*?

"Tom!" she shouted. "I'm coming down!"

The wet breathing sound stopped. Something deep inside told Jenny to leave, to drive back to her sister's place and forget that Tom had ever existed, to have her baby and never come back to this goddamn house ever again.

Instead, she descended the stairs.

When she reached the step with the ragged-edged hole, she stopped, set her jaw, and looked into the gap. She thought she could make out things wriggling in the darkness. Tom had told her about the seemingly endless number of millipedes and spiders in the basement, saying that he couldn't bring himself to kill any of them. She tried to convince herself that that was what she was seeing. But the things half-visible in the shadows looked too large to be regular insects. She told herself, *They aren't really there, Jenny—now, keep moving,* and sure enough, after she closed her eyes and opened them to look again, the moving shapes were gone.

This was one of the only times she had ever ventured into the basement in the entire time they'd owned the house. *Why?* she asked herself. *Did I know, on some level, that there was something evil down here?* She put her hand on her stomach and thought about the object that Abigail had mentioned finding "on the other side of the world." Thought about Tom's behavior and her own. Had he found Abigail's artifact in the basement and unintentionally infected Jenny somehow? Or intentionally infected her?

She expected it to be pitch black beyond the bottom of the stairs but was surprised to find that Tom had hung Christmas lights, creating a path through the farther shadows of the basement. The colorful lights flickered on and off, creating a strobelike effect.

"Tom?" she said quietly, barely making a sound.

He was nowhere to be seen. She looked around the basement, shocked again at how packed it was with stuff. Had it been this crowded before? It was a hoarder's paradise, a jumble of boxes and garbage, with piles reaching the ceiling and others spilling everywhere. She wondered if Abigail's artifact was hidden somewhere in one of those piles.

"Tom?" she said again.

Walking along the makeshift path, Jenny realized that it had been traveled many times. All the detritus was pushed back, and the edges of the pathway had been strung with old bottles and ornaments that caught the gently flashing colors of the seemingly endless Christmas lights. It was beautiful, a certain part of herself had to admit. For a second, she allowed herself to hope that this was Tom finding a new way to showcase his art. Yes, he'd let his behavior spiral out of control, but he wasn't the first man to break down under the strain of house, kid, and career.

Hell, she felt like she was panicking half the fucking time, too. She imagined reaching the end of this maze of lights and finding Tom with a huge canvas, or a series of canvases, illustrating his struggles in breathtaking oil paints, his way of explaining, of apologizing. An unbidden smile flitted onto her face, but she forced it away. *No.* If that was true—and it would be a huge step in understanding at least a *fraction* of what was going on with her husband—he would still need to atone for, and explain, so much.

But the lights and the careful array of glass, ceramic, and metal objects that caught and reflected color—they gave her a glimmer of hope. At the same time, part of her insisted that she turn around and run up those stairs as fast as her pregnant body would allow.

Resolute, Jenny pressed on.

As she got closer to the back walls, the lights became sparser and the shadows darker. The breathing sound had grown louder and more high-pitched, like an animal struggling for air after being badly hurt. Had Tom gotten a pet? No, from all indications, the man could barely take care of himself. Realizing she was approaching two vaguely human-looking shapes, Jenny stopped and tried to make out what she was looking at, waiting for her eyes to adjust to the darkness.

Finally, she was able to determine that she was gazing at Tom. He was facing away from her, toward the other dark form, which appeared to be stuck to the wall. To Tom's left was an old refrigerator, its mechanical guts jutting out from the back, coiled metal and frayed wires, as if it had been sliced open for dissection. The thing on the wall caught the light in a strange way, glistening slightly.

"Tom, what the fuck? Are you okay? What the hell is going on down here?"

He didn't move at the sound of her voice, but she could have sworn she saw the thing on the wall expand slightly, the breathing sound seeming to swell as it did.

Sweat beaded on her forehead and down her back. It was blazing hot back here, despite how cold the rest of the house was. Haltingly, Jenny reached out to grasp her husband's shoulder. He was wearing a thin T-shirt; she could feel the intense heat of his skin right through the fabric. *He must have a fever,* she thought.

"Tom? Please."

Either her touch or the softness of her voice, or both, seemed to have an effect. As he slowly turned around, her arm naturally fell away. When his face was revealed, she barely recognized him.

Her husband looked like a skeleton wrapped in a facsimile of human skin, hair, and clothing. Huge black circles hung beneath his eyes, flesh pulled taut across the cheekbones. Old bruises and cuts peppered his face, and his nose looked . . . different. His hair was long, almost as long as before he'd cut it to go work with Kevin, and was visibly dirty and greasy, with chunks of . . . she had no idea what . . . hanging from it in many places. A graying beard covered the lower part of his face.

His eyes were still beautiful—they looked larger than ever due to his shocking weight loss—and she stared into them for a moment. Though everything else about him had changed, those eyes still belonged to Tom Decker, the man she'd loved for years. But they—he—looked at her without recognition.

"Is this what you've been working on down here, Tom? Is that . . . *thing* . . . your art? I'm trying to understand. I . . . still love you. But I'm worried. You . . . you don't look healthy, Tom. Can we go upstairs? And talk? Please?"

He opened his mouth, uttering one word, louder than she expected, and perfectly clear. "Jenny . . ."

She smiled at the sound of her name coming from his cracked lips. Despite her worries—was he shooting heroin while working on some kind of bizarre mechanical sculpture?—hearing his voice gave her hope. For him. For them. And for their baby. As if in response to her surge of emotion, she felt a kick in her stomach.

"The baby . . . *our* baby is kicking. Do you want to feel it?"

She placed one hand on her stomach and reached for her husband with the other. The gesture or the idea of touching his wife seemed to bring him to his senses. He blinked several times, tilting his head, his eyes focusing.

"Baby . . . ?"

"Yes, Tom. Our baby. We've missed you so fucking much. Come upstairs with me. Please. I'm begging you. I know we have a lot to work through. But let's go upstairs and talk. You can feel the baby kicking. I'll make coffee and we'll figure everything out."

Tom's eyes welled with tears, and her heart broke yet again for her husband. She'd always known that he was a tortured soul, but this was almost too much to bear. Finally, he reached a trembling arm out toward her. Forcing a smile, she took his hand. Slowly, not wanting to spook him, she drew his hand to her stomach, causing him to stumble forward a couple of steps. As his fingers touched her abdomen, his face crumpled with emotion.

They were closer to each other than they had been for a long time. His presence. His hand on her body. It all felt amazing, especially juxtaposed with the insanity of the basement. Even if he looked like shit. Even if he smelled awful.

The baby was making them wait.

She placed her hand over his. "Give it a second," she whispered.

He stared, wide-eyed, until the baby kicked again. Then his eyes widened sadly, as if the experience had been excruciatingly painful. He tried to pull his hand away, but she wouldn't let him. She was surprised by his strength, considering how frail he looked, but she was surprised by her own strength, too. She was *not* letting him go. She wanted her goddamn husband back.

"What is it?" she demanded. "I don't understand. I need you to explain it to me. *Please*. What's the matter?"

He stared her in the eyes, tears streaming down his face now. "I'm sorry," he sobbed. "I am *so* sorry. I love you, Jenny."

"I love you, too," she said, refusing to cry. "But why are you apologizing? We're here. Together. We can fix this. Please, let's just go upstairs."

"I'm sorry," he repeated, then clamped his free hand around her upper arm and pulled her closer to him. She thought he was going to hug her, but he twisted her around so he was behind her and she was facing the dark mass on the wall. This close to it, she could see that it was expanding and contracting regularly, its surface crisscrossed with dark veins. It was huge, bigger than either her or Tom, at least seven feet tall and several feet across. The breathing sound had grown louder again. This, she realized, was no high-tech sculpture. This was Abigail's artifact. And the fucking thing was *alive*.

"Jesus *Christ*, Tom!"

"I love you, Jenny," he murmured as he pushed her toward the object on the wall. "I'm sorry. I'm sorry."

The dark mass breathed out, pulsing. At its greatest point of expansion, a spot on its surface lightly grazed her cheek, and an incredible burning sensation seared through her face. She thought about the baby inside her.

No!

She threw an elbow at Tom's head, catching his left cheek. A horrible, dull crack rang out, and blood gushed immediately. It was easily the hardest blow Jenny had struck in her entire life.

Her husband gasped in surprise, reeling back and losing his grip on her. She tripped over her own feet and fell into him, and they both went clattering down into a pile of ancient garbage. Metal rods and wadded paper fell around them as they crashed to the floor, Tom winding up on top of her. Jenny's head hit the concrete floor and she saw stars.

Tom stared at her with a strange look in his eyes, as if he was trying to figure out what they were doing. The breathing sound got faster again.

"Get the fuck off me!" she yelled.

The urgency in her voice seemed to partially snap him back into the present. He raised one hand to his cheek, touching the blood, then stared at his fingers, confusion rippling across his face.

"Jenny?" he said, barely audible.

A moist, ripping noise echoed from behind him, and Tom shivered so hard that he fell off his wife. On his knees, he looked at the thing on the wall as if he were praying to it. A fissure had appeared in its skin, and dark, thick fluid was gushing out; a horrible smell began to fill the basement. Terrified, Jenny tried to back away, still on the floor, but was stopped by the piles of stuff that surrounded them. Staring as it opened wider, she came to understand what the thing was: a monstrous chrysalis. She knew she should run but was completely unable to move.

A bizarre smile filled Tom's face as he stared up at the dark mass. It continued to split open, fluid now covering the ground and running along Tom's feet. He raised his arms higher, caught up in what looked like religious fervor.

"Yes . . . ," he said gently. "Come on. . . ."

As if on cue, a large purple-black form fell from the chrysalis, landing right in front of Tom with a wet smack. It was curled up in a fetal position, so it was hard to make out any details, especially in the darkness of this corner of the basement, but Jenny could tell at once that it wasn't human. As the creature began to stretch out, Tom backed away, on his knees, to give it room. It resembled a giant insect, like a cockroach fused with a scorpion, with multiple sectioned limbs and a long, spiraled tail that ended in a vicious-looking point. Its many eyes were still closed, and its angular skull was covered in short, thick, bristly black hairs. There was no visible nose, and its closed mouth jutted out sharply.

Jenny couldn't get her legs to respond, found that she had no voice.

Tom leaned forward, putting his hand on the thing's head and rubbing gently, as if comforting it.

In response to his touch, several of the eyes popped open. Tom's smile widened.

"There you go," he said quietly.

The creature wobbled to its full height, towering over Tom, and stared down at him. Jenny wanted to get up and run, but it was as if she were glued to the floor. She could barely even catch her breath. In some distant part of her mind, she realized that huge stabs of pain had been radiating up her body for the last few minutes.

Tom gazed, mesmerized, at the thing. He got to his feet, then slowly reached up and put his hand on its face. All its eyes were open now, and it seemed to be studying Tom with what looked almost like curiosity.

"My baby . . . ," he said.

Jenny felt like she was going to throw up from the horrible earthy smell of the fluid running beneath her and the sight of muscles rippling under the creature's leathery skin.

The tail slowly unraveled and flexed. In the next instant, it shot out, its razor-sharp end piercing Tom straight through his stomach and out his back, sending blood splattering everywhere, including all over Jenny. Tom's eyes went wide; he stared at the creature in confusion, then looked down at the black append-age that had just put a large hole through him.

"Oh," he said.

"Tom!" Jenny screamed, shuddering in terror.

The creature's head swiveled as it noticed her. The holiday lights behind Jenny continued to blink on and off, their colors merrily bouncing off the monster's still-slick skin.

When the thing withdrew its tail, Tom crumpled to the dirty floor with a dull thud, his blood flowing even more freely. The sight of his broken body and the sound of his head hitting the concrete shocked Jenny out of her stupor. She leaped to her feet and bolted for the stairs, scrambling back along the narrow path through the basement, the ornaments and bottles jingling as she frantically brushed past them.

She could hear the thing's limbs clattering as it scrambled to catch her, smashing clumsily through the piles of junk. She hoped it was too newly born to have full control of itself.

As she reached the bottom of the stairs, another wave of pain ripped through her abdomen, and her pants darkened with a surge of wetness. Despite her terror, she knew she hadn't pissed herself—her water had just broken.

Racing up the steps, Jenny almost put her foot into the jagged hole that had wounded her months earlier. Twisting herself aside, Jenny threw her hands out to catch herself and kept heading up. The clattering sound on the basement floor, a million times worse than nails on a chalkboard, was getting closer and louder. She glanced back; the creature's head appeared in the pool of light at the bottom of the stairs and swiveled up to stare at her with its dozens of opaque black eyes.

Terrified, Jenny yelled in fear and lurched up the last few steps, into the brightly lit kitchen. She doubled over as a strong contraction hit, then gritted her teeth and hobbled forward. She could hear the monster making its way up the stairs. *Maybe it'll get caught in that stupid fucking hole,* she thought, and laughed hysterically.

The pain eased and she limped into the darkness of the dining room, then began running for the front door, cursing herself for not going out the back door in the kitchen. Old habits died hard.

"Just get to the car," she said out loud, a command that she hoped would override what her body was telling her: *Stop. Lie down. You need to stay put and have this baby.*

As she put her hand on the doorknob, she heard the horrible clattering behind her, followed by a bloodthirsty shriek. A shadow loomed over her, and she instinctively ducked. The creature smashed into the door above her, wooden fragments shattering all over both of them. The force of the impact seemed to stun the thing, and Jenny wasted no time in dashing toward the door to the second floor. In her panic, she crashed into the massive oak dining room table, causing even more pain. Fighting through it, she quickly made her way around the table until she had a clear path to the upstairs door. Moving as quietly as she could, she raced through the door and shut it behind her—anything to delay the monster another second or two.

She wondered if it had seen where she went. *Maybe its eyes don't work that well yet,* she told herself, desperate to believe it, her entire body on fire. Despite her panic, she forced herself to creep up the stairs as slowly and quietly as possible, thanking Abigail or Spencer or whoever the fuck had covered the risers with this horrible dark pink carpet that she had always hated but now loved with every molecule in her body. At the top, she stopped to catch her breath, straining to listen.

The house was silent. There was a small window at the top of the stairs with an antique table beneath it, something Jenny and Tom had seen at a yard sale back in early September, a million years ago. They had bought it excitedly, knowing it would look perfect in this spot. Staring at it now, an overwhelming sadness nearly crushed her. Tom was bleeding in the basement, maybe already dead. She had to help him, but how?

Looking out the window, she realized the second floor was higher than she remembered. The backyard was covered in a white, uncompromising sheet of ice and snow, and the drop was at least twenty feet. Jumping probably wouldn't kill her, unless she was unfortunate enough to land on her head, but she'd most likely break an arm or a leg, and who knows what would happen to her baby. As if on cue, another contraction made her shudder, and she let out a loud, unintentional gasp.

She clamped her hand over her mouth and held her breath, trying to wait out the pain. With her other hand, she got her cell phone out of her jeans pocket and punched in 911. She was about to hit Send when the creature slammed against the door at the bottom of the stairs. She could hear the wood splintering. Startled, she dropped the phone, which skittered across the floor and bounced down the stairs, out of reach.

"No . . . ," she whispered.

Jenny sprinted down the hallway, listening as the monster continued its assault on the old wooden door below. The rooms flashed by—the master bedroom where she and Tom had been so happy for a fleeting time, the bathroom, the guest room, and finally the nursery. Jenny slowed for a second, smothering a sob. Tom had "finished" the nursery, but it didn't look anything like what they had planned. There was absolutely nothing in the room except the crib, and the walls were painted in shades of black and gray, resembling rocks . . . or a cave. Jenny didn't have time to fully take in the insanity of the room.

She reached the winding stairs that led to the third floor just as the door below was audibly destroyed, the creature letting out an animalistic howl at its success. Jenny couldn't hear its appendages skittering up the carpeted stairs, but she could picture them. The image drove her up to the top floor faster than she thought possible even as another contraction seized her.

Stepping into the still-empty room, she slowly closed the door behind her. The latch made a tiny click, and Jenny realized for the first time that there was a push-button lock on the door. She pushed it in with a trembling finger, knowing it was a pointless gesture but doing it anyway.

The moon had come out, and its rays were filtering through the stained-glass window, filling the room with eerie light. Jenny had never spent much time up here, though she'd thought about eventually turning it into some kind of office or possibly a play-room. But she knew the location of the hidden door to the secret staircase. Assuming the monster took a few minutes to search the second floor before it realized Jenny wasn't there, she might be able to get downstairs and outside before it came after her again. She would go to Andrea's and beg to use her phone.

She doubled over as her body was racked with another con-traction. Were they supposed to be so close together already? Her mind was blanking on the details of the end of pregnancy, though she had read enough books on the subject. And who knew how the stress of the current situation was fucking with the way things were *supposed* to happen.

As she caught her breath, Jenny found herself staring at the large black-and-white photos framed on the wall. She'd wanted to get rid of the bizarre photos covered with red scribbling, but Tom insisted on keeping them. Jenny had assumed he was draw-ing inspiration from them for his art, but now realized there must have been another reason.

Had it been Abigail who wrote on the pictures, images of her final dig? Looking at them now, Jenny saw that the crazed lines and arrows formed a pattern, a series of clues leading to one pic-ture in particular and to one specific part of that picture.

Stepping forward, she tried to make out the image, squinting through the colors thrown across it by the stained-glass window. The photo showed the interior of a cave, bathed in shadow and light. It was difficult to determine which shadows were real and which were captured in the photo, a visual memory of shadow.

There, almost completely hidden against the wall of the cave,

Jenny saw a chrysalis. Much smaller than the one Tom had attempted to feed her to, but obviously the same one.

The door to the room suddenly smashed in, the creature bursting through in a tangle of limbs, issuing a shriek of otherworldly rage. How the hell had she not heard it clacking up the wooden stairs? Had she been that mesmerized by the photographs?

Realizing she had blown what was probably her last opportunity to escape, Jenny bolted across the room anyway. She heard the thing righting itself behind her.

As she threw open the hidden door, the creature slammed into her, its teeth and claws raking her body. Falling forward, she screamed, and they tumbled together down the stairs, Jenny doing her best to protect her belly.

They hit the door at the bottom of the stairs with enough force to slam it open and send them rolling away from each other. The monster's claws drew fresh blood from Jenny's face and arms as they were separated.

She frantically reached up and opened the knife drawer, grabbing for a blade and luckily seizing the largest one she and Tom owned, a carving knife. Getting to her feet, Jenny lunged forward and stabbed the creature in one of its multiple eyes; green fluid spurted out, covering her and the floor. She stumbled back, leaving the knife stuck in the thing's eye.

It bellowed, louder and more ear-piercing than anything Jenny had ever heard. It flailed about wildly, its tail striking blindly, smashing the wall, then hitting the oven with incredible force and knocking it clear off the wall. Two of the monster's many appendages clawed at the knife sticking out of its eye.

Gas flooded the kitchen, filling the room with a rotten-egg-like odor.

Part of Jenny's mind shouted at her to escape, but she was out of control, her heart pounding, her vision going red. Filled with an oddly calm fury, she scrambled to her feet and pulled out the next-biggest knife. She rushed forward and stabbed the monster in what looked like its neck, between two of its armored-looking sections, sending green and black fluid shooting out.

"Get the fuck out of my house," she said through clenched teeth, stabbing it again in the same spot. A horrible screeching noise emanated from the creature as its tail speared Jenny in the shoulder. She gasped in pain as the tail-tip hit her shoulder blade, sending a burst of agony through her but failing to run her through. Jenny screamed and pulled away, feeling blood streaming down her arm. Another contraction hit, that pain competing with the one in her shoulder.

The gas smell was nearly overwhelming now. Jenny coughed repeatedly.

The monster didn't seem bothered by the odor. It gave up trying to remove the knife from its eye and rose to its full height, looming over Jenny.

She gripped the knife tighter, the blade and her clothes and her skin covered in green, black, and red blood.

"Come on, you motherfucker. *Come on!*"

The monster adjusted its legs, preparing to rush toward Jenny. She braced herself for the fight, knowing this was most likely the end but determined to destroy the thing if she could. Before either of them moved, a pair of bloody human arms wrapped around the monster from behind, gripping the leathery skin hard enough to tear the wounds in the thing's neck farther open. The monster's inhuman screeches increased in volume, threatening to shatter Jenny's eardrums.

A human face appeared behind the thing—it was Tom. Alive. Barely.

"Tom!" Jenny shouted, torn between delight and terror.

He met her gaze and she saw clarity in his eyes. He gave her a sad, loving smile and opened his closed fist slightly. Something glinted inside. With horror, she realized it was his Zippo.

In that instant, she knew what he was planning. What he intended to do. For her. For their baby.

"No!" she yelled.

The creature drove itself and Tom into a nearby counter, shattering the wood. More multicolored blood flowed, dripping onto the floor and obscuring the original stain. Tom struggled to hold on as the claws slashed at him.

"Go!" he shouted.

"No!" Jenny repeated, stepping forward with the knife held up, ready to fight.

"God damn it, Jenny!" Tom said. The thing's tail drove through his leg, and he fell to one knee without letting go of the monster.

"Please," he said. "I love you. Take care of our baby. Please." His voice was full of tenderness. He was *her* Tom again.

He was shaking so badly, Jenny knew he had to be coming to the end of his strength. How he'd managed to hang on for so long, she didn't know. Her eyes filled with tears that she refused to let fall, and she nodded, defeated, knowing she couldn't save herself, her child, and her husband. She had no choice.

"I love you, too."

Bolting out the back door, Jenny doubled around toward the front of the house, barely staying upright on the ice and snow. The cold, clear air tasted better than anything she had ever experienced and was a huge relief after the mercaptan-filled kitchen. Another contraction hit her as she reached the sidewalk, this one much worse than any she'd experienced so far.

She fell to the ground as the pain rolled on. Something in her brain told her to push.

On her hands and knees, she crawled past the rental car, into the middle of the street, determined to get to Andrea's house. Waves of pain washed over her. She flipped over onto her back, unable to move anymore. Somehow, she managed to turn around so she could see her house, the home she had bought with Tom just eight months earlier. They'd hoped it would be the first step in a brand-new life. Now it was the place where the man she loved had been changed beyond recognition, where her marriage had died. A flash of light came from the back of the house—the kitchen—accompanied by a muffled thump, quickly followed by a horrible noise and a huge bloom of light as the house exploded. Shards of wood, glass, and metal rained down over the cul-de-sac, multiple pieces landing on Jenny.

Neighbors streamed into the street, surrounding Jenny, talking at her, brushing away the debris that covered her and gasping at the sight of her bloody injuries. Some asked if she was okay, what the hell had happened, and where Tom was. When a couple of people tried to help her up, she yelled at them to get their hands off her. From remarks others made, at least one person called 911.

By then, Jenny's entire being was focused on giving birth. She experienced the arrival of official vehicles in a fog as an ambulance, police cars, and fire engines streamed onto the street, sirens blaring, lights blazing. Andrea placed a folded blanket under Jenny's head and a second one over her, and someone in an EMT uniform began talking her through her contractions, asking if they could put her on a stretcher. Jenny smiled and shook her head and said, "No, I'm not going anywhere," and kept watching the house. She wanted to be looking at Tom when she gave birth to their child.

When the police and medics tried to lift her and move her to the nearby ambulance, she fought them with a violent rage that shocked her, and them. If she hurt anyone, she decided, she would apologize later.

One of the medics, the young woman who had been the first to talk to her, made eye contact, silently telling Jenny that she understood. That she was going to help Jenny deliver the baby right here in the middle of the street as the house burned to the ground in front of them.

The cops backed away, keeping the growing number of on-lookers away from both the blaze and the laboring woman. Some of the neighbors left, but others stayed to gawk. The firemen worked to contain the raging fire.

As the young medic coached Jenny, the world seemed to fall away, the pain becoming a distant thing. Jenny followed the woman's commands dutifully, but her attention remained on the house as the blaze consumed it. She was looking for living move-ment within the flames. Praying for one version of it. Dreading the other.

As an icy dawn broke feebly against the sky, Jenny gave one last push, and her baby entered the world. At last, Jenny's tears flowed. They were not tears of sorrow or anger. Jenny wept with joy. Her daughter . . . *their* daughter was here.

The young medic cut the umbilical cord and wrapped the baby in a blanket from the ambulance.

Jenny sat up slightly as the medic placed a silent bundle into her arms. Panic raced through her—was the baby dead? Had all her effort, everything she and Tom had been through, both good and horrible, been for nothing?

She looked down and saw that her daughter's eyes were open;

the baby was staring at her mother with naked curiosity. More tears streamed down Jenny's face.

"Congratulations," the young medic said, crying, too. "It's a girl."

Jenny nodded, staring at her daughter's gorgeous face. The breath suddenly hitched in her throat, her joy hiccupping briefly.

The baby had Tom's eyes.

ACKNOWLEDGMENTS

Let me start off by saying that basements have always kind of freaked me out. The idea of descending into the ground to watch TV or get something from the backup freezer or tools to hack away at the nature that is overgrowing the backyard . . . it's weird and cool and always a little terrifying.

I remember with clarity the basement of my childhood home. It was segregated into two sections. The first held our only television set and either one or two couches, depending on . . . I'm actually not sure what it depended on. I spent a lot of time down there, watching bad/amazing 1980s television shows and sorting through my comic book collection. The other half of the basement, cordoned off from the rec room by a wall and two slatted wooden doors, was unfinished. There, one would find the constantly running (at least during the winter months) woodstove, the gray concrete floors, the piles of stuff that we kept hidden from polite company, and, of course, the old, giant chest freezer and the even older backup refrigerator.

The refrigerator was close to the back wall of the creepiest part of the basement. Sometimes when I was down there, getting something from that ancient fridge, my "spider-sense" would go off, and I'd get light-headed. (Does this happen to anyone else when they're in a new/strange place? No? Uh . . . me neither.)

So, I'd like to start these acknowledgments by thanking my house on Hayden Avenue in Windsor, Connecticut, where I spent the first eighteen years of my life as well as a couple of months and years during and after college. I love that house. Even my bad memories in that house, like the creeptastic parts of the basement, are pretty amazing.

I'd also like to thank my wife, Kim, for supporting my writing since we met at the University of Scranton in 1994. During the writing of the first draft of this book, we were at a family camp in Upstate New York with our two young daughters, and I managed to steal some time to work on *The Chrysalis*. At one point, while my younger daughter was playing in a bouncy house, I sat down in the shade, got out the notebook in which I was handwriting (yep!) the novel, and got to work. I think I was writing the Ray section. Poor Ray. Anyway, after a little while, Kim and my older daughter pulled up on their bikes, and Kim said that I looked the same as I had back in college when I was writing angsty short fiction. That made my day. I guess writing really can keep us young! Thank you, Kim. I love you. And I love our daughters, Eloise and Charlotte, too. I just hope they don't read this book anytime soon.

I'd like to thank editor extraordinaire Melissa Ann Singer for recognizing the cool idea at the heart of my original proposal and promptly tearing it to shreds, then building it back up with me. It was originally her idea to have the book take place over nine months, and that was frickin' *brilliant* (among many brilliant insights). Thank you, Melissa!

David Field also deserves a big thank-you. I first came up

with the idea for *The Chrysalis* way back in 2006. I was working for Miramax, and Kim was about eight months pregnant with our oldest daughter. We moved out of New York City and bought our first house out in New Jersey. I remember entering the place and feeling overwhelmed by everything: the high-pressure job, the impending baby, the big house with the equally big mortgage payments. At that moment, for reasons still unknown to me, I imagined a creature growing in the basement, a not-so-subtle manifestation of my stress. I had almost immediate interest from *Cemetery Dance*, but I couldn't write the book—there were too many other things going on in my life and career.

Cut to a couple of years ago. I had done an interview about my publishing and movie/TV career, and I guess I mentioned *The Chrysalis* offhandedly. Not long after that, I got an email out of the blue from a young director/photographer who wanted to meet and discuss books, movies, and specifically, *The Chrysalis*. That was David Field. I was dubious at first, but I watched the short films that David had included with his email and realized that the guy was incredibly talented.

When we met face-to-face, we got along instantly. His thoughts on *The Chrysalis* were shocking, mostly because he totally understood what I was going for with the project. Thank you, David, for the additional inspiration!

I'd also like to thank Brian Freeman and Richard Chizmar from *Cemetery Dance*. You guys showed interest in this book long before I was ready to actually sit down and write the damn thing. I appreciate your patience and your belief in me.

My neighbor, Louis Wells, inadvertently made a big impact on this book. When I started writing in earnest, I lamented that I needed some good mood music to write by. He casually suggested the album *Ghosts I–IV* by Nine Inch Nails. That album became the soundtrack of the novel as I wrote . . . and I'm not sure I'll ever be able to listen to it again. And I consider that the highest compliment. (Thanks for everything, Trent Reznor!)

I'd also like to thank author and friend Nate Kenyon, for some great suggestions.

There are so many people at Tor who made this book possible, including Kirsten Brink, Irene Gallo, Jamie Stafford-Hill (who created the amazing cover), Devi Pillai, Elizabeth Curione, and Eliani Torres (whose copyedits were both terrifying and amazing).

Finally, I would be remiss if I didn't thank my parents, Rich Deneen and Irene Murray. Ever since I was a kid, creating issue after issue of my original comic book, *Marvle Man* (sic), and writing disturbing short stories, they supported and encouraged me. Now that I have kids of my own, I see even more clearly how important that kind of support and encouragement is. Mom and Dad, *thank you*!